A Son's Tale

TARA TAYLOR QUINN

W9-ASM-169

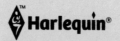
Harlequin®

TORONTO NEW YORK LONDON
AMSTERDAM PARIS SYDNEY HAMBURG
STOCKHOLM ATHENS TOKYO MILAN MADRID
PRAGUE WARSAW BUDAPEST AUCKLAND

Recycling programs
for this product may
not exist in your area.

ISBN-13: 978-0-373-60717-4

A SON'S TALE

Copyright © 2012 by Tara Taylor Quinn

www.Harlequin.com

Printed in U.S.A.

Cal pushed the button on his office answering machine.

It wasn't as if there'd be any news about Morgan Lowen's son already. Just because her urgency was coursing through him like a river with a broken dam didn't mean he was in any way privy to her personal information.

But he couldn't just sit still. Morgan's child was missing. Something had to be done.

He told himself he was overreacting. Kids went missing every day, and almost every single time they turned up. Morgan was probably with Sammie at this very moment. Maybe scolding him for having given her a scare. Or taking him out for fast-food hamburgers.

The message began. "This is for Dr. Caleb Whittier. Dr. Whittier, my name is Detective Ramsey Miller. I'm with the police department in Comfort Cove, Massachusetts. It's important that you return my call—"

Cal cut off the message before the man recited his phone number. Cal hadn't been anywhere near Comfort Cove in years, not since he was a kid. Not since the accusations that had forced him and his father out of town...

"Tara Taylor Quinn writes with wonderful assurance and an effective, unpretentious style perfectly suited to her chosen genre."
—Jennifer Blake, *New York Times* bestselling author

Dear Reader,

I was lucky growing up. I had great parents. My mother was there—always. She cooked and cleaned for us, bandaged bruises and kissed away tears. She also taught us. She stood for right and good and kindness. She didn't tolerate lying or meanness. She was strict with us…and she spoiled us. She woke us up in the morning; each of us kids had our own personal welcome to the day. She was at the door telling us goodbye when we left for school. And there waiting for us when we got home. She was our sounding board and our listening post. She is still a voice in my head that I take with me every place I go.

And my father—he was the one who told us (and showed us) that we could be anything we wanted to be. We could do anything we wanted to do. We just had to put our minds to it. Stay focused. He was not a lazy man and he did not tolerate laziness in others. He was goal oriented and demanded the same from each of us. My father gave me the stick-to-it-iveness to reach my goal of becoming a writer for Harlequin Books.

And that brings us to Comfort Cove, a small coastal fishing town in Massachusetts. Something happened in Comfort Cove that changed the lives of two sets of parents and children. In *A Son's Tale* we meet Cal and his father, Frank. How far will a father go to give his son a good life? And how far will a son go to protect the father who sacrificed so much for him? Do we ever quit owing those who gave us life? Or serving those to whom we gave life?

I don't have all the answers, but I am very happy to be bringing you this story of one father and one son. I care very much about these men—and about the woman who enters the son's life. I hope you do, too.

Watch for *A Daughter's Story,* coming in October 2012 from Harlequin Superromance. I think mothers and daughters are even more complicated than fathers and sons!

As always, I love hearing from you! You can reach me at staff@tarataylorquinn.com. Or at P.O. Box 13584, Mesa, AZ 85216.

Tara Taylor Quinn

ABOUT THE AUTHOR

With over fifty-five original novels, published in more than twenty languages, Tara Taylor Quinn is a *USA TODAY* bestselling author. She is a winner of the 2008 National Readers' Choice Award, four-time finalist for an RWA RITA® Award, a finalist for a Reviewers' Choice Award, Booksellers' Best Award and Holt Medallion and she appears regularly on Amazon bestseller lists. Tara Taylor Quinn is a past president of the Romance Writers of America and served for eight years on its board of directors. She is in demand as a public speaker and has appeared on television and radio shows across the country, including *CBS Sunday Morning*. Tara is a spokesperson for the National Domestic Violence Hotline, and she and her husband, Tim, sponsor an annual inline skating race in Phoenix to benefit the fight against domestic violence.

When she's not at home in Arizona with Tim and their canine owners, Jerry Lee and Taylor Marie, or fulfilling speaking engagements, Tara spends her time traveling and inline skating.

Books by Tara Taylor Quinn

HARLEQUIN SUPERROMANCE

HARLEQUIN SINGLE TITLE

MIRA BOOKS

*Shelter Valley Stories
‡Chapman Files

Other titles by this author are available in ebook format.

For my father, Walter Wright Gumser, and big brother, Walter Wright Gumser, Junior. Together as angels just as you were together on earth. I miss you both so much!

CHAPTER ONE

W<small>HEN HE FIRST OPENED</small> his eyes, Cal Whittier had no idea what time it was. Squinting against the light from his bedroom window, he focused on the ceiling above him.

Memory came back in bits and pieces. Piling on top of him, weighting him down to the bed.

He'd had dinner with Joy the night before. Their standing Thursday night date. He and the petite banker had been dating for four months—longer than usual for Cal. He liked Joy.

But then he'd liked all of the women he'd dated. One thing he'd never had a shortage of was women.

He and Joy had each had a glass of wine at the restaurant—a steak place, he thought. He could remember ordering his medium-rare. They'd had patio seating. Joy had commented about the misters—an outdoor staple during Tennessee summers—making her hair frizzy.

She'd ordered a salad. And they'd decided to try the house wine.

He'd overindulged.

Cal was careful about his drinking. He had a nightly ritual. A glass of whiskey before bed to help him sleep. And if that didn't work—if he was still up writing—

he allowed himself another. But he never got drunk. And he almost always drank alone.

Last night he'd broken both self-imposed rules. After dinner, he'd consumed most of a new bottle of wine back at Joy's place—and done it in front of her.

Like a bad movie, the reasons for his rudeness replayed with what seemed like sarcastic clarity in his mind's eye.

Thursday had not been a good day from the start.

A promising student had appeared in his office the morning before, just weeks before her end-of-the-summer graduation, to tell him she was dropping out of school to join her boyfriend's band. He'd been Courtney's undergraduate adviser all four years of her college career. He'd had her in several of his classes, as well. She was carrying a perfect grade average. Dr. Caleb Whittier, Wallace University's youngest English professor and department chair, was all for love and togetherness—as long as it didn't involve him—but to throw away a lifetime of work, a more secure future, because of a new relationship?

And then his father had called to tell him that he'd canceled his fishing trip that weekend. It had taken Cal months to get the old man to agree to go—a thousand nonrefundable bucks to hold his spot for the seniors' adventure holiday and to reserve a private room at his father's behest—and the old man didn't go.

He'd rushed home to load the car with the things he'd helped his dad pack the day before, determined to get the old man from the home they shared to the center where Frank would be loaded into a van and whisked away for the time of his life—only to discover that he'd have had to restrain his dad and then haul his ass out of bed, dress him and physically carry him to the Durango to get him out of their neighborhood.

The man might need Cal to prepare his food to get him to eat, but he was not in any way weak or disabled. He could still take Cal if he had a mind to.

He'd had a mind to when it came to him going on that fishing trip.

Then, because of Frank's bullheadedness, Cal had been late for the lunch meeting with some bankers—possible supporters of the young artists' league—Joy had arranged for him. It was hard to beg when you'd just kept your targets waiting for half an hour. He'd left the meeting without any kind of commitment for the scholarship money he'd been hoping to win for some very talented kids.

His body might be slow to move this morning but his mind wasn't giving him any breaks. The day before continued to play itself out—as if living through it once hadn't been enough.

After lunch he'd come back to his fourth-floor office at Wallace University in Tyler, Tennessee, to find an unwanted message on his answering machine.

Some dude named Ramsey Miller. A detective from Comfort Cove. The man gave up no other details about himself or the reason for his call, but he'd said that it was imperative that Caleb Whittier contact him immediately. Cal would bet his life the call he didn't return regarded a cold case. A twenty-five-year-old ice-cold case.

Comfort Cove, Massachusetts. The place where two-year-old Claire Sanderson had lived when she'd been abducted from her home.

It was about that time in his mental wanderings that Cal realized he was lying on top of his still-made bed. And wearing the shirt he'd pulled from his closet the morning before.

His pants were undone; they'd slipped a bit, but he hadn't taken them off, either.

And then he remembered.

Joy's expressive green eyes.

The cups of coffee.

And the short drive home.

Alone.

MORGAN HADN'T SLEPT well. They were having their annual summer sock-hop and picnic on Saturday at the day care where she worked, and Morgan, as the nondegreed employee with the most seniority, and as executive assistant to the director, was in charge of most of the physical details, like organizing the game and food committees, the table setup and decorating.

She'd spent most of Thursday night cutting and pasting many mediums of primary colors because the woman who'd volunteered to do so several weeks before had forgotten. In spite of the many calls Morgan had made to ensure that the party's decor was on track. She really should have asked to see some finished product when the woman had offered to provide samples.

But with her university courses, the day care and

schoolwork she did in the evenings, she hadn't had time to babysit a parent.

And rather than letting anyone else know that she'd done it again—she'd placed her faith in someone who hadn't proven trustworthy—she'd taken care of the fallout on her own.

Someday she might learn not to always think the best of people, not to be so quick to believe they were going to do what they said they would—but she doubted it.

"Let's consider Twain's 'The Man That Corrupted Hadleyburg,'" Dr. Whittier said, looking straight at Morgan at that Friday morning's lecture. She was sure he was looking at her because she'd been working on day-care decor yesterday evening rather than rereading the short story as she'd intended. You'd think, with only one last class to complete before graduation, she'd be able to keep up with the homework. He'd assigned the reading material at the end of Wednesday morning's class, and although she'd read everything by her favorite American writer, she hadn't read "Hadleyburg" since before Sammie was born.

Her son was ten.

"Twain was sixty-three years old and in Vienna when he wrote this story," Whittier was saying. Didn't matter how blistering the Tennessee sunshine made their city, the man always wore a tie. He'd left his jacket and long sleeves at home, but still…

Of course, the man did things—sexy things—to that ordinary tie. Things she was convinced no man had ever done before.

"Someone provide us with a quick overview of the plot," Whittier said. He glanced her way.

Morgan's stomach gave an irritating leap. She remembered the basics, but...

His gaze moved on. Her stomach didn't settle.

Yes, she was attracted to her English professor. She and every other female student at Wallace University.

"It's about, um, the corruption of an honest town." One such female creature quickly grabbed the opportunity to snare Whittier's attention. Bella Something-or-Other was thin, blonde, about twenty, and didn't have one responsibility on those perfect shoulders or one line on her equally perfect face. "Hadleyburg is known for its honesty. Then some guy sends money to someone in town for a good deed and everyone in town tries to claim the good deed to get the money."

The Richardses, Morgan remembered. They were the old couple in Hadleyburg that the stranger sent the money to for safekeeping.

"Right," Whittier said, and Bella preened. Sick. The girl was just sick.

Morgan tried to let her sleepless night catch up with her. To be bored in English class just for once. More to the point, she tried to be bored with the man who taught her favorite class.

"Hudson Long, a Twain biographer, claims that Twain uses this story to depict the pessimistic attitude that he had toward himself and the human race in general. Would you agree with that?"

He was asking the class.

"No." Morgan blurted the word against her better

judgment. She was as bad as the kids, preening for the man's attention. Her better judgment had deserted her sometime between leaving her mother's womb and landing in her cradle.

"Why not?" Whittier's gaze was all hers.

In four years of being in the man's classes, she should be over getting warm every time she had his attention.

But, recently, they'd been talking more.

"Because I think it's unfair to label the man as pessimistic just because he had the ability to see deeply inside the human condition and then was giving and talented enough to bring out his vision in such a way that we can all take honest looks at ourselves."

"So you think you know more about Mark Twain than an official Twain biographer?" His brown eyes were not unkind as he met her head-on. Instead, they had that peculiar light of enjoyment that kept her up nights.

"I'm not saying I know more than a Twain scholar," Morgan replied, aware of the other, mostly younger students watching her. She felt ancient at twenty-nine. "But I agree with another Twain biographer, Jerry Allen, who says that Twain wrote 'Hadleyburg' because of all the maliciousness that he saw in mankind and the hopelessness that was our plight if we didn't change. I think Twain was giving us a view of ourselves, exaggerated, as an analogy."

Whittier's responding smile did it to her again. "Good answer," he said, walking back over to the other side of the room.

His legs were long and firm and he moved with the grace of an athlete.

"I happen to agree with Ms. Lowen…" he was saying when Morgan's phone vibrated against her hip.

She never went to class without that phone. Being the single parent of a strong-minded boy wasn't easy work. Sammie always came first.

Morgan tried not to be too obvious as she glanced down at the screen, although Whittier knew about Sammie. Knew why she kept her phone on during class, and encouraged her to do so.

The vibration signaled a text from Julie Warren, the office administrator at Rouse Elementary where Sammie was in summer school taking art and swimming. Julie was also Morgan's friend.

The message was one word: Call.

They had a lunch date. Maybe Julie had to cancel. Wouldn't be the first time.

She typed her response.

In class. Emergency?

She sent the text off with one hand, leaving the phone in its clip.

The reply was almost instantaneous. Like Julie hadn't waited for her reply before sending it.

S missing!

The phone vibrated again, but Morgan didn't take the time to look down. Closing the lid on her notebook computer without shutting the thing down, she threw it on top of its case in her backpack. She had the bag slung on her shoulder before she was completely standing and was already digging in the side pocket for her car keys.

"My son…" She wasn't even sure what she ended up blurting out as she ran from the room.

CHAPTER TWO

SILENCE HUNG OVER the classroom for thirty seconds or more after Morgan Lowen's dash from the room. Her frantic words—"My son is missing from school!"—occupied the space, squeezing out all the excess air.

And then the rumbling started—low voices emanating from seats all across the room. His students' wide-eyed glances darted between one another, the door, him. One kid—"Jackass," Cal had privately dubbed him—sat there staring at his electronic tablet, looking bored. That's when Cal noticed the wireless device mostly concealed by the kid's long, unkempt hair. He had an earphone in. And was listening to God knew what on Cal's time.

"Class dismissed," Cal said, filing away a mental reminder to pursue wireless Jackass at some future date.

Yeah, this was college. Yeah, students were responsible for their own education at this point. But he had more to teach than knowledge of American literature. He had the minds of tomorrow in his sphere and he took his job seriously.

He answered a couple of questions about a two-thousand-word paper due at midterm and confirmed that they'd be covering *The Adventures of Huckleberry Finn* all of the following week as the syllabus stated.

"You think her kid's going to be okay?" Bella was standing by the long table that served as his desk at the front of the window-lined classroom.

"I do," Cal said, ignoring the thread of alarm trying to take up residence within him. "She said he was missing from school. He's probably just playing hooky. Or hiding out with a friend in the bathroom. It's summer school so things are a little less strict and kids have more of a tendency to roam."

"Some jerks once locked my little brother in his locker," Bella said, sliding her electronic notebook into her backpack. "He was there for an hour before anyone knew he was missing."

"His teachers didn't miss him?"

"They had a sub and it was during lunch break."

And someone should have noticed he was gone. Like they'd obviously noticed Morgan Lowen's son was missing.

"They should check the lockers for him," Bella added, standing in front of him with her backpack slung over one shoulder.

"I'm sure they'll find him." Cal slid a couple of folders, notes, into his soft-sided leather briefcase.

"I didn't even know she had a son."

Cal had. He knew, too, that she'd given birth to and raised the boy completely on her own, but he wasn't going to gossip about another student. What he wanted to do was get back to his office in case she contacted him. He and Morgan had never crossed the line between teacher and student; he'd kept his interest in her completely professional, but he'd be kidding himself if he said he wasn't attracted to her.

And Cal did not kid himself. He couldn't afford the luxury.

Morgan had been having some troubles with her son. He knew because she'd missed class in the spring due to some antics the boy had pulled at school.

He hoped she'd also let him know that Sammie was fine.

"She doesn't wear a wedding ring." Bella was still standing there.

Again, Cal said nothing and Bella, after staring at him for another several seconds, shrugged.

"Well, I just hope everything's fine. Have a great weekend, Dr. Whittier. See you Monday."

She walked out, allowing Cal to hurry to his office.

MORGAN COULDN'T REMEMBER the four-block drive from Wallace University to Rouse Elementary. She'd run out of class and ended up in the parking lot of her son's school. She'd called her mom. But only to ask her if she'd heard from Sammie. Grace Lowen was going to be taking Sammie to Little League practice Saturday while Morgan officiated sack races at the day care. Morgan had told Sammie that morning to call his grandmother and remind her of the next day's practice.

Grace hadn't heard from him.

The call with her mother lasted about thirty seconds. Morgan didn't let on that anything was amiss. She didn't know for sure that it was.

And she couldn't deal with her father at the moment.

Julie was pacing the sidewalk at the entrance of the parking lot when Morgan pulled up in her eight-year-old Ford Taurus, purchased used the year before. Julie jumped in and Morgan pulled into the closest parking spot.

"Oh, God, Morg, I have no idea how this happened," Julie said, glancing toward the door of the school. "Mr. Peterson has already called the police."

The school principal. A man Morgan had always thought was calm and rational, ready to call the police?

"He's got to be hiding someplace," Morgan said, swallowing panic. "Did they check the bathrooms? The girls', too?"

Julie nodded.

"What about the shop? Did you check the shop? You know he wanted to finish that little wood car he'd started last session."

Julie was already shaking her head. "He asked to use the restroom," she said. "The hall security camera shows him going into the boys' restroom at the end of the hall, and in twenty minutes of tape, he never came back out. But he's definitely not in there."

"What about the grounds camera?"

"It's broken at the hinge, but we can't tell if the break is new or not."

"How long ago did he leave class?"

"He asked to go to the bathroom half an hour ago. As soon as his teacher reported that he hadn't come back and wasn't in the bathroom we went to the security camera. I texted you as soon as I saw the film."

"Have they checked his locker?"

"Yeah. His suit and towel for swimming are in there."

"What about his lunch?"

They were out of the car, hurrying toward the walk.

"Today is picnic-on-the-lawn day, remember? We provide brown-bag lunches."

"Oh, yeah, right." Picnic-on-the-lawn day had seemed so far away.

"They've locked down the school, Morg. Come on. We have to get in there. They're waiting for you...."

The fear in Julie's eyes held Morgan frozen for a split second. And then she ran.

CAL PUSHED THE BUTTON on his office answering machine before he'd taken his seat behind his desk.

As if there'd be some news about Morgan Lowen's son there already. Just because her urgency was coursing through him like a river with a broken dam didn't mean that he was in any kind of loop that would be privy to her private information on an immediate basis.

Still, he couldn't just sit there. A child was missing. Something had to be done.

He was overreacting, of course. Kids went missing every day, and almost every single time they turned up. Morgan was probably with Sammie at this very moment. Maybe scolding him for having given her a scare. Or taking him for fast food hamburgers, which she'd told Cal she'd done last April after Sammie's problems at school. She'd wanted her son to talk to her. Rather than punish him, she'd wanted to know why he'd acted out.

"This message is for Dr. Caleb Whittier. Dr. Whittier, I left a message yesterday. My name is Detective Ramsey Miller. I'm with the Comfort Cove Police Department in Comfort Cove, Massachusetts. It's important that you return my call...."

Cal cut off the message before the man recited his numbers, including one for a private cell, a second time. He hadn't been anywhere near Comfort Cove, a coastal town not far from Boston, since he was seven years old. Not since the accusations had forced him and his father out of town.

He'd be damned if he was going to waltz back there of his own accord. Other than this office line at school, his numbers—landline and cell—were unlisted. His father's cell was a pay-as-you-go with an untraceable number. They rented instead of owning so that there was no tax record of the residence. They used a P.O. box for mail. He paid taxes, but Frank didn't. His father worked at the local nursing home, doing handyman and janitorial work, and the rent on the home they lived in was free in trade. Cal hadn't lived thirty-two years without learning a thing or two about protecting his father from the stalkers who'd all but ruined his life.

Bile rose in his throat as he thought about the tall, proud man who'd once stood at the helm of one of Massachusetts' most prestigious private high schools, getting up every morning to fix bathroom plumbing and mop piss off floors.

His father had not only been one of Massachusetts' most respected educators, he'd also been a damn good basketball coach. And in the past twenty years the only ball he'd touched professionally was the float ball in a toilet.

There were two other messages. One confirming that while the adventure vacations group had sympathy with Cal's plight, the thousand bucks he'd put up for his father's fishing trip was not going to be refunded, regardless of the circumstances. The second one was from the assistant of one of yesterday's bankers informing him that she'd sent a list of questions that he would need to answer, in writing, before her boss could consider Cal's scholarship request for the young artists' league.

Voice mail over, he sat down. Opened his email.

And saw the message in his in-box that Joy had sent the day before, confirming their date the night before. She'd said she had something to speak with him about. He'd thought she wanted to deepen their relationship with spoken commitment. To talk about some kind of future.

It hadn't gone that way....

"Hi, hon. How was your day?" he'd said as he'd met her outside the restaurant. He'd bent down for a kiss, which she'd returned as though everything was fine. It hadn't been until later, back at her place, that she'd let him know how she was really feeling.

He'd pulled her into his arms. She'd pushed him away.

"I don't want to do this, Cal," she'd said. "It's like

I'm on your list of things to do, not like I'm the person you need in your life. When you kiss me…I don't know…I don't feel like I do it for you anymore."

"It's not that," he'd hastily assured her. "I want you."

"I'm not talking about sex, Cal. All your working parts are in perfect order, as I'm sure you're fully aware. You're the best lover I've ever had and then some."

"So what's the problem?" His tone was purposefully light. But he knew. In the end, the story was always the same.

"You don't give enough of yourself, Cal. You bring gifts. You take me to concerts and the theater. You've introduced me to some great restaurants that I'd never been to even though I've lived in Tennessee my entire life. You entertain me. You bring me physical pleasure I didn't even know I could feel. But you never talk to me. I know more about what's playing and who's cooking than I do about you."

Different words, but same story. As he'd predicted.

"What's there to tell?" he'd asked, as much out of habit as anything. And he'd waited for her answer with more curiosity than hope. Would her answer be any different than any he'd ever heard before?

"If I knew that, we wouldn't be having this conversation."

"Did it ever occur to you that you know what there is to know?"

"It did. But I don't believe that. You have too much insight, too much consideration and too much understanding to ever pass for a shallow man."

Her words made him uncomfortable. "You get more of me than anyone else in my life gets."

She'd wanted more.

He wasn't going to give it to her.

Her next words replayed themselves loud and clear—their echo joining the chorus of others in his mind. "I think we need to start seeing other people, Cal."

"You're breaking up with me."

"Were we ever really going together?"

"I was seeing you exclusively. You know that." He only had exclusive sex.

She'd paused.

Two months prior they'd had "the talk." The one that said she was important to him. As he was to her.

And what more was there? They'd established in the very beginning that neither was interested in marriage or family.

None of the women Cal dated were. That criteria was at the top of his list when considering whether or not he should ask a woman out. "I know you care about me, Cal. And I'll always care about you," Joy had finally said. Then she'd added, "And no, I'm not saying I don't ever want to see you again. I just think we need to see other people, too. You know, to keep things from getting too…personal."

They were done sleeping with each other. "I understand."

"We've had some really good times."

"Agreed."

She'd offered him coffee to sober up so he could

drive. He'd had several cups. The silence had gotten awkward.

Then he'd stood.

"Call me, okay?" she'd said, standing there in her banker's conservative shirt and jacket, her arms wrapped around her middle.

He'd pulled the knot on his tie up. "I will. You do the same."

"Of course."

He'd left her house pretty certain that he and Joy would never speak again.

There was another message from her in Friday morning's incoming email. She was sorry for how things had gone the night before. But she really thought their decision was for the best. She hoped he understood that she wouldn't be referring any more of her clients or associates to him for his fundraising efforts. And she wanted the earrings back that she'd left in his car the previous week.

Cal would have been a lot more bothered about Joy if he'd known that Sammie Lowen was with his mother, safe and sound.

CHAPTER THREE

SHE WAS LIVING a nightmare. She'd wake up any second.

Longing for the quilt on her bed, to be able to pull it up over her head and warm her freezing body, Morgan sat in the chair at the police station and waited for her parents to arrive.

She'd already answered all of the officers' questions.

"Let's go over things one more time, Ms. Lowen." The female detective sitting across from her in the little room with only a table and four chairs emanated sympathy. About ten years older than Morgan, Elaine Martin didn't look any more like a cop than she did. She wasn't even in uniform.

"The smallest things can make a difference," Detective Martin said. "Tell me again everything you can remember about this morning."

"I got Sammie up at seven, just like always."

"Did he get right up? Or did you have to nag him?"

Was the woman calling her a nag? Did she think Morgan wasn't a good mom? That she'd somehow failed her son? Failed to see that someone was watching him? Out to get him? Or...

"Ms. Lowen? You okay?"

Morgan focused. Detective Martin's brow creased with concern.

No, I'm not okay. How can I possibly be okay? My son is...where? What are they doing to him? God, was Sammie even still alive? Or...had he run away? Was he that unhappy with her? Was he in with a bad crowd and she'd somehow missed evidence of that fact? "Yeah. I'm fine."

The detective covered Morgan's hand with her own. "We're going to find him," she said. "Stay with me, okay?"

Morgan nodded "He got right up. He always does. Sammie's like me. A morning person."

"Then what?"

"I got his breakfast. Rice Krispies with milk."

"Did he eat it all?"

"Yes."

"Does he always?"

"Yes."

"What about toast? Or fruit?"

"No. He hates fruit." And she didn't make him eat it. Did that make her a bad mother? Did they think Sammie's missing was her fault? That she had something to do with this? They were asking her so many questions over and over and...

"Just cereal," she said, meeting Detective Martin's gaze again. "He went upstairs to dress. I heard him brushing his teeth. He left the cap off the toothpaste just like always. And he spit six times..." Her eyes welled up. She'd limited Sammie to six spits and, bless his heart, he always complied.

She smiled, not seeing anything but her son's skinny little face, his lips puckered up. "He loves to spit. Sometimes I think that's why he loves baseball so much. Of course, he loves basketball even more and you can't spit on a basketball court...." She stopped. She was rambling. Did that make her look guilty?

She searched for signs of accusation in the detective's expression and couldn't determine if there were any there or not.

"What was he wearing when you left the house?"

"His oldest pair of cutoff shorts. The ones with the ripped pocket. They were going to get to play around with oil on canvas today and I didn't want him to ruin any of his good clothes."

She couldn't afford to replace them. She and Sammie lived on a tight budget. They had his whole life. Was that why this was happening? Because she couldn't provide well enough for her son?

"And a Phoenix Suns T-shirt," she said. He had four of them. "The oldest one. It's his favorite sports team. They play basketball...out in Phoenix. We've never been there."

"What was he wearing on his feet?" Detective Martin's voice was a gentle reminder that this was all real. She wasn't having some horrible nightmare.

"Sneakers. The ones with the rip in the toe. They're black. Converse." The Converses had been a Christmas gift from her mother. He'd worn them out by March. She'd bought him a new pair of sneakers. A bargain brand. They looked the same to Morgan but Sammie loved Converses. He said all real basketball players wore them. And so he'd continued to wear them even though they were worn through.

"You said he doesn't know his father?"

Morgan shook her head.

"Are you certain about that?"

"Yes, of course. Sammie's never met Todd. He knows we were divorced and he thinks his father is dead, that he died before Sammie was born, which is why Sammie has my last name." She'd told him Todd was dead. She hated lying to her son but felt that in this case, she had no other choice. Because the alternative, the truth, was unthinkable. No one told a little boy that his father just didn't want him. That he wasn't worth the money it would have cost Todd to have Sammie in his life.

"I'd know if Todd wanted to see our son." She could bet on that. If Todd wanted something, Todd got it.

"But what if he thought you wouldn't let him see Sammie? Do you think he'd take him?"

Her blood ran cold. "As in kidnap him? You said there was no sign of struggle at the school—nor any forced entry or exit. You said that a good majority of missing-child cases are runaways and that was what Sammie's case was looking like...."

She heard how crazy she sounded, to be accusing a cop of misleading her. But she felt crazed. "No." She forced herself back to the question. "Todd wouldn't do that," she added, trying to calm down. "I wasn't eager for Todd to have a part in Sammie's life, but I never told him he couldn't see his son. Todd was the one who wanted nothing to do with him from the very beginning. Sammie's father is a thief and a liar who wants nothing more than to wallow in money. And he's doing that now. He's married to an heiress who actually has money to share with him. On the condition that he doesn't bring a kid into her life. She hates them."

Morgan was heiress to a large fortune, too—unless her father had changed his will and left all of his money to the investment firm he owned and loved more than life—but she'd been cut off from access to the money when she'd married Todd.

Her father had forbidden the marriage. He'd said that Todd was a gold digger. She'd believed Todd loved her, so she'd gone against her father's dictates. Her father then made certain that she didn't have any money for Todd to use.

And as it turned out, her father had been right.

"We ran a check on him," Elaine Martin said, and Morgan stared at her. They'd run a check on her father? Already?

"On Todd Williams," the detective clarified. "Turns out he's got a record, both juvenile and adult. He did time for burglary and theft."

"That's right." Though she hadn't known about the juvenile stuff until after he'd broken into her parents' mansion and tried to steal what was "rightfully" his. His prison time had come after their divorce.

"We've got a call in to his parole officer. They're going to be bringing Williams in for questioning."

Again, Morgan nodded. They could question the devil for all she cared. She just wanted her son found.

"What kind of relationship does Williams have with your parents?"

"After he stole from them and they prosecuted him, you mean?"

"They were one of the counts in his conviction?" She nodded.

"Before or after your divorce?"

"He stole from them before. The conviction came after."

"What kind of relationship do your parents have with Sammie?"

"My mother sees him regularly. My father never comes to our home or takes Sammie anywhere."

"Your parents are divorced?" The woman looked down at her paperwork. "I'm sorry, I thought…"

"They aren't divorced," Morgan clarified. "My father sees Sammie when my mother brings him to their place, but he and I have been in a standoff since before Sammie was born. After my marriage to Todd broke up, he offered to take me back into his fold, but only if I live at home with him and my mother and do exactly as I'm told. If I don't live by his dictates, he has nothing to do with me. He won't go to any of Sammie's functions if I'm there. Though, to be fair, I believe that if I was incapable of providing for Sammie, my father wouldn't let us starve. As it is, he's content to let me penny-pinch, drive a used car and live in a smallish duplex. And I'm perfectly happy to do so if it means I can be my own person and live my life and raise my son in the way I feel is best."

"Mmm." The detective's compassionate glance, her

knowing tone, left Morgan feeling far too exposed. And ready to spill all at the same time.

She wanted her son found. No matter what embarrassing and humiliating shortcomings she had to confess.

"So your parents don't help you out financially at all? Not even with Sammie?"

"No. My mother buys gifts for Sammie occasionally and my father doesn't object, as long as I don't benefit financially. It's his way of teaching me a lesson. My father isn't evil. He's just cold. And certain that he's always right."

But he would not do anything, ever, to hurt his grandson. Or Morgan, either, in a physical sense.

"You have no siblings, right?"

"Right."

Morgan jumped as a knock sounded on the door to the small room.

"Excuse me." With papers in hand, Detective Martin left Morgan alone.

She was back in a couple of seconds.

"Todd Williams is here. We're going to question him."

"You really think he could have taken Sammie?"

Elaine Martin shrugged. "If his money pool is running low. I know you said his wife is rich but he could be into gambling. Or he could have taken your son if he wants to get back at your folks for rejecting him to begin with and then pressing the charges that sent him to prison. Either motive is solid. It's our job to find out who has motive and to investigate every possibility as quickly as possible."

Morgan felt like she might throw up. This couldn't be happening. "But if he took him, he'd have to do something with him." She swallowed the lump in her throat. "He couldn't take him home...."

Sammie? Oh, God. Her breath caught. *Where are you, Sammie?*

Does your father have enough of a parental instinct to at least keep you alive?

Thinking of the man she'd once thought she loved with all of her heart and soul, Morgan couldn't be sure what he'd do. He'd been quite willing to turn his back on her, in spite of the adoration he'd professed to have for her, so how well could a child he'd never met fare with him?

"What about an Amber Alert? Did you issue one of those?"

"Not yet." The detective looked down at the pages in front of her. "We have to be reasonably certain that there's been an abduction before we can do that, which is why we're questioning your ex-husband. As I told you already, there's been no sign of foul play."

Her ten-year-old son was missing! That was foul. Morgan resisted the temptation to jump up and run. To make up for what others weren't doing. Not that she knew what that was.

Had Sammie really run away? Was he that unhappy with her?

As bad as that seemed, it was still better than thinking that her son had been taken against his will. That he was scared or…worse…

"But you're still pursuing the possibility that he's been kidnapped, aren't you?"

"Of course. We have to consider the worst if we're going to be assured of getting him back."

"What about his backpack, his things? His baseball mitt? He took that to school with him this morning and he wouldn't leave it behind."

She'd just remembered. She'd told him he had to leave it at home, but when he'd said he wanted to show Jimmy how to catch during the picnic lunch and he'd promised to keep it in his locker the rest of the day, she'd given in. She'd told Detective Martin she'd forgotten about the mitt when she and Julie had discussed Sammie's locker.

"There was no mitt in his locker," the other woman said, frowning. "Or backpack, either. Who's Jimmy Burns?"

"He's a boy in his regular class at school and he's in Sammie's summer school art class. He just moved here last spring. He's got Down syndrome, but he loves baseball and Sammie was going to teach him how to catch at lunch."

"Does Sammie spend much time with Jimmy?"

"Yeah, a fair amount. His mom sometimes watches Sammie for me when I'm in class. Daddy only lets Mom see us a couple of times a week."

Blind fear made her continue, to tell the detective everything. Her son's life was in danger. She wasn't going to spare herself. "According to my father, I'm a bad influence on my mother."

"And on Sammie, too?"

"Only because I'm teaching him how to disrespect a parent and go against a parent's wishes. If I'd conform to his way of thinking and move home and be pampered and protected, he'd think I'm a great mother."

She didn't want to stop talking now. If she kept talking she didn't have to think. Could Sammie really be with his father? He'd never even met the man.

Already divorced by the time Sammie was born, she'd put "father unknown" on her son's birth certificate to protect the boy from finding out who and what his father really was. And lost any chance for child support in the doing.

If Todd had her son, Sammie would be scared to death. And Todd? What would he do with him? How could he possibly keep the boy's existence a secret? If Sammie didn't turn up soon, his picture was going to be all over the evening news.

Todd had friends in low places, though, in spite of the moneyed crowd he now ran with.

She glanced up at Detective Martin, her entire body frozen with fear. "If Todd is behind this, he might turn my son over to associates from his old life for safekeeping until he gets the ransom."

"We're already checking on that. We're also finding out who he knew in prison and if anyone is out or has contacts in the area.

"We also aren't ruling out a nonrelation kidnapping."

Morgan wasn't sure which was worse—Todd or a stranger. "Even if ransom is paid, kidnappers don't return victims who can identify them. And they don't just take kids for ransom money." She was killing herself and couldn't stop. "I watch TV."

Oh, God. Please don't allow Sammie to pay for my sins....

Elaine Martin squeezed her hand, quieting the screeching in Morgan's mind enough for her to hear the detective when she said, "We get them back safely, too. And we're getting way ahead of ourselves. At this point it doesn't even look like Sammie's been kidnapped. We just don't want to leave any rocks unturned."

The detective was right. Sammie was probably hiding out someplace, just to see if he could.

"I'm going to go see what, if anything, they've learned from Williams." Detective Martin stood again.

"I should never have married that jerk," Morgan said. "My father was right."

He was also right outside the door. She could see him through the window that looked out into the reception room through which she'd been led. He was staring straight at her.

And she recognized that frown.

Her father was angry. Really angry.

And blaming her. Again.

Please, God, this time don't let him be right.

CHAPTER FOUR

ON AN ORDINARY DAY, Cal would have emailed Joy back. He'd have tried to make things right for her. He was sad to see this one go. Joy was fun. Intelligent. Witty. Conversationally she'd kept him on his toes. In bed, they'd been plenty good enough.

He'd kind of been hoping that she'd become a semi-permanent fixture in his life. He'd even thought about introducing her to his father some day.

On an ordinary day, he might even have called Joy.

Instead, Cal finished up a requisition request that was due that day for books for the fall semester, filed his class notes, found notes for Monday's class and watched the time—and the phone.

Two hours had passed since Morgan Lowen had run from his class. She hadn't called to apologize for interrupting class. To explain. To tell him that all was well.

She hadn't called to relieve him—or anyone else in his class who might ask him—of any concern regarding her abrupt departure from the lecture that morning.

She'd been his student for four years, one of his favorite students, but beyond the teaching they'd talked a few times over the past several months, about her plans for the future since she was soon to graduate, about her son. About being a single parent, a student and working full-time. He'd meant it when he'd told her he'd help in any way he could.

He hoped she'd call.

Cal kept busy. He knew how to take his mind off from that over which he had no control. He'd perfected the art by the time he was ten.

Still, a child was missing. And Detective Ramsey Miller of the Comfort Cove Police Department had called him twice in less than twenty-four hours. It had been years since they'd heard anything from or about Comfort Cove.

And a child was missing.

Morgan Lowen—and Sammie—had nothing to do with Rose Sanderson, the mother from Comfort Cove, Massachusetts, who'd once been engaged to Cal's father, and then accused him of kidnapping her daughter. Morgan and Sammie had no connection to Claire Sanderson, the little girl who'd been abducted, or to Claire's sister, Emma.

The timing was coincidence. Bizarre coincidence. He knew that. Was completely, calmly certain of that.

But a child was missing...

His hands were typing before Cal had made a firm decision to access confidential student files. He typed his username. His password. Clicked a couple of times and then entered Morgan's full name as he had it on his class register.

The wait was seconds but seemed interminable. The screen flashed. Renewed. He couldn't see everything. Her social security number, for instance. But her classes were all there. Her grades. Her petition for graduation—she was due to collect a B.A. degree in early childhood development with a minor in business and another in English in less than six weeks, right after completing his class. He knew from their conversations that she wanted to open her own day care someday.

And there was her address.

He'd been mentoring her, educationally, for years. And more recently, since her trouble with Sammie in the spring, he'd thought they'd become more than just teacher and student. Closer to friends...with the professional distance mandated by their positions, of course.

She was a woman carrying a huge load, alone. She worked hard. Did all she could. She never asked for favors or special consideration. She never made excuses.

He tried to focus on the rest of his day. On lunch, and the afternoon and evening ahead. Papers he could grade. Calls he should make.

There was a mother whose child was missing.

Something Cal knew far too much about. He could still remember the sense of panic. The horror and disbelief. The pain that never healed...

No.

This was Morgan Lowen. Not Rose Sanderson. This was Tyler, Tennessee. Not Comfort Cove, Massachusetts. This was 2012. Not the 1980s.

He decided he was going to do a quick drive-by to make certain that she was okay. Then he'd head straight home. Due to his slow start that morning, he hadn't left lunch prepared in the refrigerator for his father and chances were that the older man wouldn't bother to fix something for himself.

Frank was a good cook. Better than good. If his father cared enough to get up and get out to the kitchen, they'd be eating much better meals than the ones Cal provided for them.

If Frank cared what he ate, or if he ate...

A child was missing. Frank would care about that....

All thoughts of his father fled when Cal turned the corner of Apple Road and saw the cars parked outside the small duplex in the center of the block. Could be a woman having a Friday luncheon. Or a kids' play group. Could be, but his gut told him it wasn't.

People were walking the neighborhood. Calling out. Some had fliers already. He pulled up slowly, stopping his blue Ford Flex right behind a Cadillac Escalade—the vehicle he would have bought if he'd had the money.

A woman who looked to be about forty stood just off the sidewalk a couple of units down from the front door bearing the number he'd pulled from his computer. She had her arm around a young girl, holding her close, as she surveyed the street.

Moms would all be holding their kids close in that neighborhood tonight. There'd be no more summer nights playing tag on the streets. No more summer days playing tag, either. The fliers would be hung, and when they faded, they'd be rehung. People would watch carefully as they came and went. New locks would adorn doors that would remain tightly shut to the summer breeze.

Fear would become a family member.

No, this was Tennessee, not Comfort Cove, Massachusetts.

Flashes of knowing accompanied Cal as he approached the screen door of Morgan Lowen's small home and knocked.

A woman appeared almost immediately. She was about his age, early thirties, with long dark hair pulled back into a ponytail. Her face was pinched, her green eyes void of any makeup at all. She opened the door with an expectant look.

"Is Morgan here?" he asked.

"She's in the living room." The woman kept herself placed between him and the inside of the home.

"I'm Caleb Whittier, her English professor. She was in my class this morning when she got the call about her son."

"Dr. Whittier?" She said the name like she knew it. Like it would be followed by "*The* Dr. Whittier?" He couldn't tell if recognition was a good thing or not, but he nodded.

"I'm Julie Warren," the woman said. "I'm the secretary at Sammie's school. And Morgan's friend. I'm the one who called her out of class."

"Have they found him?"

After seeing the cars on the street, the shake of her head was no surprise. He shoved his hands into his pockets.

Julie Warren stood back. "Come on in."

"No. I don't want to bother her. I just…"

Just what? He could have called to find out if she

was all right. If Sammie was. Or waited until class on Monday.

He could have watched the news tonight and known, if nothing was there, that the boy had probably been found.

"Morgan's told me about you. About your talks," Julie said, still holding the door open. "That's unusual for her, the way she talks to you. Morgan doesn't open up to people much." The woman was talking fast, as though running away from something, or trying not to think about someone who couldn't be found. "You may not realize it, but your support has helped her a lot," Julie said now. "I really think she'd like to see you." The woman's brow was creased with worry.

She held the door open farther and Caleb moved forward.

SHE'D HEARD THE KNOCK on the door a few minutes ago. Could see the people traversing the street through her living room window. She knew her mother was sitting next to her on the sand-colored faux-leather couch she'd picked up at a moving sale several years before. Her father was just around the corner in the kitchen, talking on the phone. His tone brooked no argument or refusal.

His first time in her home and he'd already taken command of the place.

Sammie was still gone. Todd had been questioned and released.

Detective Martin was around someplace. Outside, maybe, directing the canvas of the neighborhood.

They'd tapped her cell phone. And her father's. Morgan didn't have a home line. But they wanted her there, anyway. In case Sammie came home. Or someone brought him home. Or tried to contact her there.

Morgan listened to the flapping sound of Julie's flip-flops out in the foyer where she'd gone to answer the door. Her friend had been sitting on Morgan's other side on the couch for most of the afternoon. She was wearing the sleeveless, long, tie-dyed cotton dress that she'd bought the year before at a clearance sale. Her husband hated the dress. Morgan loved it.

The couch was nice. Soft. And clean. Morgan had gone over it twice with leather cleanser and antibacterial cleanser, too, when she'd purchased it. She wanted to make certain that it was safe for Sammie. Should she tell Detective Martin she'd done that? It proved how much she loved her son, didn't it? Proved that she was a good mother.

Jumping up, Morgan stood at the window. Staring out. No matter how tightly she wrapped her arms around herself, she couldn't seem to get warm.

Julie flapped in, flip-flop, flip-flop.

"Morgan?"

She heard her friend. She just didn't turn around. Watching the flurry of activity on the street was as close as she could get to *doing* something. The inactivity was driving her crazy.

For a second she imagined herself and Sammie on the beach. In Florida. They couldn't afford the Hilton Head vacations she'd taken as a child with her parents. Florida's beaches were more fun. Less stuffy. She and

Sammie were holding hands, screaming as they took a big wave together....

Outside, a man she didn't recognize moved into her line of vision.

She should be doing. It was her job to see to her son's needs. To look after him. She was always the one who was doing for Sammie. The only one...

"Morgan, Dr. Whittier's here."

She turned. Still outside looking for her son. Still on that beach in Florida.

The man standing in her living room was as unreal as the rest of her current world. Dr. Whittier? In her home?

"Hi, Morgan," he said. "I looked up your address. I hope you don't mind my stopping by, but after the way you left class, I just wanted to make certain you were okay."

She shook her head. "My son's missing."

"I know."

Of course he did. The whole class knew. Maybe the whole town did. She hoped to God the whole town knew.

"Dr. Whittier? Are you Sammie's doctor?" Morgan heard her mother's voice as if from a distance greater than the couch across the room.

Morgan looked back outside.

Surely someone would have seen a ten-year-old boy wearing cutoff shorts, a Phoenix Suns T-shirt and black sneakers with a hole in the toe. Sammie was small, like her, but he wasn't invisible. That blond hair, and those big brown eyes of his...

"...her English professor..." Cal Whittier's voice infiltrated briefly.

Sammie had wanted her to practice catch with him the night before. She'd been too busy cutting decorations for Saturday's picnic. She'd started at the day care when she'd been pregnant with Sammie. The job had offered free child care, which saved her enough money that she'd been able to get them the duplex in the nicer neighborhood rather than settling for an apartment in a less safe part of town.

She'd worried, at first, that she wouldn't qualify for the job, but Tennessee law allowed you to teach in a day care with only a high school diploma. She'd started out as an assistant teacher and then was offered the job of executive assistant to the director. She liked teaching, though, and she substituted for the full-time teachers whenever she could. She'd lucked out. She got to spend the first five years of Sammie's life with him and earn money, too. And once Sammie had started school, Morgan's boss had allowed Sammie to come to the day care after class to play and help with the little kids until Morgan was off work.

As a bonus, she'd loved working with the preschoolers—she'd been a natural—and had found a career.

"Morgan was in my class when she got the call about her son...." She assumed Dr. Whittier was still addressing her mother and she turned back around.

The three of them—Morgan, Whittier and Julie—were standing in the middle of her tiny living room, while her mother perched on the edge of the couch, her thumbs rubbing back and forth across opposite palms.

"I'd just seen Sammie half an hour before he went missing," Julie was telling Whittier. "I'd gone into his classroom to take a message to his teacher and he'd called out to me, flashing that big grin of his."

He'd just run away. Sammie was doing this to prove he could. To prove that he was old enough to be on his own. To prove…

"They're going over her computer now…" Julie continued, filling in the newcomer, just as they'd all done every time someone new arrived on the scene.

Morgan had caught Sammie on the internet again the night before.

She'd yelled at him. He knew that he wasn't allowed to be on the internet without her. It wasn't safe for kids.

"I have parental controls in place but he knows how to hack through them." Her voice sounded far away— a disconnect from the cottony haze of unreality that had her in its grip.

"You think he might have met someone there?" Whittier's piercing gaze confirmed that she was in the conversation.

Morgan held on to that look. To him. And touched ground for a second. "No." She shook her head again. "I caught him before he could clear history and cache. He was looking at basketball shoes." She repeated what she'd told Detective Martin an hour before. And her mother and father when they'd arrived at the police station.

"Does he clear history and cache regularly?"

"He used to, before I caught on to the fact that he was sneaking on to the computer behind my back.

Then he figured out that if I saw everything cleared, I'd know he'd been on."

"Do you have any idea what he was looking at?" His tone held the same deep concern he'd expressed the previous spring when she'd first told him about the son she was raising alone and struggling to let go of enough to give him some independence, but hold on to enough to keep him safe.

"Basketball," Morgan said, breathing normally for a moment. "Stats, schedules, shoes, basketball video games, autographed balls..."

Whittier frowned. "If that's all he was into, why delete the history?"

"So I wouldn't know he'd been on the computer without supervision."

"Because he thinks you baby him too much."

She'd appreciated Whittier's conversation regarding her son these past months. Appreciated his male perspective.

"I know you agreed with him when it came to showering. I have to trust him to get himself clean enough and to give him his space to grow into a young man. But there are just too many dangers on the internet. I still won't let him go on unless I'm sitting there with him."

"And he probably sees that as more proof that you don't trust him."

"Right. I can't budge on this one. But I make sure that I put aside time to let him surf to his heart's content. I want him to learn the internet, to know how to get around and to be privy to the wealth of good information out there. Seems like we've been to every basketball site ever uploaded. We look at all the baseball sites, too, but basketball is his first love. Did you know that in the history of the NBA only eight players were born on May 3? And that the most recent was in 1977? That was Tyronn Lue. He was drafted by the Denver Nuggets and played for ten years. Sammie's birthday is May 3...."

"Morgan, Detective Martin needs to speak with you." The booming—and openly reproving—voice rent through her like a shard of lightning. She should have been more focused on the moment, should have known the second the detective had reentered her residence, seeking her attention.

She'd been rambling. Her father thought she talked too much. That she took a hundred words to say what could be said with ten.

The detective was waiting for her in the foyer. "No one in the neighborhood has seen your son since the two of you left this morning." Elaine Martin's tone was all business now. "But we found one eyewitness, a seventy-year-old woman who says she saw Sammie on the corner of Bohemian and First."

Heart pumping, Morgan took a step back until she was almost leaning against the man who'd sired her. Bohemian was four blocks from school.

"He was speaking with a man."

"What man?" She couldn't stop the shaking that had control of her body.

"We don't know. We're hoping you can help us." Detective Martin pulled an eight-and-a-half-by-eleven-inch copy of a hand sketch from the portfolio under her arm. "Do you recognize this man?"

Morgan stared at the chiseled features. The longish hair. And the tattoo on the muscled shoulder. Some kind of spiked something.

"I've never seen him before in my life."

"Look closely, Morgan. Take your time," Elaine Martin said. "Our witness says the man was in his mid-thirties and was well over six feet tall."

She wanted to know the man, wanted to find her son, and choked back tears as she shook her head.

"Look again, Morgan." Her father's voice jarred her further. "You must have seen him someplace."

She stared at the photo, studying the tight cheeks, the shoulders. The tattoo. Eyes that were…human. Trying to place them all. Running the image through her mental memory bank. A coach? A relative at the day care? Someone at the grocery store? The mall? Or the pizza place?

"I don't know him…." Her voice was only a thread—a thin thread—a testimony to the fragile hold she had on her composure. And as she turned and looked directly at her father, tears filled her eyes.

"I swear, Daddy, I don't know him. I wish to God I did."

Morgan glanced back at the freehand drawing. If that man…that fiend…had her son…

If he touched him…

Sammie could already have been—

No, he'd run away. He was fine. Just hiding from

her. And they'd find him. Sammie wasn't as grown up as he thought.

"What about an Amber Alert? Can you issue one of those now?" Did they have reasonable belief that Sammie had been abducted? If they issued an Amber Alert anyone who saw him would know that he was missing.

"We issued it half an hour ago."

Which meant they no longer thought Sammie had just run away.

The words struck a new chord of fear that Morgan couldn't ignore.

CHAPTER FIVE

Caleb knew long nights. He'd lived with them for most of his life. Which stood him in good stead over the next several hours as he stayed with the Lowens and Julie Warren and waited for news of Sammie's whereabouts.

He'd offered to stay. Morgan had accepted his offer immediately, with none of her usual assurances that she would be fine. He made coffee and small conversation when fatigue and panic threatened to get the best of the women. He sat quietly, a steady breath in the storm when detectives reported in or the phone rang.

And he studied Mr. Lowen with the outside eye of a scholar. Or so he told himself.

"I didn't realize George Lowen was your father," he said softly, sometime after ten that evening as Morgan accepted his invitation to step outside for some fresh air.

He'd thought the man heartless when, two years before, Lowen had bought up a block of real estate that included the city's oldest library and the complex that held the young artists' league studios and small gallery and tore it all down to replace it with a gated community of luxury condominiums. His perusal of

George Lowen over the past few hours hadn't softened his opinion of the business mogul much.

With her hands hugging her upper arms, Morgan shrugged. "We don't associate much."

He hadn't realized she had parents in the area until a few hours before.

"He's here tonight."

"Yeah."

Her expression blank, she gazed out into the darkness.

"You have to keep hoping, Morgan. Hope gives you the strength you need to take the next breath."

They were walking on the sidewalk in front of her place. While the curb was lined with cars—his, Julie's, her parents', and the detective's who'd replaced Elaine Martin and was going to sit with them through the night to monitor any possible contacts from kidnappers—the street was quiet. Searchers would resume looking for signs of the young boy at daylight.

And every hour that passed made it less likely that they'd be able to return Sammie safe and sound.

"It's so dark out."

"Is Sammie afraid of the dark?"

"No. It's just…I know that the first hours are critical…."

The first three hours were the most critical if Sammie had been kidnapped. Most child murders happened within three hours after abduction. Not that he was going to tell her that.

"You hear about children being taken, you know to keep your kids safe, and you do everything you can.

But still, it's one of those things—you just don't ever think it'll happen to you."

He'd never seen it that way. Or if he had, he'd been too young to remember a time when it felt like the world was a safe place for kids.

"Eight hundred thousand kids go missing each year in the United States. That's two thousand a day or one every forty seconds. But most are safely returned."

She stopped pacing in front of her house and faced him, studying him in the blackness. Light from the streetlamp shone on one side of her face, giving it a white hue that was almost sickly, and throwing the other side of her into shadow. But he could see the panic in her eyes.

"I… Are you sure you want to be here?"

"I can go if you'd like."

"No!" Her hand reached toward him and then hugged her arm again without ever making contact with him. "I… You can stay if you want. I just…I'm not sure why you'd want to. It's late. You have to be tired."

"I wouldn't sleep if I went home. I'd be thinking about you and your son. Wondering if you'd had any news."

"You don't even know Sammie. And I'm just a student…."

"It wouldn't matter to me if you were a stranger, Morgan, I'd still want to help if I could. But you are far from a stranger. I've been reading your essays for four years. I got to know you through them. And…

I've enjoyed our recent conversations. I'd like to help if I can."

"Don't you have someone at home waiting for you?" she asked, looking down the street in one direction and then the other before glancing back at him.

"A Mrs. Whittier, you mean?" Had she been hoping she'd see Sammie walking up the street toward them? He'd been looking for that very thing all night long.

"No, everyone knows you're single. But that doesn't mean you live alone."

"I live with my father. He knows where I am and why."

"Oh."

He'd never felt such an urge to talk. To share. And just as compelling was the reticence that had become a natural part of him.

"I...we...knew someone once. A woman in the town where we lived. Her child was taken. It's not something you ever forget."

"Did you know her well?"

Thinking of Rose Sanderson, of things the woman had done and said, he told the complete truth. "No."

"How old was her child?"

"Two." He wanted Morgan to know that she wasn't alone. That other people knew exactly what she was feeling.

"A boy or a girl?"

"A girl."

Her eyes filled with a painful mixture of compassion and fear and too late he knew what the next question was going to be.

"Did they find her?" Was the child returned safely to her mother's waiting arms?

"No." With a finger under Morgan's chin, he held her face gently aloft, looking her straight in the eye, and said, "Of those eight hundred thousand kids that go missing each year, only one hundred and fifteen of them are stranger abductions and less than a hundred of them are victims of homicide."

"Says who?"

"Washington, D.C.—the U.S. Department of Justice."

She looked at him—and kept looking—as though the connection of their gazes was holding her upright.

She wasn't Rose Sanderson. And this time he might be able to help.

TWELVE HOURS BEFORE, her greatest dream would definitely have included Caleb Whittier as a key player—in her home, with her.

Tonight he was included in her darkest nightmare. And her only dream was holding Sammie, safe and healthy, in her arms again. Her education didn't matter. The day care and Saturday's festivities were trivial. Nothing mattered if Sammie was gone.

Someone ordered pizza. The smell made Morgan sick to her stomach. Julie left, going home to be with her husband and twin daughters. Everything else stayed the same. Alarmingly the same.

Nothing was happening.

Until the phone rang just after midnight. Morgan's

body suffused with weakness even while her heart pounded so hard she could feel its beat.

"Wait," the detective on duty, Rick Warner, said, looking at her. The hand Morgan held suspended over the receiver, ready to pick up, was shaking. The call display flashed Unknown Caller.

"Remember what they told you, Morgan." George Lowen stood over her, having come in from the business papers he had strewn all over the kitchen table as soon as the phone pealed. "Keep them talking. Stay calm. Be agreeable..."

She tuned out the voice. She couldn't deal with her father and kidnappers at the same time.

"You'll do fine." Cal Whittier dropped quietly onto the couch next to her. Not touching her. Just there.

The detective nodded and Morgan picked up, the call broadcast to the room on a special speaker they'd hooked up. "Hello?"

"Your father killed my wife. I got your kid. Fair trade." Click.

She couldn't breathe. Couldn't move.

No one spoke at first, as the caller hung up far too soon for anyone to put a full trace on the call.

"What the hell?" George Lowen turned his back just as Grace came into the room. Morgan's mother had been lying down on Morgan's bed. Her usually immaculate, tastefully dyed brown hair was mussed. Her eyes were swollen, her lightweight navy slacks and white blouse wrinkled.

"Who was on the phone?"

Detective Warner spoke into a cell phone. And hung

up. Caleb Whittier took the receiver out of Morgan's grasp.

"The call came from a prepaid cell phone. No way to trace it," the detective said. "But they got the tower the signal came from. First and Main."

"Fifteen miles from here," George bit out.

"He's still in the area?" Hope shot through Morgan even while she was falling apart at the seams.

"We know the area the call came from," Detective Warner said softly, his brown eyes warm but tired looking. He didn't try to hide the graveness of the situation from her.

Morgan couldn't move. "He said he has Sammie."

"I know."

"So what do we do now?"

Those dark eyes were so hard to take. "We wait."

"We wait." How could her voice sound so calm when she was screaming inside? Seething with panic and dread and anger and fear and… "For what?"

"For him to call again." Detective Warner's voice was as calm as hers. Did the man also have feelings underneath? Things she couldn't see? Or was this all just another job to him? Did he know what his words were doing to her?

Did it matter?

"What about that tower?" George demanded, standing halfway across the room. "I want every inch of that area canvassed. I'll provide the resources. If you people can't man the search I'll hire someone who can."

Her father's autocratic tone cut through her—and gave her hope at the same time.

"It's a multiple base station site. The call likely came within a mile or two of the tower, but the range could extend as much as thirty miles or more, depending on the strength of the phone used. It's late at night so there are fewer transmissions going out, which means that range is wider."

Oh, God. is there no hope?

"Calls connect through to the closest tower."

So they could narrow the search dramatically?

"Not always. And that depends on the phone's operator, as well. Cars and alerts are already out, Mr. Lowen. Believe me, we've got every resource possible on this one."

"I want more."

"We're doing all we can."

"Then I'll do it myself." Her father's dismissive tone followed him out of the small living room.

Grace and Morgan exchanged looks but Morgan was no longer sure what they were saying to each other.

"You said we wait," Grace addressed Detective Warner, who was working at a card table set up along the front wall of the duplex. Morgan's mother was sitting in the armchair where earlier she'd gone through address files, making notes regarding run-ins her husband had had over the years.

George Lowen, when questioned by Detective Martin, had put his wife on that job.

And apparently Detective Martin had been right on cue, looking for people who had it in for Morgan's father. Now they could narrow the search more. To a male who'd lost a wife—and blamed her father.

"Right now this guy is in control," Detective Warner was saying. "Until we know more, we have to wait for the next call."

Caleb Whittier sat beside Morgan throughout the exchange. It was as though he was her hard drive, taking in everything and storing it in meticulous order for her to call upon later.

"What makes you think he's going to call back?" she asked Warner.

"Because it fits the profile. This man is out for revenge. One phone call isn't going to satisfy him."

Okay. There'd be another call. Another chance. She had to make it count.

"The next time he calls, you need to ask to speak to your son the second you pick up. This guy's playing with you. He's letting you know he's in charge. And now he's going to bait you. He's going to wait until he knows you're on the line, give you another one-liner and hang up."

"And then what?"

"Profiling suggests that he'll get around to asking for a ransom. Eventually. When he's satisfied that you've suffered enough. Or when the satisfaction of torturing you runs out. For now, the only chance for communication you're probably going to get is when you first pick up the call."

"So instead of saying hello, I ask to speak with Sammie."

"Right."

Foggy-headed from exhaustion and stress, Morgan studied the detective. "You think he'll let me talk to my son?"

"I doubt it. Not at this stage, in any case. He's not out to give you any comfort. Just the opposite, in fact. So we play on his need to make you and your family suffer by letting him hear how desperate you are to speak to your son."

"Why would she give this guy what he wants?" Grace asked.

"So he'll give us what *we* want, proof of Sammie's existence. He has to get pleasure out of giving us the information or we aren't going to get it."

Morgan's stomach threatened to give back what little she'd eaten. "What kind of proof?"

"He'll call back with a tape recording, maybe. Or a description of Sammie's clothing. The idea is to keep him calling back. Every time we get him on the line we have that much more chance of pinpointing where he's calling from. And every bit of communication gives us more clues to go on in helping us figure out who this guy is."

"You said he'd be calling back, anyway."

"That's right and we want to take control of his plan."

She nodded. And would do exactly as she was told.

She wanted to ask what the chances were that Sammie was still alive. Wanted to ask Detective Warner his professional opinion regarding her chances of ever seeing her son again.

Not trusting her ability to handle the answer, she withheld the question.

They'd had the dreaded call. Sammie wasn't just a runaway. He'd been kidnapped.

CHAPTER SIX

"Do you mind if I sit outside on the front step for a few minutes?" Morgan directed her question to the detective sitting at his makeshift desk. Cal watched her, taking in the whiteness around her too-tight lips, the glossiness in eyes that normally glinted with eagerness, the strands of hair surrounding skin that had been devoid of makeup since she'd first cried it off more than twelve hours before.

He recognized the signs of a woman at the end of her rope. He'd watched the same thing happen to Rose Sanderson when she'd transformed from his future mother to the stranger who'd thrown him and his father out of their home.

"If my phone rings, I'll come back in...."

"Stay close." Detective Warner's tone held warning more than acquiescence.

Morgan nodded and stood. Unlike the last couple of times she'd left the room for some fresh air, she didn't glance at Cal. Didn't invite him along.

On a hunch, he went anyway.

And was glad he had as soon as he stepped out the door and saw his star student bent over, one side of her propped against the corner of the building as she sobbed.

It was the first time he'd seen her lose control all day. There'd been tears, plenty of them, but they'd been slow, silent drips down her cheeks, not this full-out explosion of anguish.

Cal went to her, pulled her away from the building and against him, half carrying her over to the steps and settling her against his body as they sat. He didn't say anything. There were no words that could help. Nothing anyone could do to ease the pain that was eating her alive, short of returning her son to her.

But he could share the pain with her. It helped not to suffer alone. That much he understood.

He didn't take it personally when she turned her face into his chest. Or when her hands worked their way around his neck and clung to him. He held her. Stroked her hair.

And cried inside—a little boy manifested into a man who'd outgrown the ability to shed tears.

"They're hurting him, aren't they?" Her words, muffled against his chest, were completely clear to him.

Cal had no sense of how much time had passed. His arms didn't loosen their grip on the body he held. "We don't know that."

"But…" A dry sob interrupted her. "If his goal is to torture us…"

Wanting to tell her not to let him win, not to torture herself with what-ifs, Cal said instead, "We don't know his ultimate goal." He'd read everything he'd ever found written about child abductions. He knew the profiling as well as any detective.

"And we don't know who we're dealing with. Some

people just aren't killers, no matter what life has done to them. They just don't have it in them to hurt someone else physically. So they retaliate with mental and emotional abuse." He wasn't educating her. He was just talking in case hearing another voice made her situation better. He wasn't even sure she could comprehend what he was saying at that point. Or that it mattered.

"If his ultimate goal is ransom, as is probable, chances are good that he won't do anything to hurt Sammie. At least not until he's made his deal."

He had to be honest with her here.

"And chances are also good that the authorities will catch the guy before he gets to close his deal.

"Less than one hundred out of eight hundred thousand abducted children die each year," he reminded her. "Sammie's chances are very, very good. More than 99 percent."

"But the girl you knew about—she had those same chances."

"Which is why I've always believed that she's still alive."

Morgan's breathing slowed. She pulled back slowly, dropping her arms, sitting up on her own. Hands wrapped around her stomach, she stared downward.

"Do you know how many kids are taken that aren't found dead, but are never seen by their parents again?"

"The less than one hundred that are killed includes those that are assumed dead."

Which, technically, included Claire Sanderson. She was one of the less than 1 percent who weren't safely returned. But... "In the case I knew about, they never had contact from the kidnapper," he told her. "There were no calls. Nothing for them to go on."

Except a young boy's testimony that he'd seen the little girl in his father's car earlier that morning. And the child's teddy bear, which had been with her the last time anyone had seen her, had turned up in Frank's car later that day.

"They focused the investigation on one man. They weren't ever able to find enough evidence against him to press charges. And in the meantime, whatever other clues might have been there had grown cold and whoever took the little girl got away with the crime."

"Did the family have money?"

"Enough to be comfortable. Nothing comparable to your father."

But he and Emma and Claire had had everything a kid could want. And then some. They'd had a close, loving, happy family. At least for a while.

"As I recall, there wasn't ever much talk about ransom calls," he added, for her sake—and because for the first time in his life he was talking about the incident that had sealed his fate in a world filled with inner darkness. "The girl was only two. She wasn't like Sammie, able to fend for herself, or to understand that she'd been abducted. And sick people don't take two-year-old girls from middle-class neighborhoods in hopes of ransom money."

He couldn't go any further than that. Couldn't let his mind travel down the road that Claire Sanderson had probably had to travel. He couldn't save her from a twenty-five-year-old fate.

Perusing child pornography photos was one job he'd left solely up to the authorities. But the fact that there was no evidence that Claire was taken for that sordid lifestyle didn't ease his emotional burden any. There'd been no internet twenty-five years before. No global access to illegal practices. No way to find most of the scumbags who practiced or made money from under-age sex.

"Dr. Whittier—"

"Cal," he interrupted. "I'm not here as your college professor, and as we established last spring, there's only three years' difference between us…." His voice faded off. What in the hell did names or ages matter?

"Cal, then," Morgan said. "I just wanted to thank you." She drew a deep breath. "For being here. It helps."

He nodded, in spite of the darkness that probably prevented her from knowing that. "Julie offered to stay." Her friend had left hours earlier to go home and put her twin five-year-olds to bed.

Morgan rubbed a hand down her face just as he'd seen her do countless times over the past hours. "I know," she said. "But she's like the rest of us here, shocked and hurting and…besides, I think she needed to be with her kids. To hang on to them."

"I'm sure she did." Like Rose had clung to Emma, frantic to keep the four-year-old in sight at all times. Cal hadn't even had a chance to say goodbye to the girl he'd loved as his little sister.

He glanced around the dark and too-quiet neighborhood. "I'm pretty certain all the parents around here are keeping a close hold on their children tonight.

Thanking the Lord that they're home. And they're probably also scared to death that whoever took Sammie could come for their kids next."

Up, down, up, down, up, down. He could feel the rhythm of her knee's movement.

"They'll be relieved to know that Sammie was scouted out specifically. That this is someone after my father, not some sicko after kids." Shoulders hunched, she shuddered.

"Maybe. I figure the heads-up that children really are at risk of abduction will stick with most of them for a long time to come. You can't witness something like this, even peripherally, and go back. You don't ever become unaware again."

"You really understand...."

"Some things you don't ever forget."

"How long ago was that little girl taken?"

"Twenty-five years."

"What?" She sat up, turned to him. "She's been missing for twenty-five years? With no trace of her at all?"

"That's right."

"You had to have been just a kid then!"

"I was seven."

"And yet you remember..."

"Like it was yesterday. I...knew the little girl. Her mother worked with my father." He spoke slowly, choosing his way carefully. Like each word landed on a minefield and risked imminent explosion.

Rose and Frank had met at an educators' conference. She'd been an elementary schoolteacher, while

Frank was a high school principal and basketball coach. A match made in heaven.

Or could have been.

"Where did this happen? Here in Tyler?"

"No." She seemed to be waiting for more. "It was in Massachusetts." He was saying too much.

"What happened to the parents? Are they still there?"

"I have no idea where they are." Claire's father was dead. A shady man from the docks who'd run off when he'd found out that Rose was pregnant with Claire. Sanderson, Sr., had died in a bar brawl less than a year later, killed by the husband of the woman he'd just bedded.

And Rose? He didn't want to know. "We moved away shortly after that and all we knew was what was on the news, which wasn't much."

"But you know she wasn't found."

"I was an impressionable kid. The incident stuck with me. I still periodically check the missing-persons database."

"You don't ever go back to a state of unawareness."

She understood. And in a strange way, on a night when his only purpose was to give a measure of support, he'd found a moment of peace.

"When I get Sammie back...he won't... I... Neither of us will ever be able to go back. We'll be different."

"Yes, but different might be better, too." He knew with all of his being that she had to think that. Had to believe. To hope.

"Julie said something this morning shortly after I

got to school. She apologized for not watching over Sammie more closely. She felt so guilty. And so do I. It's my job to protect my son. And I didn't. How can he ever forgive me?"

"Hey." He nudged her arm, wanting to take her hand, but not doing so. "You have absolutely nothing to feel guilty about." Guilt ate a body alive with insidious tenacity. "Your son was at school right where he belonged. You aren't allowed to be there babysitting him even if you wanted to."

"My son left class." Her voice had dropped an octave. "He misbehaved and put himself in harm's way and that is my fault. I'm the only one in charge of teaching him. Training him. I try so hard but he butts heads with me on a constant basis. Probably because he doesn't have a father around and that's my fault, too."

Cal debated his response in terms of being kind to her. And then spoke. "He left class, with permission, to use the restroom. That's all you know. The kidnapper has it in for your father. He obviously planned this whole thing. He didn't just happen to be in the right place at the exact time that Sammie misbehaved. And while Sammie doesn't have a father, you've been discussing things with me, getting male perspective and allowing Sammie some freedoms based on our conversations."

Her silence gave him pause. He sure as hell hoped he hadn't made things more difficult for her.

"You think this...this monster was watching Sammie? That he'd have taken him, anyway, the first chance he saw?" Her leg bounced up and down. Continuously. Getting faster.

"Probably."

"I keep a close eye on him. As you know, that's part of what he complains about."

"You obviously do a great job if this guy thought his best chance of getting to your son was while Sammie was in a secure school situation being watched over by trained professionals."

The bouncing stopped. She rocked forward. And back. And then forward again.

"Sammie says I don't let him grow up and be a man, but this is why…" Her voice broke with the threat of more tears. "I'm so sorry," she said on a sigh. "I'm losing it here."

"You have absolutely nothing to be sorry about and you are not losing it. As a matter of fact you've held up astonishingly well, considering. This is the first time I've seen you really cry."

"It's not something I do in front of my father." She sounded stronger again.

"In front of your father? You're kidding." He said the words, and yet, thinking of the man inside the door behind them, what she'd told him made sense.

"From the time I was little I learned to hold back my tears around him," she said softly. "Crying pisses him off. He says it's a tactic females use to try to control men. It's a sign of weakness. Of victimization rather than accountability."

The guy was a first-class bastard.

But he was there. Insisting that mountains would

move and his grandson would be brought home to them. From what Cal had seen, George Lowen was willing to get out there and move the mountains himself if need be.

"I must respectfully disagree. Crying is normal. Healthy. And part of being human."

"When's the last time you cried?"

He didn't answer, knowing that his silence was an answer in itself.

"You just said it's part of being human."

He wasn't surprised that she'd called him on the inconsistency.

"Which is why I've always envied people who could cry," Cal said, the night, the circumstance, putting him in strange territory, making him a stranger to himself.

This night, these circumstances—it wasn't real life.

It was a snippet of time outside of ordinary living. An anomaly that would seem surreal once Morgan's son was home safe and sound.

"So why don't you cry?"

"I'm not sure. It's not like I sit around and try," he said, giving her a sideways glance, glad he seemed to be distracting her. She was listening so he continued. "Might have something to do with the fact that I never knew my mother. She died when I was six months old."

"That's horrible! What happened?"

"She taught a program for accelerated students and was on an oceanography field trip. She went into the water at night with a couple of other teachers, on an ocean life study, and she and another teacher got tangled in the reef and drowned."

"I'm so sorry! That's awful."

For his father it had been. Cal didn't have any memories of her at all. But he missed knowing a mother—her absence had made him particularly eager to accept and return Rose Sanderson's motherly care.

"Do you have brothers and sisters?"

"Nope. It's just me and Dad."

"He never remarried?"

"No."

"So you went into teaching because of her? Because of your mother?"

It wasn't that simple. "I teach because I enjoy it." And because his father—who'd lost his prestigious career in education because of something Cal had told the police that had incriminated an innocent man—lived vicariously through him.

"You're sure good at it."

Before he could say more and risk crossing the boundaries between teacher and student and professionalism, the receiver in her hand pealed, splintering the quiet of the night.

CHAPTER SEVEN

"PLEASE...LET ME SPEAK to my son...." Morgan's voice broke as she started to cry, something she couldn't help in spite of her father standing over her as she answered the phone.

Cal was there, too, somewhere behind her in the living room. Her knees were weak and wobbly as she stood at the card table, watching Detective Warner's face.

He nodded, mouthed that she was doing fine, and then the voice that she recognized from earlier that night—a voice she somehow knew was going to live within her forever—spoke again.

"Good, you're begging for the life of your loved one. Just like I did."

Click.

Morgan's stomach felt like lead as Detective Warner listened to the earbud that connected him to his people and then shook his head.

"They got the tower," he announced. "A different one. It's forty miles away."

"He's moving," George Lowen said.

"Or his cell phone provider has good range and other towers had conflicting signals," Grace said from the doorway leading into the bedrooms. "You heard

what he said earlier, George, depending on cell pro-
viders—"

"It's the middle of the night," George interrupted,
his impatience evident in spite of the soft tone he used
to address his wife. "There can't be that much business
out there. He's moving south." George left the room,
cell phone to his ear, barking orders to someone to get
cars on every road going south out of Tyler.

Cal Whittier was behind her, a steady presence, and
still Morgan struggled to maintain composure as panic
surged through her. She looked at Detective Warner.

"We've got officers combing south, as well, Ms.
Lowen. And we've notified law enforcement within
a six-state radius. The Amber Alert has gone out na-
tionally. We'll find him."

She nodded. "You have to bring him home to me.
You have to."

"We will, ma'am."

She wanted to believe him.

ANOTHER CALL CAME in an hour later.

"Your son is crying for you." Click.

Looking helplessly at Detective Warner, Morgan
was crying, too.

BY 6:00 A.M. Morgan had fielded a total of five calls
originating from towers on a southward route. Sometime in the small hours of the morning another detective, a woman, had shown up, offering to relieve
Detective Warner. He'd declined.

George had spent the night in the kitchen, except

for the occasional trek into the living room to confer with Rick Warner or to witness a phone call.

"I've got half a million sitting in wait," he told Warner just after six. "I can put my hands on another two and a half by noon."

The look of relief on Morgan's face was palpable—as if that money sitting out there would ensure her son's safe return, when, in fact, there hadn't been a single request for ransom.

Only a slow and cruel torture of a beautiful young woman whose biggest sin, as far as Cal could see, was allowing herself to believe that she was in any way to blame for her son's abduction.

"I've arranged for a press release at seven," George continued, the more pronounced lines on his face the only visible sign of having spent a sleepless night. He'd shed his jacket at some point. Cal had seen it draped over the back of a kitchen chair when he'd made a trip to the bathroom. And the knot of Lowen's tie was a little loose, but neatly so. His black wingtips still glistened as though they'd been freshly polished and the obviously expensive slacks bore few wrinkles. "I'm going to be offering a million-dollar cash reward to anyone who provides the information that brings my grandson home."

Detective Warner stood. "Let me talk to my captain," he said. "As you know from our conversation last night, he's planning to go to the press in a few hours. We can't stop you from making your own announcement, but I know he's going to want you to coordinate the press release with the department. We're trained to deal with these types and know the things to say that get the best response the most times. And regardless of that, it would be best for us to make a joint statement—puts more pressure on the perp if he knows we've joined forces—and the captain's going to insist that you run the responses through us. Anything else will jeopardize our investigation and potentially put your grandson in more harm."

Cal stood next to Morgan, whose weary gaze moved between her father and the detective with whom they'd all spent the night. She turned to Cal and he lowered his head to catch her whispered, "This is so my father, and I hate it. What if his high-handedness makes things worse? But I'm grateful, too. Am I nuts?"

"No. He's out of line. But if he gets results, then he's doing the right thing."

Grace, having come in from the bedroom each time the phone rang, raised her head from the back of the chair to follow her husband's exchange.

"Tell your captain that I'll agree to a joint conference if your people can be ready at seven. And he cannot insist on anything. However, if you can have a contact response team ready to begin receiving calls within the hour, and will agree to let my representatives be privy to each and every response as well, I will agree to sending all possible leads to the care of the police. We realize the offer of a reward will bring out false leads and we'll need the manpower to follow each of them until we can weed them out. I want my grandson back."

Warner nodded and reached for the cell phone he'd been using all night to confer with his team.

"And tell him that I will make available to him any monies he needs to get this done," George added, leaving the room without a glance at his daughter.

He motioned for Grace to join him, though, and with a quick squeeze of Morgan's shoulder as she passed them, the older woman followed her husband from the room.

Morgan's lips and chin were trembling and Cal knew that unless Sammie Lowen was found safe and sound, this was one of life's pains that would not get better with time.

DETECTIVE RAMSEY MILLER from the Comfort Cove Police Department in Comfort Cove, Massachusetts, didn't believe in anything as certain as fate. Spending his days and nights viewing gruesome details of crime scenes had taught him one thing for certain—life was a crap shoot. Sometimes the bad guys got it. Sometimes the good guys did.

And sometimes a guy just happened to be at the right place at the right time. Since his divorce he'd taken to drinking his morning coffee in bed, reading national and local news via the laptop computer that was always either on his nightstand or, if he'd fallen asleep while working, sharing the covers with him.

The thing about internet news sources was that they were so plentiful he was never without company, even if it meant that he was reading about an Issaquah couple caught having sex in their car. This time on the fifth floor of a Park and Ride. It was news to someone. And as long as there was internet and people to talk about, there would never be a time, no matter how late in the night or early in the morning, when he would have to settle for his own thoughts.

The second Saturday morning in July was when he was the lucky guy who ended up in the right place at the right time. He'd taken an extra hour in bed to surf other people's troubles instead of working on the pile of unanswered questions waiting for him on his own desk. Sort of.

He'd been perusing a local news site from Tyler, Tennessee, but he hadn't been there just randomly. He'd chosen the town because he was trying to reach a man there who wasn't returning his calls. Caleb Whittier. The guy worked as a professor at the university there, he'd discovered from tax returns. He needed some answers from Whittier so he could lessen the pile on his desk and instead all he was getting were more questions.

That was until he got lucky.

A kid was missing from Tyler—which wasn't lucky. He'd seen the Amber Alert go out because he was on the internet looking at Tyler news. He'd called Lucy Hayes immediately. He and the detective from Aurora, Indiana, were long-distance compatriots—they'd both, for different reasons, dedicated their lives to missing children.

And then a live video feed flashed on his screen. Pursuant to the missing child. It was a press conference that was taking place. Ramsey clicked.

The kid hadn't been found. Damn.

And more bad news—the kid was the grandson of some local millionaire who was offering half a mil in reward money.

If Sammie Lowen had been kidnapped for ransom, chances were his family wouldn't see him alive again. Of course, there were other reasons kids were snatched that weren't any better. He'd hoped the kid had just run away. He was ten, after all.

And Ramsey had his right-place-right-time moment.

There on the screen. The guy standing behind the mother of the missing boy—his image was also on the file on top of the stack waiting for him at work. Granted, the photo on Ramsey's desk had been gleaned from the department of motor vehicles, a driver's license shot, but he was certain that he was looking at Dr. Caleb Whittier. A grown-up version of the seven-year-old boy whose photo was also in the file.

Sitting up straight, Ramsey held the portable computer with both hands and stared. He still had questions. Just different ones.

Like, why was a man who, as a boy, had been involved in a missing-child case, involved in another missing-child case as an adult?

Whittier had only been seven when the two-year-old daughter of his father's fiancée had gone missing. The boy could hardly have been a mastermind child abductor at that point.

He watched the rest of the video. The kid's mother never spoke. She just stood behind the grandfather and Captain Dennison, who was representing Tyler law enforcement, with an older woman Ramsey assumed was her mother. Caleb Whittier was farther back than they were, probably unaware that he was on camera. Others were with him. Neighbors, maybe.

And maybe that's all he was. Maybe there was no connection to him and the missing boy at all. Maybe he'd never even met the kid.

But there was definitely a coincidence here.

And to Ramsey Miller a coincidence was like a toothache. It bugged him until he did something about it.

"YOU REALLY DON'T have to stay." Morgan found herself alone in her living room with Cal Whittier after the press conference Saturday morning. "You haven't slept at all."

"Neither have you."

"He's my son. My mind isn't going to relax enough to allow me to sleep." Detectives Warner and Martin and Captain Dennison were in the kitchen conferring. Her father and mother had left to shower and change and would be back within the half hour. Detective Martin had suggested that Morgan call her doctor and request a sleep aid, but she wasn't planning to heed that particular piece of advice. At least not for the next twenty-four hours.

"I'll go if it will make it easier on you."

They were sitting on opposite ends of her couch. "No!" The volume of her emission embarrassed her. "You've…helped. I just don't want you to think you have to stay. I'll be fine."

She didn't want him to leave. Ever.

And that wasn't fair to him. Or right.

Cai Whittier owed her nothing. And had no idea she'd had a crush on him for years.

"You aren't fine," he said, his gaze so understanding Morgan almost broke down again. "But I'd like to stay. At least until you've seen the fallout from the press conference."

"You've been on the phone several times. I figured you had something going on and…"

"My dad asked me to keep him up to date."

Hearing that a perfect stranger cared threatened her composure all over again. Strangers came to your aid when things were really bad.

And the world really did have good in it because strangers came to your aid.

Her thoughts rolled around one another, presenting themselves and then rolling off again. She couldn't focus. She could only feel.

And other than an inexplicable sense of comfort from having her college professor sitting with her, Morgan felt nothing but out-of-control bad.

HALF AN HOUR LATER Morgan was thirty minutes closer to flying out of her skin. Her parents were back. Grace was frying bacon in the kitchen. The smell nauseated Morgan. George sat at the dining room table with a phone to his ear, whether on one conversation or many, she had no idea. Every man he had out looking for Sammie was to report to him directly. He had charts and maps and was keeping a detailed account of every move everyone made.

Her phone hadn't rung since the press conference an hour and a half before.

Was this the fallout, then? Nothing? This man who had Sammie really didn't want money? He only wanted to make them suffer as he had? To hurt as he had?

His wife was dead.

What did that mean for Sammie?

Her stomach swarmed, her joints felt too weak to support her, and Morgan had to fight not to give in to the thick cottony fog encasing her mind. She had to stay coherent. To believe in Sammie. For Sammie.

"You said your dad lives with you."

Caleb Whittier stood at the living room window, watching the street. He was looking out for her and she knew she was never, ever going to forget this man.

The crush she'd had on him in class seemed so menial now. The man had become her angel, holding her suspended just slightly above a hell that would burn her to ashes in seconds were she to fall.

"That's right, he does." Cal turned around, his face darkened with stubble, his eyes slightly puffy from lack of sleep, and still his smile was warm and nurturing and filled with a peculiar understanding—as though he not only saw her but felt her, too.

"Does he work?"

"Yes, but he's on vacation this week."

For years she'd wanted to know more about this private man who was so generous with his time and advice. And right now, she could hardly focus on his words.

"On vacation? So he's not at home?" She'd thought his father was at home. That Cal had called to tell his father he wouldn't be home. But maybe she was wrong. The night before was a bit of a haze to her right now.

"He's at home. His fishing trip was…canceled."

Something about the way he said the word was a little different. Morgan couldn't bring forth the effort to be curious. She nodded. "Where does he work?"

"Green Pastures."

"The nursing home?"

"Yes."

"Is he a doctor?" No, wait, they visited nursing homes; they weren't usually on staff there. Were they? Did Sammie need a doctor? Was there still time for a doctor to help him…?

"No, my father is a janitor."

A janitor? She looked at him. Had she heard him right? Cal was so…genteel. So self-possessed. Like he'd been raised in wealth. She'd just assumed he was like her.

"Did you grow up here in Tyler?"

"No."

His responses weren't eliciting any invitation to continue the interrogation, but Morgan didn't stop. He was special to her. She needed to know him better. Knowing him meant that Sammie was okay. No, getting to know him better helped take her mind off the possible torture her son was experiencing. The fright he had to be experiencing. If he was still…

"Where, then?" she blurted.

"We moved around a lot."

"But you got a good education." Obviously. He was a college professor at thirty-two.

"My father was a teacher. He made certain that I had all the schooling I could get."

Oh. "So he's retired?" That made more sense. The elder Whittier was supplementing teacher's retirement.

Cal shrugged, and a car drove past out front but didn't stop and sent a sharp stab of fear through her. Oh, God. Sammie...

"Have you ever been married?" She pushed the words out quickly and too loud, sounding half-crazed. Which was better than she felt.

"No."

There was another car out there somewhere. One that had had Sammie in it. Could still have her son bound and gagged and...alive? Please, please. Alive.

"You and your dad have always lived together?" The question ended on a high note. A prelude to tears.

She felt Cal's approach. She couldn't look at him anymore. Couldn't look at the window. "Yes, we've always lived together." His words, filled with compassion, were just above the back of her neck and when he touched her, gently pulled her into his arms, Morgan fell apart.

CHAPTER EIGHT

GEORGE WAS ON the phone throughout breakfast. The man's tone was a bit too curt for Cal, but there was no doubting that Morgan's father cared deeply about finding her son. He was not taking no for an answer. From anyone. To the point of being in denial of any outcome but the one he ordained.

"Here, Cal, have more bacon." Grace handed him an inexpensive but colorful serving plate filled with what looked to be a pound of meat left on it. The bowl of lightly fluffed scrambled eggs and plate of home-fried potatoes were equally laden. George was the only one of the five of them sitting there who'd eaten his share.

Cal took bacon he didn't want.

"Detective Warner?"

The uniformed man who'd been ordered by his captain to go home and shave and get some rest took some more bacon as well, in spite of the untouched piece still on his plate.

"Are you going to be in trouble for staying?" Grace asked the man.

"Captain's a good guy. He'll get over it," he said, adding, "and I'll go home and shower. I just wanted to wait a bit longer with the press conference and all."

Grace put a piece of bacon on Morgan's plate. She

didn't seem to notice. Her gaze traveled from speaker to speaker, as though she was following the conversation, but Cal didn't believe she could have repeated a word that had been spoken since her mother had called them in from the living room to eat.

She'd dried her eyes before her father saw her tears. She'd stiffened her spine—and her features—and she'd taken her place at the table like a dutiful daughter. Cal admired her strength. Her determination. And he worried about her, too. She was on the verge of collapse and neither of her parents seemed to recognize that fact.

"This is good, Mrs. Lowen, thanks," Cal said, thinking about a happier Morgan choosing the dishes with primary-colored flowers all over them. Trying to picture her in the store, making her choices. Had Sammie been with her?

When he started to picture himself there, watching her deliberate, he caught himself. He was more tired than he'd thought.

George's voice droned on. Cal leaned over to the fragile woman sitting up so regally beside him. "You need to eat some of that, not just play table hockey with it," he said softly. "Without sleep that food is your only source of energy…."

He couldn't promise her that Sammie would be walking in the door needing things from her that she had to be able to give. He didn't want to tell her she had to be strong—he had an idea she'd been hearing that one all of her life. He just told her like it was.

She glanced at him for a long moment. Cal studied

those weary brown eyes and would have given much to be able to give her every bit of energy he'd ever had.

She ate a forkful of egg. And then another. And…

"We've got him." The words were staccato—more so than usual. George's intense look was focused, not on his daughter, or his wife, but on the detective seated opposite Cal and Morgan at the table for six in her small dining room.

Warner stood. Without asking he grabbed the phone from George Lowen. George didn't hesitate to turn it over.

"This is Detective Rick Warner from the Tyler Police Department," he said. "I'm here with the Lowens. What have you got?"

As the man listened, an intent look on his face, Cal reached for Morgan's hand under the table. She grabbed hold, clutching him so tightly her fingernails dug into his palm. He barely felt the pain. He was that glad to be there for her.

He prayed that the news would be good. Over and over he prayed. Forgetting that praying was something he hadn't done since he was seven years old.

He'd stopped because praying didn't work.

MORGAN COULD HARDLY stand the waiting. "I should have gone with them," she said for the tenth or so time. Cal came up behind her as she stood at the living room window, staring out into the early-afternoon sunshine. He rubbed her shoulders, his hands warm and alive and keeping her blood flowing.

"They weren't going to take you, Morgan, even if you'd insisted on going."

He'd patiently repeated his response every single one of the times she'd voiced the thought that continued to race through her mind.

Detective Warner had explained it all to her. They didn't know for sure if the guy her father's men had found was the one making the phone calls. They were reasonably sure, by some means that probably wasn't legal, but they weren't positive. Even if it was the guy, they had no proof that he really had Sammie. He'd never let her talk to the boy or given an indication that he had Sammie with him. He'd never asked for anything in exchange for the boy.

And if he had Sammie, and Sammie saw her and reacted, she could be putting his life in danger.

"Still, I should be there. He's going to need me."

"He needs to be brought safely out of the situation and then he'll be brought straight to you."

She nodded. He was right. They'd been over this two hours earlier when her father's phone call had ended the most excruciating breakfast of her life. Her mom and dad had gone home to rest while the detectives went in for the man George's team suspected had Sammie. Detective Martin was going to contact her father the minute they got the guy.

Cal had opted to stay with Morgan. Maybe it was weird, having her college professor be such a good friend all of a sudden. But with his past, his understanding, it felt right. Besides, right now she couldn't take being around anyone else who was emotionally attached to Sammie. She needed an outsider—some-one who could hold it together and be strong for all of them. Just in case…

No. No just in case.

"He's going to want macaroni and cheese for din-ner," she said. "I'm not sure I have any."

"You do." Cal continued to rub. "You checked an hour ago."

He was right. She had.

Detective Martin was in the dining room, having set up shop on the table her father had vacated. Giv-ing Morgan some space while she waited. And man-ning the phone.

The suspect didn't know they were on to him. He'd called twice more since breakfast. Both times exactly the same as before. Short. Cruel. And then gone.

"You really need to get some rest," she said now. She'd changed yesterday's jeans for a fresh pair. Changed her top for another short-sleeved pullover. And washed her face.

"I will. As soon as this is done. I can sleep all day tomorrow."

Right. Hopefully she and Sammie would be able to sleep, as well. As long as her ten-year-old would consent to sleeping in the same room with her like he'd done when he was little. Before he'd gotten the idea that sleeping in the same bed as your mom was for sissies.

If he wouldn't consent she'd stay away until he was asleep and then camp out on his floor beside his bed.

"Julie sounded like she hadn't slept all night." She'd

called her friend before the press conference, just to let her know it was going to air, and then again after arrangements were made for a team of local area detectives to meet with her father's men, to close in on the motel in southern Alabama where they were pretty sure the man who'd been making calls to her was staying. The Tyler police wanted someone with local jurisdiction on-site to make the arrest.

"She probably didn't."

"It's hard talking to her." She didn't blame Julie for what had happened. But Julie seemed to blame herself.

"There's no way to control the emotions that attack you when a child goes missing." Cal's voice was soft. Calm. "And no way to predict them, either."

"I know it's not her fault," Morgan said, still staring outside. She felt closer to Sammie when she was looking out the window. He was out there. Somewhere. "She's the office administrator at the school. Watching the kids isn't her job."

But there was a screen in the principal's office. A monitor showing the halls and bathrooms—identical to the one in the office of the school security guard.

Julie could see the principal's monitor.

"That doesn't stop someone from feeling like there's something he or she could have done."

Maybe that's why Cal's presence was such a godsend. When it came to missing kids he seemed to know so much.

And the comfort she took from his presence stemmed from more than just his knowledge. The detectives could have given her statistics.

Cal gave her something far more personal—something she had no business taking from him because he had no idea she was taking it.

"I think it's more than that." She couldn't believe she was saying this. That she was allowing herself to think it about her friend. "I don't blame her, but I can't help wondering what would have happened if she'd been watching when Sammie went to the bathroom. If she'd seen him walking down the hall, she'd have noticed when he didn't come back. And then we'd have known to look for him before he had a chance to get away."

"The what-ifs are unavoidable, Morgan. They're a natural human response."

She hoped so and turned to tell him so. He was unshaven. Unwashed. His shirt and slacks were wrinkled and his eyes were red-rimmed. And he looked so... right. So strong and capable and reliable.

"I—"

The phone rang. Detective Martin's line, not hers. Morgan froze for a split second.

And then she ran.

Cal stood in the archway between the living room and the dining area just behind Morgan.

"Okay," the redheaded detective, dressed in brown slacks, a blouse and matching tweed jacket, said for the fourth time. And then, "You're sure?"

There was no expression on her face and, taking that to be a bad thing, Cal moved a little closer to Morgan, pulled out a chair and helped her to sit.

Martin hung up the phone.

"They got him," she said, looking Morgan straight in the eye.

"And?" His student's voice held none of the life he heard in his classroom. Her question was anticipatory, but her tone was deadpan. He hardly recognized it.

"Derek Gunder was in the hotel room, just as suspected. There was no sign of Sammie."

"So maybe he wasn't the one. Obviously Daddy's men were wrong."

The detective was shaking her head even before Morgan finished. "Gunder admitted to making the phone calls. He had identification on him. And he was on the list of people who could be out to get your father that your mother provided. Gunder's wife was fired from one of your father's investment companies—a data collection company where she was an office supervisor—for excessive absence."

The older woman's voice was even, her facial features straight and unchanging. "Turns out she was terminally ill but hadn't said so, because she was afraid that if the company knew she was dying she'd lose her job, and her husband was out of work. She hadn't figured on being fired, but when she was, she lost her insurance and didn't qualify for a new treatment that might have saved her life. Gunder sued your dad, but lost the lawsuit because his wife had not been honest about her illness. The guy swears he never had Sammie. He only found out Sammie was missing when he saw the Amber Alert. That's when he started making the calls. They were strictly to get back at your father for, what he considers, killing his wife."

"He's lying. He has to have Sammie. Why would he admit to kidnapping if no one can prove anything yet?" Morgan's tone was tremulous now. And angry. The second stage of grief, or so several of the many counselors Cal had contacted on behalf of his father had told him. Anger followed denial.

Detective Martin covered Morgan's fidgeting hand on the table. "They're still investigating, Morgan, but it looks like this guy is telling the truth. He was at work yesterday when Sammie was kidnapped. He worked all day and then was seen in a restaurant, eating dinner. A gas station attendant saw him after midnight, on a southbound exit, and he was traveling alone."

"Sammie could have been in the trunk or—"

"They checked his car and there was no sign of your son. Or of any kind of struggle. No body fluids. The crime lab's going for the car, checking for fingerprints, among other things, but it's only a formality at this point. It's pretty clear this is not our guy."

"Then…" Cal felt his throat tighten as Morgan's sentence fell off and her shoulders started to shake. She couldn't take much more of this.

And she could be facing a lifetime of it.

He'd never felt so helpless.

Watching his star pupil, watching the woman who'd become more than a pupil to him, Cal Whittier's life altered course.

For the first time since he was seven years old he

had a glimpse of understanding into the cruel actions—the *reactions*—of Rose Sanderson.

For the first time since he was seven years old, he felt an ounce of forgiveness.

CHAPTER NINE

SOMETIME IN THE EARLY afternoon on Saturday numbness set in. Morgan had finally agreed to lie down for a bit. But only on the couch. She'd tried her room, but hadn't been able to stay put. She'd spent a few minutes in Sammie's room, too, but being surrounded by his things, by the feel of him, only brought tears.

The couch had brought some physical relief to a body that was aching with tension and fatigue, but her mind still had not allowed her the bliss of unconsciousness. She'd doze, only to wake herself up immediately with attacks of fear. If she let go, left her vigil for one second, Sammie might give up, too. She had to send him strength every single second, to stay tuned in on the only level she could right now, a soul-deep level, a mother/child level. She had to help him hold on.

She'd kept her eyes closed, though, for the sake of anyone who might be looking in on her. Cal was still there, but he'd finally given in and fallen asleep in the reclining chair adjacent to the couch.

Detective Martin was in the other room doing whatever a detective did while waiting for word. The Tyler Police Department was still canvassing the neighborhood where Sammie had been seen last. They were still looking for the man her son had been seen talking to. They were setting up larger-scale searches of the area and already had dogs out.

She'd wanted to join them. Needed to be out there looking. Her job, she'd been told, was to stay home in case someone tried to contact her. They wanted her voice on the other end of the line. It was when Elaine Martin had mentioned that they might put Sammie on the line that she'd agreed to do as they'd ask and stay put.

At the moment, staying put was the hardest thing she'd ever done.

Hearing a rustle, Morgan opened her eyes to see Detective Martin in the archway from the dining room, her phone suspended in her hand. She'd said she was putting the ringer on silent when Morgan had agreed to lie down.

"They found the guy who was speaking with your son," Elaine said. Morgan flew off the couch as the clank of the recliner lowering sounded. "He says Sammie was asking him directions to the bus depot," the detective continued as Morgan followed her to the dining table. Cal was beside her in an instant, and Morgan's heart pounded as she and her college professor exchanged glances.

"Do they like his story?" Cal asked.

"Yeah. The guy's alibi checks out. He's got no record. He plays basketball for UT," Elaine Martin said, naming the well-known state university. "He said that Sammie recognized him."

Morgan's eyes filled with tears yet again, and she blinked them away impatiently. "That sounds like

Sammie," she said, pulling out a chair and placing herself in it. She had to stay calm. Focused now.

"We've got people at every bus stop in town and down at the station, too," Detective Martin continued. "We've also pulled surveillance tapes. They've been on red alert down there since yesterday morning. We've passed around Sammie's photo to every shift and posted it on the walls, too, but it's possible that he slipped by unnoticed."

"A ten-year-old kid boarding a bus alone would go unnoticed?" she asked, incredulous.

"It's summer. The sad truth is that a lot more kids than you know are put on buses alone to travel between parents over the school break."

"You think Sammie might have gone alone, then?" Cal asked. "He might have run away?"

"It's possible."

She'd ground him for life, Morgan thought. Right after she hugged him to death and slept for twenty-four hours. "Where would he get the money for a bus ticket?"

"Apparently your mother told Detective Warner this morning that she'd given Sammie money for new basketball shoes a few weeks ago. He'd been so excited about the shoes, it had never occurred to her that he'd use the money for something else. I guess she didn't realize he was still wearing the shoes with the hole in the toe until she heard the description of him read at the press conference this morning."

Thank God. Oh, thank God. Relief was heady. Making her dizzy. She'd be angry with her mother later.

And Sammie, too. Right now she was just so thankful to have hope that she didn't care about expensive shoes and gifts behind her back.

"She told Detective Warner, but no one else because she didn't want your father to know," Elaine Martin continued.

Morgan nodded, her lips trembling.

"You think Sammie would get on a bus by himself? And stay out all night?" the detective asked.

Morgan nodded again, fighting a fresh flood of tears. And Cal helped her out.

"Sammie's been rebellious lately," he said. "He thinks that Morgan babies him too much, that he's the man of the family and that she should listen to him more. He's completely wrong. She's a great mom. But he's a kid pushing his boundaries."

Morgan listened, so thankful that Cal was there, sharing the burden of parenthood with her, even for the moment. She was giddy with relief. And sick with worry, too. Sammie might think he was a man but the little boy was only ten years old and had taken himself on a bus to God knew where. Had he been there all night long?

Had he arrived safely? Had he been left alone once he got there?

Or had he met with ill fate on the other end of his journey?

There were so many creeps out there, sickos who did horrible things to young boys. And Sammie was small for his age....

An HOUR LATER Morgan was climbing the walls and Cal was pretty much scaling them right beside her. Even having only seen pictures of Sammie Lowen, after months of hearing about the boy, going to bat for him regarding a male point of view, Cal felt like he knew the boy. He certainly cared what happened to him.

"It's not good, is it?" Morgan asked from her perch on the front step. "The fact that we haven't heard anything yet?"

"You can second-guess this all day long," Cal said, fatigue slowing his mental processes, but not his desire to be there for her. To find a way to make things turn out right this time. "Try to envision Sammie safe. And coming home to you."

Like it was that easy. Just picture it and it will be. Not.

Or Claire Sanderson and Cal Whittier would have grown up as brother and sister.

"He's really a good kid," Morgan said now. "I know it sounds like I'm always talking about him fighting me, but Sammie isn't a troublemaker. He isn't belligerent. He's always in the kitchen when I'm making dinner, helping out. He stays around for cleanup, too, unless he has homework to do. He puts his clothes in the hamper and makes his bed. He gets good grades. He's the type of kid who befriends a boy with Down syndrome the other kids were making fun of. He's just not real fond of his mother watching out for him."

"Morgan, it's okay. I know what a good kid he is. Whether you're aware of it or not, you talk far more about the good times than you do about the struggles."

"I do?"

"Yeah. It's gotten to the point where I look forward to Mondays because I'm going to hear about what you and Sammie did over the weekend. You're a great mother—you don't just take care of your son, you share your life with him."

"I love having Sammie in my life."

"What about his dad?" He hadn't ever asked. And while it had been obvious that the boy's father wasn't around, Morgan had never talked about the guy.

Strange that in the past twenty-four hours no one had even mentioned the guy's existence.

"Todd Williams was the worst case of bad judgment I ever had," Morgan said now, staring out at the street.

"Your worst case?" An odd turn of phrase from a woman who was so levelheaded and insightful.

"According to my father, I'm good at misjudging people," she said. "I take people at face value. I give them the benefit of the doubt."

"All good qualities. We should all be more like that."

She shook her head. "My father thinks I don't discern well. My choice of husband didn't help my case any."

She'd been married to Sammie's father.

A strange feeling swamped him for a second. Only briefly. An unfamiliar and most unpleasant sensation. It took Cal another moment to realize he was jealous of the unknown Todd, which was absolutely ludicrous. Must be the lack of sleep.

"What happened?" he asked, telling himself that he

was just helping her pass the time while they waited for Sammie to be found.

"I met him in high school. Was certain that he was the love of my life. Looking back I see that he was just the opposite of my father. He relied on me. He let me call the shots. He listened to me. The complete antithesis of the life I had at home. The life that was driving me crazy. By the time I met Todd my father and I couldn't be in the same room for five minutes without having horrible fights."

"Todd treated you like the smart and savvy woman that you are."

She looked at him, almost with curiosity, and then she shook her head.

"He was after my father's money, but I didn't get that at all. Not even a hint. My father saw through Todd the first night he met him. He tried to tell me. When I wouldn't listen, he forbade me from marrying him. I defied my father and ran away with Todd to get married, as anyone would do for the love of their life. I was promptly disowned by my father, and then, as soon as Todd realized that I wasn't good for my father's money, he was gone, too."

"He turned his back on Sammie, too?"

"He didn't know about Sammie then. Neither did I, actually. I didn't find out I was pregnant until after Todd was in jail."

"In jail?" If the guy had hit Morgan, hurt her, jail was too good for him.

"He borrowed my car to have access to my key ring and promptly made a duplicate key to my folks' place.

He went through my private papers, found where I'd written the new code to my folks' security system, and the next night when he was supposed to be at work, he broke into their home, stole everything of value he could find and trashed the place. Ostensibly he did it all to get what he believed was coming to him, owed to him, for having taken on a life sentence with me. Unlucky for him, he was caught. Daddy pressed charges and I saw the light."

She showed very little emotion. A bit of self-deprecation was all. As though the bastard's shortcomings were somehow her fault.

"Is he still in jail?"

"No. He got out a couple of years ago, on good behavior. He's married again, to some older heiress who has full control of her fortune."

"And he's never tried to see Sammie?"

"Nope. His wife can't stand kids. Anyway, Sammie thinks he's dead. I was divorced and had reassumed my maiden name before Sammie was born. I listed his father as unknown on his birth certificate. I figure I'm going to have to explain that to him at some point but it hasn't come up yet."

"And once you divorced, your father acknowledged you again?"

"Technically I'm not sure he ever disowned me. I don't know whether or not I was ever written out of his will. Or, if I was, if I'm back in it. But no, I'm still not welcome in their home. Not unless I'm willing to move back into the house and allow him complete control over Sammie's upbringing. And me."

"Surely he couldn't expect you to do that."

Another glance from Morgan, this time meeting his gaze head-on, and Cal was angry all over again. This time at the man he'd spent the night trying to like for Morgan's sake. "I'm certain that right now my father believes I am fully to blame, in whatever way, for Sammie's disappearance. He doesn't believe I'm capable of making sound decisions, proven by the fact that I'm twenty-nine years old and still an undergrad working for little more than minimum wage."

"You're a single mom who works full-time and goes to school full-time, too."

"But, you see, I wouldn't have to work at all, or go to school for that matter, if I'd only do what I was born to do and be a Lowen, representing the Lowen family on various charities and boards. If I'd married right I'd be living in luxury, and my father would have two-point-five grandchildren by now and would be molding them to follow in his footsteps."

"In today's world? That kind of thinking went out a long time ago."

"Not really. Not in the society my father keeps."

"Was your father born into money?"

"Yeah."

"Do you miss it?"

"I don't like having to watch my son walk out the door in shoes that have a hole in the toe. I don't like lying in bed at night counting pennies in my head over and over, trying to find a way to make them add up differently. But no, I don't miss a life of privilege. I'd rather worry about money than give up my right to think my own thoughts and live my own life. I love kids. And teaching and—"

"Ms. Lowen?" Detective Martin was at the door.

Cal helped Morgan up and they turned together to face the detective. "Yes?" Morgan's voice held hope. And dread.

"We've heard from our people at the bus station. There is absolutely no sign that your son was there. Either yesterday or today."

She held the door open and Cal followed Morgan inside. The three of them sat in the living room—Cal in the chair he'd dozed in, Detective Martin on one end of the couch and Morgan on the other.

"Are you certain there's no place else you can think of where Sammie might have gone? Any favorite place he's visited in the past?"

Morgan shook her head. "Not that I haven't already told you."

"Have you checked the University of Tennessee?" Cal asked. "Maybe he's hanging out around the basketball courts."

"We've been watching courts all over the city," Martin said. "And baseball fields, too, just in case he shows up. We're getting calls on the number we gave at the press conference, but so far all the leads have been false. Most of them usually are. We just wait for that one that isn't."

"I can't stand much more of this," Morgan said, looking like she might be sick.

"We've still got teams out canvassing, but if there's

anything you can think of, anything else we can go on..."

Morgan's cell phone rang. Probably Julie checking in.

She pulled it out of her pocket and glanced down.

Her head shot up and the frenzied look on her face as she stared at Cal had his heart beating faster. "It's an unknown number," she said. Her hand was shaking.

"Put it on speaker," Martin directed.

Pushing a button on the cell and then another one, Morgan said, "Hello?"

"Mom? It's me, Sammie."

Martin stood. Cal sat forward. Morgan turned white. "Sammie? Where are you? Are you okay?"

"I'm fine, Mom." The little boy sounded tired, but not panicked. Or in pain.

"Where are you?"

"I'm not far from home. I'm actually on my way there, but I wanted to call first to let you know I was coming."

"Where are you?"

"On the corner of Vine and Banta. I'm borrowing some kid's phone."

Morgan looked at Martin, who nodded and dialed her own cell. Speaking softly she gave Sammie's location to whoever was on the other end of her call.

"Keep him talking. A squad car is two blocks away and they are on their way to pick him up," Martin told Morgan.

"Where have you been?"

"Just around," Sammie said. "I had a plan, but then

I saw you on TV with Grandpa, and I didn't know what to do. I was just trying to show you that I was old enough to make it on my own...."

His voice broke. "I'm sorry, Mom...I swear, I didn't mean to scare you."

The boy was crying openly now.

"I... You looked so weird and all and I...well, I'm in big trouble, huh?"

"Yes, Sammie, you are," Morgan said, but she was crying, too. And shaking so hard the phone was not steady at her ear. "I love you, sweetie."

"I love... Mom?" Fear entered the child's voice. "There's a cop car stopping right by me. Am I being arrested?"

"No, Sammie, they're bringing you home to me. Just get here quickly, okay?"

"Maybe they'll put on the lights and siren," Sammie said earnestly. And then added, "That'd be cool. Before I get in trouble for life."

"They've identified him," Martin said, her phone still to her ear. "He's wearing the same clothes he had on yesterday and there's another kid with him, on a bike. Let Sammie know that the officers are going to approach him."

Morgan did so. "Thank the young man for sharing his phone with you and go with the officers, Sammie."

"Okay, Mom. I'm in trouble, huh?"

"Just come home, Sammie."

Cal stood as Morgan hung up. He walked with her to the front door, knowing that she was counting the seconds until she could hold her son.

And when the squad car pulled up, lights flashing, and the small boy got slowly out of the backseat, his face solemn as he approached his mom, as Morgan flew down the steps and grabbed her son up off the ground, clutching him to her, Cal slipped away.

He had a life to get back to.

CHAPTER TEN

MORGAN WAS SOUND asleep Sunday afternoon when the phone rang. She reached toward the nightstand next to her queen-size bed, trying to make contact with her cell phone, cracking her knuckles on the end table at the same time that she registered the leathery texture beneath her cheek. She was on the couch.

With a quick glance at Sammie, who was asleep on the other end of the couch, his bare feet touching her, she grabbed the phone off the table, pushing the answer button as soon as she'd made contact with the device.

Sammie had had a rough couple of nights. She didn't want him disturbed.

"Hello?" She spoke in a whisper until she was outside the front door.

"Morgan, honey?"

Her stomach sank. She knew that tone of voice.

"Yeah, Mom, what's up?"

Her father's bidding, she knew that much. There'd be a price to pay for Friday night's debacle.

"I have a favor to ask you, sweetie."

"Daddy wants me to move home."

"No! Your father understands that you're an adult and that you have your own life."

He'd finally come around? She couldn't believe it.

But then, miracles happened. She'd had proof the afternoon before when she'd felt her son's skinny arms around her neck, holding on like he'd never let go, when she'd held his small body up against her heart and known that he was safe.

"What, then?"

"I want you to listen to me for a few minutes, honey." A big red ant climbed down a step.

"Okay." The ant climbed back up. She'd have to get some spray. She couldn't afford a professional exterminator right now. Not with school starting in another month.

"You know I've always supported the idea of you having Sammie. And I've done everything I could to help you two make it all right."

Everything she could within the auspices of her father's close oversight.

"I know, Mom." The babysitting over the years had helped. Her mother's emotional support had helped even more.

"I encouraged you to go to college."

"I know." The ant circled around. Looking for friends? Didn't ants travel in groups? All for one? The king of the hill?

"And I've bought things for Sammie whenever I could."

Was that was this was about? The money her mother had given her son without telling her so that he could get the basketball shoes he'd wanted? The money he'd used to buy a cheap sleeping bag and other supplies for his bid for independence?

"I know, Mom." She didn't blame her mom for Sammie's running away. She blamed herself. He'd told her he was struggling. That she was holding him too tight. She should have trusted her son on the internet. If he didn't visit any sites he wasn't supposed to visit, he wouldn't be prey to the dangers lurking there.

She'd misjudged the degree of his discontent, had driven him to the point of feeling he had to prove he was ready for more responsibility.

And she blamed Sammie, too. Whether he was right about her overprotectiveness or not, he was still underage, still her son and still answerable to her. He might not like her rules, but he was obligated to live under them.

She'd made that abundantly clear to him over the past twenty-four hours.

"You said you wanted me to listen to you, Mom."

"I…"

The ant left again, disappearing over the curve of the step.

"Tell her, Grace."

George's voice, barely audible in the background, sent chills through Morgan's entire being.

"Tell me what?"

"Oh, dear, I… It's not like you think. I…I agree with your father, Morgan. This time I believe he's right. I'm sorry."

"Right about what?"

"Sammie's too much for you, honey. He's a boy.

He needs firm control. A man's guidance. He needs a father."

"His father opted out of the job, Mom, you know that. Surely you aren't suggesting that I contact Todd?"

"Of course not."

"Or that I find someone to marry just to provide a father for my son?"

Her stomach was in knots. The ant was back. Still alone.

"I want you to pack Sammie's things and bring him home, Morgan. He's a Lowen. He's going to inherit this home someday. And the businesses, too. He needs, and deserves, your father's guidance."

So this was about them moving home.

"We've been over this a million times, Mom. I'm not moving home. You know that."

"Of course not, Morgan. That wouldn't be best for Sammie at this point. Having you here would only make things more difficult for him."

What?

"I've been up all night thinking about this, Morgan, and I think you'll find that this is best for everyone. You, included. I'll make sure that you see Sammie as often as you like—"

"Within reason." Her father's voice could still be heard.

"And you'll have the chance you never had to get solidly on your feet. You're only twenty-nine, Morgan. There's still lots of time for you to settle into a life of your own without constantly worrying about bills and babysitting. You'll be able to come and go and work around the clock if you want to. You can go out and date and travel and…"

Morgan couldn't find the ant. She couldn't see anything but a blur of gray where the step had been. Gray rimmed in red.

"You want me to give up Sammie?"

"Just to your father and me, sweetie. That's not really giving him up. He'd still be yours, still be in the family. Still be a Lowen. We'd just be helping you. Lots of parents do it, Morgan. You've done it all alone for so long. You deserve this chance to get ahead. And this way Sammie will be safe."

"No."

She had no argument. No rationale. So she hung up the phone.

CAL FILLED HIS FATHER in on the details of Sammie Lowen's safe return. He slept for almost twenty-four hours. And then, late Sunday afternoon, telling his father he was going to the grocery store, he took his shopping list and headed out.

But he made a stop first, at his fourth-floor office on the Wallace University campus.

Cal never showed up at school in shorts and sandals, but he wasn't there to work. The halls were silent in the building he had to unlock with his master key, adding to his sense of a world out of sync.

He hit Recent Calls on his office phone without taking a seat and punched in the number as soon as it came up. Sunday afternoon, maybe the guy wouldn't be available.

"Miller."

"This is Caleb Whittier."

"I recognized the number, Mr. Whittier. Thanks for getting back to me."

Cal waited.

"I'm calling regarding a case you were involved with in Comfort Cove, Massachusetts, about twenty-five years ago."

"I was seven years old twenty-five years ago."

"I'm aware of that, Mr. Whittier. The case involves a missing person."

Cal's heart started to pound as something occurred to him—something that should have occurred to him from the very beginning. "Have you found Claire?"

There was a rumble on the other end of the line. "I'm sorry, Mr. Whittier, can you hold on a moment?"

The line clicked before Cal could give his affirmative answer. He had to know.

Somehow he'd worked it out in his mind that Emma would have contacted him if Claire had been found. She'd promised. They'd made a pact—before he and his father had become the bad guys: whoever heard first would tell the other before telling anyone else.

But then, she'd been four at the time.

A lot could happen in a quarter of a century.

Was Emma even alive?

Was Claire?

Was his father finally in the clear?

Or was he...

The thoughts raced so quickly Cal could hardly keep track of them. Or reel in the unwanted ones.

He'd made himself pretty hard to find. Maybe Emma had tried to contact him.

"Mr. Whittier? Sorry about that. Had a situation here."

"Have you located Claire Sanderson?" Her body? Bones identified by dental records?

"No, sir, we have not. I called to inform you that a box of evidence from the Sanderson case has come up missing."

"Missing?"

"You wouldn't happen to know anything about that, would you?"

"Me? How could I possibly know anything about a box in police custody?"

"Where's your father, Mr. Whittier?"

"At home watching television. It's about all he ever does since you folks took away any hope he had of enjoying life." Frank had been the only suspect in Claire's disappearance. They'd hounded him until he'd left the state. And then the suspicion followed him from job interview to job interview.

"Are you sure he's at home?"

"Yes. I just left him."

"You visit him often?"

"Yes." So many years of running—of hiding facts— came to the fore and Cal protected his father's where-abouts without thought. He wasn't about to tell Miller, or any detective, that his father lived with him.

They'd changed identities for a while. Until it made Cal's education suffer. But they never registered a car, or an address other than a P.O. box. Until Cal came of age and registered in his own name.

His father had never been charged with a crime. But he'd been hounded until suicide had seemed the only alternative. For Cal's sake, his father had run instead.

Cal owed him.

"Have you or your father been in Massachusetts anytime over the past three months?"

"No." Nor for the past twenty-five years, either.

"To your knowledge have you or your father been in contact with anyone who has been in Massachusetts?"

"No."

"I'm sorry to have to ask these questions, but it's routine," Ramsey said.

Cal didn't think the guy sounded sorry at all, and he didn't bother to reply.

"It's my duty to inform you that a box containing some of your personal information is missing from the archives of the Comfort Cove Police Department, Mr. Whittier. Your fingerprints, as well as those of Emma Sanderson, were in that box. As was a shirt you were wearing on the morning of the abduction."

"What about the tape containing my testimony?" It was that tape that he'd have stolen, if he could. Stolen and destroyed. Just as the things he'd put on that tape had destroyed his father.

"That, too."

Shit.

"And you have no idea who took the evidence? Or why?"

Could the real perp be behind this?

Or someone who suspected that Claire was still alive?

"Not at this time, no."

"Have you contacted Emma Sanderson?"

"We're in the process of doing so."

He wanted to ask more questions. To know where Emma was living.

Had she gone to college? Did she have a career? Kids of her own?

"Just out of curiosity," he said instead, "how did you come to find the evidence missing?" Obviously someone was looking at the case, for some reason. Unless the Comfort Cove police had unlimited resources allowing them to randomly check evidence lists for every cold case on the docket.

"I was following a lead."

"On Claire's case?"

"I'm not at liberty to say any more at this time."

"Has someone found Claire?"

"No. And I really cannot disclose anything else at this time."

"But you'll let me know if you find the missing evidence?"

"Yes, Mr. Whittier. You can rest assured, I'll be in touch."

Cal hung up with a bad feeling in his gut. He hadn't liked the sound of that last promise.

And he was going to make damned certain that his father didn't catch wind of any of this.

CHAPTER ELEVEN

MORGAN HAD A HARD time dropping Sammie off at school on Monday morning.

"You understand that you're going to be under constant surveillance for the rest of summer school, right?" she asked as she turned the corner to approach Rouse Elementary.

"I know."

"It was either that or be suspended. It's only because you've never been in real trouble before—other than the acting-out in class last semester—and because you're a good student, and because of Julie speaking up for you, that you're even allowed to go back to summer school." She had to get through to him. To impress upon him the seriousness of what he'd done.

"I know." He looked her straight in the eye, his gaze so open and so childlike-sweet she almost choked up again.

"These are the consequences you pay for breaking the rules, Sammie."

"I know." He nodded again, looking down and back up again. "I swear, Mom, I'm going to follow the rules and I'm not going to run away again."

Pulling up in front of the school she studied her son

for a long moment. She wanted to believe him, but she had no idea if he was telling her the truth.

"I didn't think about the police part." He repeated what he'd told her when he'd come home to her on Saturday. "I didn't think you'd call them. And I didn't think about you being so worried. I just wanted to show you that I'm grown up."

His eyes were wide and moist, like he was fighting tears. A little boy trying so hard to be a man.

"And don't you see, Sammie, a grown-up would have thought of all those things—the police and the way everyone would worry. That's why you have me. To think about the things that wouldn't occur to you."

She reached over and hugged him as best she could with the console between them. He kissed her cheek, just like every other morning that they parted ways.

"Remember we have our first meeting with Amanda Rohn tonight." The counselor had come as a recommendation from Detective Martin.

"I know," Sammie said again. "But we don't need her. I just stayed out one night. I was coming home by myself. We didn't need the cops."

He'd told her all of that before, too. And it was his lack of understanding of the seriousness of his actions that scared her more than anything at this point. It was the mixture of mature thoughts with the innocence of childhood. Like the time he'd seen something on the news and thought that she could call the president of the United States and offer a solution.

Hopefully the counselor would be able to help her get through to him.

"Don't worry, Mom, nothing bad's going to happen," Sammie said, and slid out of the car, slamming the door behind him before trotting off to the closest entrance. His backpack swung behind him, almost bigger than his torso.

Maybe Sammie was right and she had nothing to worry about. Maybe she should just trust him like he kept saying. Or maybe her son was planning his next adventure.

She prayed that it was the former.

MORGAN DIDN'T EVEN get both feet on the ground at the university before people were calling out to her, congratulating her on her son's safe return.

Being older than most of her fellow students meant that while Morgan was friendly with them, none of them were really friends. She didn't hang out or go to bars or coffeehouses. She went to class and home to Sammie.

But she'd been attending Wallace for more than four years. She'd sat in a lot of classrooms, chatted with a lot of people, worked on group projects and participated in discussions. It seemed to her, as she walked to class Monday morning, that every single individual she'd ever made eye contact with, or breathed the same air as, spoke to her. Some asked questions. Some expressed relief. Others curiosity.

And all of the attention took her mind off the English class she was about to attend—off the man who taught the class.

She was a little nervous as she entered the room.
He was Professor Whittier today.

Not Cal, the man who'd appeared on her doorstep
Friday afternoon and remained steadfastly by her side
through the worst nightmare of her life, the man who'd
disappeared before she even had a chance to thank
him, or introduce him to her son. He'd arrived, and
then vanished without a trace.

All day Sunday she'd waited for his call. She'd had
no way to reach him. No home phone number. No cell.
And no permission to use either.

Her mind was filled with the things she'd say to
him, the details she'd give, the thoughts she had. Julie
had called. Morgan had been glad. But she'd kept her
internal confusion to herself. She'd been waiting for
Cal. She wanted his opinion—an outside source that
she trusted with her life, with her son's life.

He hadn't called.

It was as though Cal had existed only in her imagi-
nation. An angel to see her through the trauma. A special gift of strength when her own would have failed
her.

Prior to Friday they'd talked, but always at school—
in his office or after class. They'd never even so much
as had a soda together.

Now he'd spent the night in her house. He'd seen
her at her worst.

They couldn't go back.

She'd like to go forward.

But what did he want?

He'd been a crush. And then a best friend in her

time of greatest need. She felt something for him that she'd never felt for any other man in her life.

But was she anything more than a student in need to him?

"I was so glad to hear that Sammie made it home safely!" Bella, the thin, blonde college girl personified said, taking the seat next to Morgan's just before class was due to start.

The girl's eyes were wide and brown and brimming with authenticity. Morgan was a little ashamed at having judged her so harshly before. It wasn't like her.

"Yeah," she said now, "me, too."

"Where had he been all night?"

"He camped out in a spot he'd arranged at the back of my folks' property." Somewhere in the back forty acres. By the stream Morgan had run to as a kid anytime she needed to get away from her father's domineering presence.

"So he'd been planning the whole thing?"

"Yep." Planned it while visiting his grandparents. Food and shelter financed by her mother's basketball shoe money.

Professor Whittier had arrived, coming in through a side door in the front of the room.

Judging by the way he was looking at her, he'd overheard the last part of her conversation.

Her father had kept the facts of Sammie's escapade out of the news. A brief mention of her son's safe return was all that had been aired.

Professor Whittier didn't say a word to her. He didn't nod, or smile, or greet her in any way.

As though this was any other day, he put his leather satchel down on the table in front of him and started class.

HE'D SPENT AN UNCOMFORTABLE couple of days. The one element Cal could count on in his life was not counting on anything that he couldn't have. He didn't count on emotional support. Or happiness. He didn't plan the American dream, or even think about getting a dog. Dogs attracted attention. They barked. People were naturally drawn to them. Cal couldn't afford to have people drawn to him for any reason.

He counted on being able to work. On being a decent person and doing a good job. Helping his students to reach for *their* dreams. He counted on caring for his father. On food on his table and a roof over his head. A car to drive and things to interest him.

He counted on sex once in a while.

He counted on his alone time to write. The relationship between him and the words that poured out of him late at night were all the emotional sustenance he sought.

He counted on living peacefully.

And then Sammie Lowen had gone missing and he'd found himself facing a confusing array of conflicting internal pressures. The pressure to help one of his students who seemed to need him. And something else, too. Some long-ago something that was fighting for release.

Closure, maybe?

Or anger?

He wasn't sure what was going on, which was why he'd stayed clear of Morgan Lowen the second he'd known her son was okay on Saturday.

And it was also why he handed her an envelope at the end of class on Monday, inviting her to stop by his office if she wanted to.

He could walk away from the weekend and leave things as they were. He'd helped a lot of students over the years and then never heard from them again. She could be one more.

Yet he wanted to see her. To speak with her. Like there was some unfinished business to the weekend they'd shared.

He'd expected her to come up immediately after class.

She didn't.

And that left him uncomfortable, too.

His phone rang instead.

Seeing his father's cell phone number on the display, he answered immediately.

"How is she?"

Sitting back in his desk chair, staring out the wall of windows that looked down on the green expanse of Wallace's campus, Cal could picture the old man on the other end of the phone.

Off work for what should have been a week of fishing, Frank Whittier would be sitting in his chair in his room, probably reading, the lines on his face getting deeper by the day.

"She seems fine."

"You didn't speak with her?"

"We talked about some of the social issues that Twain raised in *Huck Finn* as part of the class discussion."

"And after class?"

"No. I had some students with questions. She left."

"You spent the night with her, Cal."

His father had asked him no less than half a dozen times since Saturday if he'd called "that poor girl."

"Not hardly."

"You felt compelled to stay with her through the trauma but didn't ask how she's holding up after?"

"It's not my business."

"You made it your business."

"You ever think of Rose Sanderson, Dad?" They didn't talk about what had happened. Ever. His father had established the rule early on. That way they never made mistakes, spoke out of turn, or were overheard.

"Yes."

The rule of silence had been established for a young Cal. But the habit had stuck. Cal wasn't sure what he was doing.

"Not a day goes by that I don't think of her."

He wasn't surprised. They didn't have to speak about the past to know that it lived with them.

"You still hate her that much?"

His father had practically spit the woman's name when he'd told Cal never to speak of her again.

Cal had hated her, too. For a lot of years.

"No, I don't hate her. If I ever did, it wasn't for long."

Cal lay back in his chair and looked to the ceiling. "But you're angry with her."

"No, son, I'm not angry with her. I feel sorry for her."

Cal wondered again why he was instigating this conversation. Why everything was changing just because a young boy had run away.

And because he'd had a call from the Comfort Cove Police Department.

Two things that didn't really affect their lives at all.

"You feel sorry for her?" He felt strangely removed from the situation.

"Of course, who wouldn't? She had her two-year-old daughter snatched away from her. Gone. And no explanation. No answers. No chance for goodbyes. Or even closure. Her whole world fell apart. I should have been stronger. More understanding."

He sat forward, his gaze skimming the files on his desk. "You're kidding me."

"No."

"Dad, she said she loved you. That she would marry you and honor and cherish you—and me—for the rest of her life. And then the first time that love was challenged, she turned on you. She didn't trust you at all. She believed you'd hurt her child! She told the police so. She threw us out and wouldn't even let us get our stuff. She ruined our lives."

"She was out of her head with grief. She had to blame someone. I was there."

Morgan had been beside herself with worry and fear, but she hadn't blamed anyone. Except herself.

"She turned on you within the first hour of Claire going missing and never changed her mind. Never came to her senses or remembered that we were family."

"We don't know that. We had no contact with her after those first few weeks."

"Because she got a restraining order." Any further contact had been up to her. If she'd ever missed them, wanted to speak with them, she could have sought them out. Lord knew, Cal had spent years hoping…

"I can understand if she just didn't have anything left to give us," he said now. "But she didn't have to take our lives from us."

"She had to do whatever it took to get her daughter back."

His conversation with Ramsey came to mind. Again. Claire was still missing. So what Rose Sanderson had done hadn't worked.

And his father, whose life Rose stole, was just waiting to grow old enough to die.

CHAPTER TWELVE

DRESSED IN A SHORT denim skirt, black tank top and black sandals, Morgan had been on the way to Professor Whittier's office when her cell had rung, causing an instantaneous flood of panic to surge through her. Phone already in hand, she opened it, weak with relief when she saw that her caller was not Julie. Or anyone else at Sammie's school.

Sliding the flip phone beneath the blond hair hanging past her shoulders, she pushed the call button.

"Hi, Mom."

"Morgan? Sweetie? We need to talk...."

IF HIS DOOR WAS CLOSED she was not going to disturb him. If he wasn't there, she wasn't going to leave a message, or in any other way indicate that she'd stopped by.

She shouldn't be there. Cal Whittier was her English professor. Nothing more.

But he'd left the note for her to come by.

Probably just something to do with the half class she'd missed on Friday.

The day seemed forever ago.

In some ways it had been.

She entered Cal's building. Looked at the bank of

elevators, any of which would take her up to the fourth floor. People were there. Waiting to cram inside the small space together.

She took the stairs.

He'd given her the note. Asked her to stop by.

She climbed a flight, her pack digging into her back. And then climbed another. Toward Cal.

At the moment, it was all she knew. To reach for Cal. And once she was with him, she'd begin to think.

ON THE LANDING at the top of the third flight of stairs, Morgan paused, pulled out her phone and hit speed dial.

"He's in class, sitting right up front, looking at the teacher," Julie's voice announced after half a ring. It was the fourth time she'd reported in that morning. She'd kept one of the surveillance screens tuned into Sammie's classroom since he'd arrived.

"Thank you." Morgan's reply was soft. Apologetic.

"Call as often as you need to. I'm on this."

Morgan was very lucky to have such a good friend.

CAL HADN'T MOVED since his conversation with his father ended. He was still in his seat at his desk, his tie firmly knotted, glancing at unopened files on his desk. He needed answers but they weren't in those files.

He wasn't sure where they were.

Cal didn't like that.

His life was neat. Orderly. It made sense.

He liked it that way.

Wanted it that way.

Intended to keep it that way.

"Professor?"

At first he wasn't sure if Morgan's voice came from the swirling thoughts in his mind, or from the door of his office. But when he looked, there she stood, looking beautiful and real and...

"What's wrong?" If her son had run off again...

"I... Nothing... You said I should stop by."

Her eyes told a different story. And concerns about his own situation fled.

"Come on in," he said, rising to usher her to a seat on the couch that sat in front of a floor-to-ceiling wall of books—dark bound tomes and gray encased references, fiction and literature and poetry, too.

Closing the door, he joined her, sitting close, but not too close. "How's Sammie?" He asked the first, and most obvious, question.

"Fine." Head slightly bent, she glanced his way, smiled at him. Resting her elbows on her knees, she clasped her hands. Unclasped them. Clasped them again.

"He wasn't hurt, then?"

"No." She shook her head. Smiled again. "He was good as could be. Spent the night on my father's property at a campsite he'd set up in preparation for his great adventure. He ate well, had plenty of water and extra batteries for the handheld gaming device my mother had given him that they'd neglected to tell me about."

Cal didn't understand why Morgan's parents couldn't see that it was hard enough for a young woman to raise a son on her own without interference from them.

"He was at their place all night?"

"On their property. My father has a lot of acreage, with no road access, that he doesn't fence because he wants the animals to roam freely so that every fall he can hunt them down and kill them."

Her knuckles were white. He resisted the urge to cover them with his hand. Morgan was strong. Capable. She didn't need his assistance.

"He fired his security team."

"They were responsible for your father's hunting ground, too?"

"No, but he fired them anyway. For not knowing that someone had set up camp there. Thing is, Sammie was only able to do so because he had access to the land from the grounds at Mom and Daddy's place and the team had no reason to suspect he was there. They didn't see him on Friday, of course. They'd have known to report that. But his visits weren't monitored, which allowed him to get everything set up. Daddy had told his team to let Sammie run free on the property because young boys need to test themselves, to taste freedom, to become men. He believes I coddle my son too much. That I'm making him into a wimp."

"He lives and breathes sports. Basketball, baseball. Or did I misunderstand that?"

"No. You're right."

"From what I gathered, Sammie's about as much of a boy as you can get."

Gaze directed at the floor, she nodded. And he saw her chin start to tremble.

"So what did the police say? Did they press any charges?"

"No. And they didn't call child protective services as it was so obvious that Sammie was just trying to prove a point. I'd taught him well enough that he'd been able to pull the whole thing off without putting himself in much more danger than if he'd walked to a friend's house after school. He didn't hitchhike, or stay out on the streets after dark. He didn't talk to strangers—he said the basketball player *wasn't* a stranger, and he only asked directions for the bus because he was so excited to see the guy it was all he could think of to say. He went straight to his campsite on his grandfather's property and stayed put until Saturday morning. He was heading home when he saw the replay of the press conference on a TV in the window of a fast-food place and called me."

"Well, that's good."

"Yeah. The police admonished him pretty severely, of course. He wasted a lot of people's time and resources, not to mention the hell he put us through...."

"Do you think he got the message?"

"I'm certain he did. He's been apologizing ever since. Detective Martin asked that I take him to counseling, though, in exchange for letting everything else go. We start tonight."

"Is he resisting?"

"Nope. Not at all." No sign of a smile. Her face was drawn, her eyes more vacant than not.

"Hey." He moved over, covered hands that were strangling each other. "What's going on?"

Her right leg started to bounce. Slowly. Methodically. She didn't speak right away. Cal wasn't sure she was going to. And then she said, "My father's attorney filed papers on Daddy's behalf this morning. He's suing me for custody of Sammie."

"He can't do that."

"Apparently he can. Doesn't mean he'll win, but he can try."

"On what grounds?"

"He's planning to prove that I'm an unfit parent."

"That's ludicrous!" He wanted to strangle the man.

"Apparently Sammie's escapade was enough to get the attention of social services."

"You said they weren't called."

"I said the police didn't call them." She turned to look at him, her hands still clasped beneath his. "My father did."

SHE HAD FRIENDS. Close friends like Julie Warren. Women at work with whom she occasionally shared confidences. Mothers of young boys she knew from Little League and scouting and school and city league basketball practice. A boss who valued her and was always willing to listen.

And the person whose spirit called out to her, the person she needed to talk to, was the college professor she'd secretly fantasized about.

She didn't understand the calling. And she didn't

question it. Her life was imploding and she had to do what she had to do to keep Sammie safe.

"You know what I think?" Cal asked, looking her straight in the eye as he sat next to her on the couch in his office.

She shook her head.

"I think that social services will take one look at a man who would try to derail his own daughter and show him the door."

Maybe. If the father were someone other than George Lowen.

"Your son is well fed, clothed, healthy. He's getting a good education. You said he maintains above average grades. I know for a fact that his home is a place of warmth and love—and it's clean, too."

"But I'm not in control there, Sammie is. A ten-year-old needs guidance, not coddling." She wasn't playing devil's advocate so much as releasing the thoughts that were scaring her to death. As though putting them in Cal's keeping would help. "And I'm overprotective."

"Parenting style isn't grounds for a custody battle."

This was why she was here. Because she needed a fresh perspective, needed views from someone who didn't have preconceived prejudices.

"I made some pretty serious errors in judgment in my past. I was young. It's behind me now. But my father is dragging it all out. And he's claiming that I put my son in danger by not being more aware of his state of mind."

"Have you been served papers? Maybe your father is bluffing."

She should move across the room, away from Cal Whittier. Her college professor should not be holding her hands. Especially not when the touch made her feel so close to him.

"My mother called as soon as everything was finalized. She wanted to tell me firsthand that the papers were coming. I called social services immediately. I'm not sure they were supposed to talk to me, but the guy who answered knew who I was from the news on Saturday. He told me he'd seen the Amber Alert and had been out looking…"

She swallowed. Another perfect stranger who cared. Who wanted to help.

"Anyway, when I told him why I was calling he did some checking and found out that a file was opened for Sammie this morning. We'll be assigned a court-appointed counselor for Sammie by the end of the day. I'm to expect a call no later than tomorrow, and then to plan for a series of in-home visits and interviews before our court date, which has been set for two weeks from tomorrow."

Cal frowned. "When did you get the call from your mother?"

"Right after class."

He glanced at a big, dark analog clock that dominated the wall behind his desk. It was still a few minutes before noon. "And they just filed this morning? That's some fast work."

"That's my father for you. I'm sure Young Stoddard, my father's attorney, asked for an audience with the judge when he filed the papers this morning. Daddy doesn't like to go through clerks and assistants. Sammie played right into Daddy's hands by running away. He was on the news. Wasted thousands of dollars in city employee resources. An Amber Alert was issued. Which makes our situation serious."

He didn't release her hands. Instead, he gave them a soft squeeze. "Your father may have a lot of money, Morgan, but he's not God. He's not even a politician. So he gets a look into your life with Sammie. You're a great mother. It should be an open-and-shut case."

If only life were that clean. Easy.

If only a woman were judged on her heart, her intention, not solely her deeds...

"My mother called to warn me. And to deliver a message from my father. He said that unless I cooperate and give up custody without the battle, my father is going to dig up dirt on me until he wins."

CHAPTER THIRTEEN

"You've got to be kidding!" Cal inwardly cringed. Morgan had just told him that her father was set to cremate her alive, and that was the best he could do?

Cal wasn't used to having students in his office with problems he couldn't solve.

"Do you really think he'd do that?"

"I think he'll do whatever he has to do to get his own way. How far will he go? I'd like to believe he wouldn't totally undermine me, but I'm just not sure…."

"What kind of parent would cut his own child off at the knees?"

"One who believes that he's doing what's best for everyone involved," Morgan said, her tone softening just a bit. "You saw my father in action, Cal. He makes up his mind and he pushes forward, regardless of the cost—to himself or anyone else. He's certain he's always right. And equally sure that it's his job to think for the rest of his family.

"He believes I'm going to buckle and he's going to get his way. And if I don't, if I call his bluff, he'll have been pushed into a corner and he'll move forward. Because he's George Lowen and that's what he does."

"Is he willing to create dirt where none exists?" he asked. He'd not only been reading Morgan Lowen's essays for four years, he'd been listening to her critical insights in class. The woman was gifted. And full of heart.

She always saw the deeper meaning and championed the moral choice.

"He won't have to make stuff up. My mistakes are several years old, but they're there. I have very few secrets from my father. He sees to that."

He sat back, holding on to one of her hands as he did so.

"He has you followed?"

"Not that I know of, but it wouldn't surprise me. My father has a way of knowing everything he wants to know."

"That's almost creepy. And could be considered stalking."

Shrugging, she sat back, too, her shoulder touching his. Not a big deal. But he noticed.

And didn't mind.

"I'd bet a month's pay that he knows how many open accounts I have and with who, if I'm paying my bills on time, that sort of thing. I'm certain he knows what I'm paying in rent."

"That can't be legal."

"The internet makes all kinds of things available if you know how to go about getting it. My father can afford to hire the people who know how to get it."

"Have you called him on it?"

"Yes."

"And?"

"And nothing. He denied doing any such thing.

We fought. Or rather, I did. He remained calm and adamantly assured in his right—or as he put it, 'his duty'—to keep tabs on his own daughter if he chose to, which he said he did not. And while he calmly lied to me, I built up to yelling at him. I was asked to leave until I could be more respectful. And I'm certain that if he was watching me, he didn't stop."

Cal wondered if Morgan had any idea how strong she was. She was heroine material if ever there was a living embodiment of fictional perfection.

Her fingers moved in his, striking an answering flicker inside of him, and he knew he had to end this.

"What evidence does he have to use against you in a custody battle?"

Her sigh sounded as though it came from her very depths. She glanced his way and those big brown eyes affected him as her fingers had. He could feel her.

Cal didn't much like to feel.

Unless he was naked with a woman.

"Like I said, I've made some pretty bad judgment calls. Not so much lately. But a few years ago I was so busy rebelling against my father's control that I did some stupid things."

The words were said so calmly, so matter-of-factly, Cal wasn't sure he'd heard them right. And then he couldn't make sense of them.

"You're a single mother with a job you've held more than ten years, finishing your last semester on a college degree. You drive a trustworthy car, live in a safe neighborhood and have a healthy son who gets good grades. I'm not seeing evidence to support his case."

"My father hasn't seen much of me in the past several years. What he's going to point out to the court is that I'm a single mother because I trusted a gold-digging son of a bitch when he told me he loved me more than my father did. I knew Sammie's father had lied to me a few times, but I put the lies down to his issues because he'd never known a secure home life. I knew he had trouble with his temper, but told myself that was a product of frustration, and understandable, considering the abuse he'd suffered in his last foster home. Mostly, I think I married Todd because my father was so adamantly positive that I couldn't. I had to prove to him, and to myself, that I could make own decisions.

"My poor choice got my parents robbed, their home ransacked, priceless memorabilia ruined. It resulted in my being abandoned and pregnant at nineteen with no way to support myself and having to testify against the father of my child in court. It garnered my son a father who was in prison at the time of his birth and who has disowned him ever since."

"You aren't the first woman to fall for a guy who didn't turn out to be who he seemed, Morgan."

"I know."

Well, then...

"Todd is only one in a long line of errors in judgment," she continued. "I trust too easily. I don't know for certain, but I imagine one of the things my father is going to claim is that it's only a matter of time before I trust someone in Sammie's life who will hurt him. I'm not sure that it matters all that much. This past weekend is pretty strong evidence that I don't have control of my son."

"Lots of kids run away just to assert their independence."

"I realize that. But my father's going to capitalize on what happened. I guarantee it."

"He won't get far without more to go on," Cal said, breathing a little easier. "Give me another example of what he might use against you." He'd do his job, set her free and move on to assessing the term papers in one of the folders on his desk.

"My first apartment, after Sammie was born, the landlord let me stay in exchange for cooking all of his meals for him until I could get a job and get on my feet. I planned the first week's meals—twenty-one of them—bought the groceries with the money he'd provided me to do so, and had to kick and bite my way away from his table the very first day when he let me know that what he wanted for breakfast wasn't the ham and cheese omelet I'd prepared."

His neck was warm. His tie too tight.

"By the time I made it back upstairs Sammie was awake and screaming for attention."

"He didn't...get what he was after...did he?" It was none of his business. He had to know.

"No. But I got a few bruises I hadn't been planning on. My mother saw them and told my father."

"I'm guessing that guy hasn't been renting out property since."

"He claimed that I'd offered my services in exchange for room and board, which Daddy might have believed, but Mom wouldn't even consider the possibility. My father's subsequent investigation turned up some questionable money practices, which led to some other things, and the guy is now doing twenty-to-life for selling drugs to a minor who subsequently died of an overdose."

So her father had been instrumental in putting away two men with whom Morgan had associated.

"You were trading honest work for honest compensation, Morgan. There's no way you'll be found an incompetent parent over that."

"I've trusted two men that ended up in prison. One of them fathered my son. The other I exposed to Sammie. And when I was serving breakfast, I left Sammie alone in the apartment."

"For the few seconds it would take you to deliver food downstairs. He was asleep and you never left the building."

"I know. And I'm telling you the truth. But if I push my father on this, he'll make it come out looking differently. He'll use the truth as a basis for his claims, and then skew it enough to serve his argument."

Cal knew only too well how that could happen. And hurt. Sometimes the truth didn't set a person free.

"What else is there?"

"When I was in high school, this girl I knew came to me crying because her mother and her father refused to let her get married because she was only seventeen. She was also pregnant and I knew her boyfriend. They were responsible, good students who'd made a mistake and wanted to do what was right for their baby. They wanted me to go to my father and see if he'd help them. I emptied my savings account instead and the money helped her and her boyfriend run away to Las Vegas, get married and pay for pre-natal care. I hear from them every Christmas, by the way. They're still married, living in Vegas, and have three kids."

"If the money was yours there was no crime in helping them."

"I gave them ten thousand dollars. My father will use that to prove that I don't understand the value of a dollar, which is what he told me at the time as justification for taking away my allowance. I can fight him on that one. I've got a ten-year history of making it on my own. But I can guarantee you he'll find a way to use that incident against me. I admit, it was dumb. But to my way of thinking, the only thing that made being the rich kid palatable was to be able to use my father's money to help people."

What kind of parents gave a kid, any kid, access to ten thousand dollars? "How in the hell did you even have a chance to establish any sense of the value of a dollar with that kind of cash hanging around?"

"I don't know. Maybe he'll say I stole it out of his and my mother's account. Which I didn't."

His fingers were growing numb. He let go of her hand.

And wished there was some reason for him not to have done so.

"When Sammie was a couple of years old, I met a young woman at the park." Morgan sounded as though she was giving a recitation now. "She was pregnant and unmarried, and off work during the last month of her pregnancy. She wanted to leave her boyfriend, but didn't have anywhere to go. Her father was dead and her mother had kicked her out when she'd refused to have an abortion."

"How old was she?"

"Nineteen."

"The same age you were when you were pregnant with Sammie."

"Right.

"Anyway, I met the boyfriend and didn't like him. He was lazy. And fat. He'd had three jobs that year and missed work if he didn't feel like getting up. He wasn't abusive or anything, but it was clear that her life with him would be a series of dead ends."

Cal knew that this wasn't going anyplace good.

"I was working at the day care by then and took Sammie to the park every day after work, which is how I met her. She and I talked every day that month, and I told her that after her baby was born she could move in with Sammie and me until she could find a job and get a place of her own. My mother warned me that it wasn't a good idea, but they're always so uppity, you know? They don't know what it's like to try as hard as you can and still have that not be enough."

"So what happened?" The woman stole from her, was Cal's guess.

"My lease disallowed me from taking in a roommate. It was just a one-bedroom place. I told Shelley to keep things low-key when the landlord was around and she seemed to be really careful. But it turns out that when I went to work, she cranked up the stereo, had people over and let her friends drink too much. A neighbor complained. I got evicted. Sammie and I ended up having to live in one of those rent-by-the-week motels until I could find another decent place I could afford on my day-care salary."

"What happened to Shelley?"

"She took the baby over to her mother's house. Her mother fell in love with her grandchild and Shelley moved back home. She talked to the landlord for me, tried really hard to smooth things over, but he wouldn't reconsider."

"And her mother didn't have room to take you in, too? Just until you found a place?"

"They didn't offer. And I didn't ask."

He wouldn't have asked, either.

"I wasn't the only single mother living in the motel. It was clean and safe. I don't think for a second that I'd lose custody of my son for having lived there. It's the spin my father is going to put on things that scares me."

"What about dating?" He told himself he was asking because her answer was pertinent to her case. If there'd been other men, her father would certainly bring them into the picture.

Morgan was a beautiful woman. One who would be certain to attract her share of male attention. "Have there been other men in your and Sammie's lives? Any that would feed your father's cause?"

"I've only dated one man since my son was born.

Sammie was three, was potty trained and old enough to talk, to tell me if something wasn't right, and so I finally felt comfortable leaving him with a sitter. Greg worked for my father, which didn't sit well with me, but I liked some of his ideas. He was a junior financial adviser, working on charities, and one night I ran into him at the grocery store. He told me that he was trying to get Daddy to get more involved in charitable work, showing my father how it would actually help his bottom line, and I liked his passion to do good. He'd been after me since before Sammie was born to go out with him. My father didn't approve, which might have been why I finally agreed.

"Anyway, it wasn't long before I figured out that he had no interest in Sammie at all. What I didn't know was that he was using his relationship with me to put pressure on my father to invest in this charitable venture he'd found. My father agreed, but what Greg didn't yet know was Daddy's thoroughness in investigating any new financial expenditure even if it came from his own people. Turns out Greg's venture was part of a tiered plan that benefited him more than the charities involved."

"Another man went to jail?" Cal asked, beginning to feel as though he'd stepped through Alice's looking glass and wondering why he was still stepping. Were the prisons filled with men who'd known Morgan Lowen?

"No, Greg's venture wasn't illegal. It just wasn't as altruistic as he'd made it sound. No one got hurt.

Daddy made sure I knew what had happened. And Greg was history."

No one got hurt? Looking at the clouds in Morgan's eyes, Cal didn't believe that for a second.

And he saw how hard it had been for her, the young, beautiful, only daughter of one of Tyler's richest men. Her mere existence made her prey to the scum of the world.

Her plight called out to him. He would be her friend. He would listen and offer support wherever he could. And when she came through this with the dignity and class she exuded everywhere she went, when she'd secured her son's future, he would see her graduate and wish her well before they went their separate ways.

What he was not going to do was touch her again. Ever.

Not even to help her up from the couch.

As soon as Morgan left, Cal picked up the phone and dialed a number that a new professor in the art department had slipped to him during a faculty meeting at the beginning of the summer. Professor Kelsey Barber was a vivacious, cute, redheaded free spirit. Cal asked her if she liked Italian food, not that the type of food mattered, and then asked her to dinner. She accepted.

CHAPTER FOURTEEN

MORGAN WAS LYING in bed, trying her damnedest to make herself sleep, when the phone rang. It was only ten o'clock. Sammie was already asleep. She could hear his breathing over the monitor she'd installed that evening despite her son's vocalized displeasure.

Not wanting Sammie to waken, she grabbed the phone. There was no one she wanted to speak with. After her argument with Sammie, one in which she heard her father's voice-over, repeating verbatim the words she used with his own negative connotation given for the benefit of the judge, she was in a pretty vile mood.

The LED screen showed a number she didn't recognize.

"Hello?"

"Morgan?"

She recognized his voice immediately.

"Yeah?" She couldn't get involved right now. Couldn't trust herself, or her son, to any more upheaval.

But God, his voice sounded good.

"Were you asleep?"

"No." She sat up in the dark, keeping her voice low

for the sake of the sleeping boy across the hall. "I'm wide awake. What's up?"

Did he have any idea how much she'd been thinking about him?

"I hope it's not too late. I'm just getting in. But I wanted to know how your meeting went tonight with the counselor?"

"We didn't go."

"Why not?"

"We had a call from Sammie's new court-appointed counselor. We have a meeting with her tomorrow and I didn't think it was a good idea for him to have to counsel with more than one person at a time. I discussed my concerns with both women and they agreed with me."

Why was she explaining herself to him? Like he was her father and she had to justify her actions.

Something she'd stopped doing with her father when she was about thirteen.

Cal's opinion didn't matter to her. It couldn't. Not now. She couldn't afford a single misstep. A single mistake.

"So you talked to this new counselor?"

"Yeah. Leslie Dinsmore. She's a certified counselor and a caseworker, too, so she's used to dealing with troubled kids. She seemed nice." But then, she thought everyone seemed nice, didn't she? According to her father, anyway.

She was not going to let him make her second-guess herself. Yes, she saw the best in people. She liked to help people, too. Both were positive characteristics.

"I also called an attorney. I'm going to meet with her tomorrow, too."

"Good. Your father has a lot of money, Morgan, but you're a good mother and you and Sammie have rights."

"I know." She also knew not to underestimate the power of money. She'd seen her father's wealth in action all of her life.

"How was Sammie tonight?"

She didn't want to tell him. Didn't want anyone to judge her son. Sammie was just struggling with growing pains.

"He was angry with me for putting a monitor in his room."

"A monitor?"

"Yeah."

"Like those things people use to hear if their baby cries in the night?"

"Yeah."

Dead air followed and when she felt uncomfortable after a few seconds she said, "I just wanted to be able to get some sleep. What if he sneaks out during the night? I'll lose him for sure if he goes a second time. I can't make him sleep with me, or camp out on his floor forever. What he did was wrong. A monitor in his room seemed like a punishment that fit the crime."

"The crime?"

"He broke my trust in him."

Another silence had her wishing she hadn't spoken quite so freely. Cal Whittier made her feel as though she could tell him anything. She'd have to watch that.

"It's not anything I would have come up with, but, you know, what you said has some merit.

"A more common punishment would be grounding, maybe," he continued. "I'm not a parent, but I am an educator and I know that taking away something that the child values for a designated period of time is a widely accepted practice. But you're right. He's lost your trust. And that's what you're showing him."

"Other than sports, Sammie values his computer. What good would taking away the computer do?" she said. "He uses it for legitimate things—schoolwork, and keeping up with his favorite teams and game scores. He'd be bored stiff without it. I heard in one of my classes once that the prisons are filled with smart people who were bored. It's more of a challenge to be bad than to be good, and when you're bored you look for a challenge. Besides, his computer use played no part in what happened on Friday. The other thing he values is his independence. That's what I'm taking away. Only until I can trust him again. He has to know that breaking someone's trust is critical."

"You're right."

Why did his saying so matter so much?

"Well, thank you for calling," she said abruptly. "I have to work early tomorrow. Covering for someone…" The words tumbled over one another as she hurried to extricate herself before she did something really stupid.

Like talking to the man half the night and getting herself in too deep. Her son's life was at stake. Morgan was not going to mess this up.

SITTING AT THE COMPUTER in the small room that served as an office at home, Cal wrote long into the night on Monday—a collection of personal notes and memories that he was putting in chronological order. And he nursed a single glass of whiskey. He'd have had something to eat, too, but he'd eaten his fill during his dinner with Kelsey.

She'd seemed to enjoy herself. And he'd asked her out again for later in the week. She'd accepted.

On Tuesday, at ten o'clock, he dialed the phone again, exactly as he had the night before.

"How did your meeting with the lawyer go?" he asked as soon as Morgan picked up. He was in the office, wearing sweats and a T-shirt, ready to write, but had to do this first.

"Good. She says that while my father has a legal right to ask the courts to consider my ability to parent Sammie on my own, the courts will put the most weight in Sammie's health and well-being. His having run away will work against us, but his good grades, good health and emotional stability will be in our favor. She thinks there's a possibility that we might get joint custody, because of my father's ability to provide for Sammie financially so much better than I can, but she doesn't expect that to happen.

"And…she said that she thinks I should represent myself in court. She said that court is all about strategy. About choosing the best strategy to win. And in this case, she recommends that I appear on my own behalf. Basically, my father is going to have me on trial. All an attorney would do for me is call me to the stand and ask me questions so that I can present my case. She said that I'm perfectly capable of giving the court the truth on my own and that I'll appear more confident and capable if I do so. We aren't going to try to fight my father, or drag him through the mud, which is what I'd need an attorney for. We aren't going to challenge him, or put him on trial because then it appears like I'm fighting with my father, not standing up for my son. And…she said that she'll continue to advise me as we go along, free of charge. She was really sweet, Cal. I liked her a lot."

"She sounds wonderful. Where did you find her?"

"She's a friend of Julie's."

"What she says makes sense. Do you think you can stand up to your father and his attorneys if you're put on the stand?"

"In this case, yes. I know I'm a good parent. And, having grown up under my father's thumb, I really believe that Sammie is better off with me."

"For what it's worth, I do, too," he said, and then continued without giving her a chance to respond. "So how did the meeting with the counselor go?"

"I'm not sure." She sounded tired.

"Was Sammie uncooperative?"

"I don't think so. She talked to him alone. And when I asked him about their meeting he said it was fine."

He wondered if she was in bed in the room he'd seen when he'd visited the restroom last Friday night. Or sitting alone on the couch he'd shared with her during that one very long night. "Boys aren't big on details."

"Or maybe she told him not to tell me."

"Maybe." He'd never dealt with child services. He and his father had always outrun them. "What did you think of her?"

"I liked her. She seemed to have Sammie's best interests at heart."

As opposed to her father's?

"That's good."

"Yeah."

"Did she ask you a lot of questions?"

"Not really. She just wanted to talk with Sammie tonight."

"When do you see her again?"

"Thursday night." He was taking Kelsey out for sushi Thursday night.

"Okay, well, have a good night."

"You, too."

Cal hung up and took a long swig of the whiskey that was supposed to last him the rest of the night.

ON WEDNESDAY MORNING, a couple of hours before class, Cal was in his office at the university reading over material for the one Monday/Wednesday/Friday summer class he had that session, when he had another call from Comfort Cove Detective Ramsey Miller.

Accepting the inevitable, he picked up.

"Whittier," he said abruptly into the mouthpiece.

After identifying himself Miller said, "Tell me again, Professor, how many times have you left the state of Tennessee in the past six months?"

Miller had already asked that question. And his reply was the same. "None."

"Would you like to reconsider that answer?"

"No."

"Then how do you explain a receipt at the Starwood Steakhouse in Lexington, Kentucky, in June?"

Cal drew a blank.

And then he didn't. "I was flying from Tyler to Nashville. We were rerouted due to inclement weather. We got meal vouchers. I went to the Starwood Steakhouse, which is in the Lexington Airport, by the way, for dinner while I waited for the storm to pass so I could get home."

There was a pause on the line. And then Cal asked, "And what in the hell are you doing looking at my receipts? Am I under investigation for something?"

"I got a warrant. We have a twenty-five-year-old cold case on a missing child that has had inexplicable activity." The detective continued. "And everyone involved is being looked at." Cal's heart sank. Not again. For the love of heaven, not again.

He'd bet his ass that they were looking at his father and him with suspicion while everyone else was just being given a fond and concerned glance. "You did your duty and informed me about the missing evidence, Detective, now leave us alone," he said. And hung up.

Frank Whittier had, in effect, been punished for a crime he hadn't commited. He'd become invisible so he could keep Cal with him, so he could make sure Cal was loved and treated well, so Cal would get the education he needed to have a career he enjoyed. And now Cal was going to make damned sure no one touched his father. Ever again.

"SAMMIE? WHAT ARE YOU doing in there?" She stood outside the bathroom door in their duplex, talking to wood paneling.

"Nothing."

"Come on, sweetie. You need to eat some breakfast before we go."

She'd wanted to run the brush through her hair again, too, now that it had dried. And to put on some eyeliner. But she'd already given up on both of those counts.

"I'm not hungry."

Staring at her unpolished toes in their plain brown flip-flops beneath the hem of her cheap, cotton tie-dyed skirt Wednesday morning, Morgan took a deep breath. Maybe the monitor had been a bad idea, after all. Her son hadn't spoken a kind word to her since Monday night.

This was the third time he'd locked himself in the bathroom where "she couldn't hear him breathe."

"You're going to be late for school." She tried again.

"No, I'm not."

Surely he didn't think he could just hide out in the bathroom and not go to school?

She had to get to her class and then to work at the day care.

The monitor in Sammie's bedroom might have been a poor choice, but she'd had to discipline him. Her father had stated in his complaint that she didn't give Sammie enough discipline, that she let him tell her what to do instead of the other way around.

And maybe she had. She was open-minded. She

listened to her son. But she never gave in when his safety or health was involved.

Anyway, she'd had to do something more than just talk to Sammie after Friday's misbehavior. Sammie had put his life at risk. She had to take firm action.

"Sammie, you and I have always at least been able to talk."

No answer.

"I thought we were always honest with each other. What you did on Friday, that was a lie in action. A big one. I can't just let it go."

More silence.

"Did Ms. Dinsmore tell you who she is and why you're seeing her?"

"She said I could call her Leslie." With emphasis on the "I."

Glancing at the large gold watch her mother had given her for Christmas, Morgan calculated distances. They had to leave within six minutes or Sammie was going to be late for school. And so would she.

Her son was ready, other than having missed breakfast, if you could call dressing in ripped denim shorts and a stained T-shirt dressed.

Sammie knew she hated it when he dressed like a homeless kid, but she'd also learned a long time ago to pick her battles with her stubborn and too-smart-for-his-own-good ten-year-old going on fifty.

"Did Leslie tell you why you're seeing her?" she asked.

"She didn't tell. She listened." His belligerent tone

let her know quite clearly what he thought of her own listening skills.

"This isn't just about Friday night's camping trip," she said. "Our troubles are more serious, Sammie."

"You said I'm not in trouble. I heard the cop tell you that they weren't going to take any action." Accusation was in every word.

Her son had betrayed her trust and now he didn't trust her? They'd gone from bad to worse.

And she still hadn't had a full night's sleep.

"She's a detective and I'm not talking about the police."

She heard some shuffling. But Sammie didn't open the door.

"Your grandfather claims I'm not a good mother." Did the responding grunt communicate agreement or disgust with George Lowen?

"He's trying to get you to go live with him." If Sammie wanted to go, her battle was pretty much done before it had begun. And if he continued with this behavior, same thing.

More shuffling.

She couldn't do this now. Couldn't have him miss any more school or he'd be kicked out.

And then she'd have to drop out of her summer class and not graduate and spend at least another semester as a slightly-higher-than-average-paid hourly worker at the day care while her son wore cheap basketball shoes and ate school-sponsored lunches. She couldn't get a promotion in her job until she had a degree.

"We have to go, Sammie."

To her shock, the door opened. Sammie was standing there, dressed in his newest old pair of navy shorts with a clean, short-sleeved, light blue shirt that matched. He was wearing the sneakers she'd bought him, too, instead of the Converse shoes with the hole in the toe. The clothes he'd put on earlier that morning were in a pile on the bathroom floor.

He glared at her as he walked past, grabbed his book bag and stormed out the front door.

Grabbing a breakfast pastry and a juice box, Morgan hurried after him.

CHAPTER FIFTEEN

THE ENTIRE TIME Morgan was in class, she fought with herself. Her life was in chaos. She had a problem larger than anything she'd dealt with before looming on the horizon.

What was she doing sitting in English class, discussing *Huckleberry Finn* and Mark Twain? It seemed so trivial compared to what was going on in her life.

And what was the matter with her that talking to her English professor made her feel so good? It wasn't like they were really friends.

Their give-and-take wasn't mutual. He knew far more about her than she knew about him.

And he had no obligation to her whatsoever.

He was just a nice guy who got caught up in a tragic situation. Sammie was home and fine, and life would go on now.

"Was Huck a hero? A good guy?" Cal glanced around the surprisingly full classroom, surprising because it was the third Wednesday in July and ninety degrees outside.

"Nooo." Bella drew out the word. She smiled at the man in his short-sleeved white dress shirt and striped tie at the head of the room. Cal's hair was styled impeccably as always. It was long enough to be attractive in a slightly rakish way but still look completely professional.

Not that Morgan was admiring him or anything. She was just imagining what Cal must look like from Bella's twenty-year-old perspective.

"Huck made poor choices."

"He flaunted societal mores at every turn," Dave Armstrong, a fellow education major and a young man Morgan had grown to respect over her college years, chimed in.

Cal's gaze bounced from student to student as comments volleyed back and forth, kind of like he was watching a tennis match. And then his gaze landed on her.

On any other day, she might have joined in the debate. Today it hadn't seemed to matter a hell of a lot.

"Morgan? Was Huck a hero?"

"I think so."

"Why?"

"He did what he thought was right even if it went against the social mores of the time. Those of us lucky enough to read Twain now can learn from Huck's choices."

"You're saying he was bad for good reason," Bella said from across the room.

Maybe. Or he'd been good and no one had seen it.

Others jumped in. Talked about the type of people we want living among us. Those who lead. And those who follow. Those who challenge the status quo and set trends. Cal watched the debate.

Morgan watched Cal.

Most of her classmates, minus the jerkoid with the headphones on, were engaged in the discussion. A couple spoke among themselves. No one was sleeping.

But Morgan wanted to sleep with her professor.

CAL WAS PLANNING to get a word in with Morgan after class Wednesday. He couldn't keep calling her up to his office, but he wanted to make certain that she knew he was there to support her through her struggles for as long as she needed him. He'd taken her on and he wasn't going to desert her.

He wasn't a therapist, but teachers often found themselves in a position of trust. He'd be there for any of his students who came to speak with him.

Besides, Morgan didn't need another therapist. She needed a friend. And he wanted to be that friend as much as he could be, considering their teacher-student relationship.

She was taking longer than usual to gather up her things after class. Waiting for him, he surmised. He was glad.

Bella, who always seemed to be the last to leave, finally exited the classroom. And then, in his peripheral vision, he saw Kelsey Barber hovering in the doorway.

"Cal?" she called out softly. She was dressed in white gauze from her ankles to her neck, her arms and shoulders bare and tanned to a freckleless golden brown. Her deep red hair flowed in natural curls down her back.

"Yeah! Kelsey, come on in." She was attractive.

Natural and a little wild, she was just his type of woman.

The free-spirited type.

"I'm on my way to the kiln—timer's about ready to go off—but I just wanted to ask if we could change tomorrow night to seven-thirty instead of seven? I have a student who needs to meet with me after she gets off work."

Morgan could hear. Which made him inexplicably tense. And more eager than ever to lock in time with Kelsey. "Seven-thirty's fine," he said.

"Good." Her smile held a promise he wanted to explore. "If you'd like, we could head over to my loft rather than having to sit in a busy restaurant and listen to the buzz of other conversations. I make a decent lasagna."

He'd asked her about Italian food the first time he'd called her.

"That sounds great," he said. And meant it.

He wanted to spend time with Kelsey. To get to know her.

He wanted to talk to Morgan, too. But by the time he turned back to her, she was gone, the back door of the classroom closing quietly behind her.

THAT EVENING, AS SOON as his father had turned in for the night, Cal poured his glass of whiskey and shut himself in his office. As far as he knew, his father never set foot in the room that had formerly been a third bedroom—insisting that Cal needed his private space—but tonight he locked the door anyway.

He was there to write, to work on the compilation of impressions and thoughts that had become a life-long project to him. Putting his life in book form. A story that was tragic. A hobby that was therapeutic.

Usually he wrote in sweats. His home office was the only place he allowed himself such casual dress. Tonight he needed the barrier more formal clothes provided. A mental barrier, perhaps, but one he chose to maintain.

Loosening his tie, he knelt in front of the wooden file cabinet his father had given him when he'd graduated from college. The solid piece of furniture had been one of the few things that had traveled with them through the years.

In its former days the cabinet had supported the middle sectional piece of the mammoth desk in his father's headmaster's office in Massachusetts.

The bottom drawer slid open to reveal the locked metal box Cal kept hidden away. He hadn't opened the drawer, or the box large enough to hold several legal pads, in years.

Tonight he pulled it out, carried it over to his desk, sat down. Using the key from the ring in his pocket, he unlocked the black metal lid and slowly lifted it.

The first thing he saw made his heart pound. Ramsey had read a list to him of evidence contained in the box that had gone missing from the Comfort Cove Police Department.

Obviously the detective had never seen the "box." It had been fluid like an envelope as opposed to hard-sided like a box. Made of some kind of durable plastic material. The kind that lined swimming pools, only a frosted clear color instead of blue.

At least that was what he'd thought when he was seven years old and had been left alone in a room with that "envelope" sitting on a counter.

The thing had been big enough to hold books.

Instead, it had been filled with his things. And Emma's. And Claire's. Taken from their rooms. Their home.

Even the clothes taken from their bodies, underwear included, the day that Claire had gone missing.

Cal stared at the small, dark tan bear lying on a backdrop of papers and old articles in the black metal box on his lap. The edges of its fur were matted, tips dirty from sticky little fingers, from tears.

The bear—Teddy, a young Cal had named it— was on Ramsey's evidence list from that missing envelope.

But a seven-year-old boy could hardly be blamed for grabbing the bear and hiding it in his jacket. He could hardly be charged with theft for rescuing a child's toy and smuggling it home.

Teddy's golden eyes gazed up at him. One of them could have had a tear seeping out from the crack down the center of it. He remembered the day the bear got hurt. They'd all been piling into the van to head out for ice cream. The sun was high in the sky and Dad and Rose were home so it had to be summer. He was already sweating even though he had on a T-shirt and shorts and the flip-flops Rose had just bought for him because they had the Boston Celtics basketball logo on them.

God, he'd loved those flip-flops. He'd worn them every day that summer. So proud he'd practically skipped when he walked.

Not so much because of the Celtics, though they were the coolest and wearing their emblem made him cool. But because he had a mom now. Someone who thought about things he liked, and not just things he needed. Someone who surprised him with gifts just because he was there, because he was in her thoughts. Because he was loved.

Rose was a teacher, too, just like Cal's mother had been.

He coughed. Took a sip of whiskey.

Teddy. The bear. Claire had been about a year old and was in the throwing-everything-all-the-time stage. It was a game she played with him, and while he grumbled, Cal had secretly loved it that she wanted his attention. She'd throw things and then laugh out loud when he picked them up. Over and over and over again.

That day she'd thrown Teddy from her car seat, over to his seat by the sliding door in the side of the van just as his dad had slammed the door shut. The bear had escaped. Claire's screams had muffled Cal's voice as he tried to tell Rose that Teddy was in the driveway.

Dad climbed in the passenger's seat of the van and Rose backed down the drive, all the while telling Claire to just hold on, she'd have her ice cream soon.

Rose had thought Claire was screaming for ice cream.

She'd been mourning her bear.

She got Teddy back. But not until after Rose had backed the van over him.

Cal had taken all the blame. He'd offered up his allowance money to buy Claire a new bear. But Rose had assured him that Teddy's injury wasn't his fault. She said that he'd done the right thing by staying put and trying to tell her what had happened.

She'd told him that he took excellent care of his little sisters and he wasn't ever to doubt that.

She told him that she was the one at fault for pulling out of the driveway without turning around to see what was wrong.

And that was how Teddy's eye got cracked. Emma was the one who pointed out that it looked like a tear was coming out of the crack in the bear's eye. It was really just a reflection from the plastic piece that was crooked now because of the crack.

Blinking. Cal swore to himself that he wouldn't cry.

He wasn't in Massachusetts anymore.

And he wasn't seven anymore, either.

Teddy was much older, too.

And there was nothing comforting about the bear now. Hadn't been for a long, long time.

Teddy was there, not because he belonged to Claire, or because Cal named him, or because part of him yearned to believe the pack of lies Rose Sanderson had told him the day that Teddy got hurt.

The bear was there because he was the reason that Frank Whittier had been the sole suspect in the disappearance of Claire Sanderson.

The morning Claire went missing, she'd had Teddy

at the breakfast table with her. There'd been a bit of a scene when she was told to put her bear away.

Just a short time later, Cal had seen the toddler in the back of his father's car. He'd told the police that, thinking they'd go to his father and find Claire. Dad always saved the day.

And Dad loved Emma and Claire as much as he loved Cal. He loved them as much as Cal did. It never dawned on him that anyone would think his father would ever, ever hurt the little girl who was like a daughter to him.

But Frank Whittier had told the police that he hadn't seen Claire after he left the house that morning. Because of Cal's testimony, they searched Frank's car anyway.

There was no evidence of the toddler there.

They found Teddy instead.

DNA technology hadn't been readily available back then. And law enforcement officials apparently hadn't gone looking for Teddy to test him once the technology became available or they'd have known they didn't have him.

Chances were good that whoever took Claire Sanderson hadn't touched the bear, anyway, or they'd have disposed of him, instead of leaving him on the floor of the car, just under the back of the driver's seat, where Claire had obviously thrown him.

But what if they had?

Twenty-five years had passed. Nothing was going to bring little Claire Sanderson back to them.

Even if she was still alive, she was an adult now, with a life of her own.

Still, if there was the slightest chance…

A rustle outside the door told Cal his father was up. Probably to take one of the sleeping pills his father relied on when the blessed relief of unconsciousness evaded him, the nights the demons attacked.

Resisting the urge to go out and talk to him—to offer some comfort to the man who'd sired him and sacrificed the rest of his life for him—Cal listened for the click of the medicine cabinet in the bathroom. For the running water that would follow.

Frank Whittier took sleeping pills often. Cal never left his writing to go watch him take them. His father would wonder what was going on if Cal walked in on him now.

And so he listened as his old man shuffled back to his room.

Cal had no idea who had stolen the evidence Ramsey was after. Especially after a quarter of a century. But he had to find out.

A resurgence of suspicion would kill his father.

Not touching the bear, Cal quietly closed the lid on the box.

CHAPTER SIXTEEN

WHEN HER PHONE RANG at ten o'clock on Thursday night, Morgan almost didn't answer it.

Partially because she'd been watching the clock. Thinking about him. And his date.

Wondering if he'd call.

Pathetic.

And partially because her heart leaped into her throat when the ringtone sounded.

"Hello?" Her greeting was slightly hurried. Had she left it too late? Had he already been sent to voice mail?

Was she weak for answering?

"It's Cal. You busy?"

"No. Just sorting buttons into color-coded compartments so the four-year-olds can glue them to the pictures they drew today. It's a spatial as well as a color-recognition assignment. The buttons are in place of crayons."

Like he cared. She was babbling.

His self-possessed, kind-looking, beautiful date didn't babble. Morgan was certain of that.

She also wasn't a student like Morgan. She'd talked about meeting a student, which meant she was a teacher, like Cal. Probably an art prof at Wallace judging by what she'd said about something drying in the kiln.

"What was their drawing assignment?"

"Full-body self-portraits. They could be standing still or doing something."

He chuckled, and she closed her bedroom door, sinking down on the edge of her bed. She'd put on her pink striped, capri-length pajamas an hour before.

"I'll bet they were interesting."

Smiling, she dug her toes into the light blue old shag carpet that she'd replace if the place were hers. And she could afford new carpet. "One little guy had himself pulling chocolate cookies out of the oven."

"You could tell that by looking at his picture?"

"No, he told me."

"Do you always have the four-year-olds?"

"No, I teach the four-year-old class on Tuesdays and Thursdays in the summer, and do administrative work the rest of the time. Officially I'm assistant to the director, Bonnie Blake, but she's really good about working around my classes. I also fill in for the regular teachers when they need me to."

"You like the work?"

Pulling her feet up on the bed, she tucked them under her legs. "I really do. Which is something my father was never able to understand. He didn't think I should work at all, but if I insisted on it, then I should get a job where I have the possibility of making real money."

"He doesn't think caring for young children is good

enough for you? Does he understand that you're shaping the future of this country?"

"Spoken like a true educator!" Morgan smiled again. And then sobered. "How was your date?"

"Fine."

That was it. He didn't offer up anything about who she was. Or how her lasagna tasted. He didn't even say the date was over. For all she knew the woman was doing the dishes while Cal excused himself to make a call to one of his students.

"How was the meeting with Leslie?" he asked when her silence hung between them.

Fine, she was tempted to say. Meant to say. What came out was, "She thinks that Sammie needs male companionship."

"She's going to recommend that your father get custody?" His incredulous tone did her heart good.

"She didn't say that. Nor did she say she wouldn't. She gave me no indication at all how she was going to weigh in at the hearing. She just talked about Sammie. She thinks he needs a man in his life."

"There are a lot of ways to accomplish that."

"I know. I've been working on it most of the evening. I've looked up the local Big Brothers organization and left a message on their voice mail, but it says that it usually takes a couple of weeks after the initial interview to find a good match. They don't want to place him with just anyone on their list. They try to find a man whose schedule not only matches Sammie's, but who has similar interests."

Bringing her knees up to her chest, Morgan hugged

them against her. "I also looked at scouting, but Cub Scouts don't meet during the summer, so Big Brothers is my best option. I'm worried about the two-week wait, though. We go to court in twelve days...."

Cal was quiet for so long, Morgan wondered if the call had been dropped. She checked her phone's display to see that their connection was still active. And then she was just plain embarrassed for having gone on for so long.

He was being kind and she was burdening him with every detail of her life.

"I have a proposal to make." Tingles slid through her when his deep voice came over the line. "Hear me out, and if you feel in any way uncomfortable with what I propose, I trust that you will let me know."

Heart pounding, she said, "Okay."

"I'm being presumptuous here, but it occurs to me that we might be able to help each other."

His words didn't settle her heart any. "Okay."

"For the next several weeks you're still my student and I am very conscious of the boundaries that places on us."

She was twenty-nine and in college. As long as he didn't fudge a grade for her there would be no impropriety in them knowing each other.

Not that she'd thought about it or anything. Ha! Just a hundred times or so over the past four years.

"At the same time, I think you would agree that our relationship has changed over this past week."

"I would, yes," she said, echoing his formal tone. Her mind was all over the place. Trying to figure out where this was going. She got stopped at the phrase "help each other." What kind of help could Cal Whittier need?

Especially when he had a sexy, earthy woman like Kelsey offering to make him dinner?

"I told you that my father lives with me."

"Right."

"What I didn't say was that he's there because if I left him to live alone, he would sit in his chair until he died."

Obviously he was exaggerating.

"My father is suffering from severe depression."

"Is he on medication?"

"No. The one time I got him into a clinic to be evaluated, they prescribed an antidepressant but he refused to take it. He also refused to go back."

"How can I help?" The question was natural. Automatic.

"I'm not sure, but it occurred to me, as I listened to you talk about Big Brothers, that maybe Dad and I could help you—at least until you can get a match for Sammie—and being with Sammie might help Dad, too."

Morgan breathed her first easy breath since she'd left Leslie Dinsmore's office.

"Do you think your father would be willing to spend time with Sammie? Shouldn't you ask him before you commit him to something?"

"I think he will. And if he doesn't, I'll still do it. I could bring Sammie over here and if Dad participates, fine, and if he doesn't, we tried."

"I take it you've tried things with him before?"

"He's supposed to be on a fishing trip this week. I might have mentioned that. I paid for the whole thing in advance, arranged transportation for him, bought him everything he needed, helped him pack, and at the last minute he refused to go."

"What makes you think spending time with Sammie will be any different?"

"I told you my father used to be a teacher. He was actually the headmaster at an affluent all-boys school. He was also their basketball coach, and in just two years got them their first winning season in a very long time. You said Sammie lives and breathes basketball."

Could life really work out so well? Was she missing something here? Was she lacking good judgment again?

She didn't think so. It seemed to her that the lapse in judgment would be to turn down her one hope of proving to the court that she could give Sammie every opportunity he needed. Even on short notice.

But…her mind raced. What would the risks be?

"Does your father have a temper?"

"As much as anyone. He's not violent, if that's what you're asking." He didn't sound the least bit put out by her question. "And his professional record is completely clean. Not a single complaint."

"Can I be there? Can I meet your dad and see how Sammie takes to him? And then I'd go. I know this is supposed to be guy time."

"Of course you can be there." Cal's voice was soft.

Understanding. It soothed her tattered nerves until she wanted nothing more than to curl up with her head on his chest and go to sleep. "We've got some curtains that need to be replaced. I could use your opinion on what to buy."

She didn't know a whole lot about curtains, but she wasn't going to let that stop her. "Sure! When were you thinking?"

"You busy Saturday morning?"

"Nope."

"The first time I meet Sammie, I'd like it to be on his own turf. My place is kind of hard to find anyway, so how about I pick you two up, say, around ten, and we'll see what happens."

"Sounds good." She was grinning from ear to ear. Feeling blessed. And stupid as hell for feeling so good.

He was being a friend. It wasn't as if she'd never had one of those before.

"I DON'T WANT TO GO over to some stupid teacher's house! It's Saturday morning. You're supposed to give me computer time."

"I'll give you computer time this afternoon, Sammie. We'll skip Saturday afternoon chores this week." She'd do all the dusting and vacuuming by herself while Sammie visited with her folks tomorrow.

A visit that had been recommended by Leslie Dinsmore so, of course, Morgan had to agree to it.

Prior to her father's lawsuit, she'd have allowed the visit anyway. She never got in the way of her parents' relationship with their grandson. Her father's lack of time spent with Sammie was strictly her father's doing.

Not that she expected anyone in the court system to believe her word against his on that one.

"I'm not going." Sammie was speaking to her through the bathroom door again. If this kept up, she was going to take the handle out of the door.

"Professor Whittier will be here in fifteen minutes," she said, trying not to lose her temper with her son, reminding herself that if Cal weren't involved, she wouldn't care how this looked. She'd be thinking about what Sammie was thinking and feeling and trying to communicate.

"I don't care." His anger was obvious, if a bit less intimidating for the fact that he wasn't all that close. She'd bet he was sitting on the toilet.

"Look, Sammie, I'm doing the best I know how to be a good mother to you. I know you aren't real happy with me right now and I'm sorry about that. But the bottom line is I *am* the parent here. By law, you have to have a guardian. You're only ten. You aren't permitted to be your own boss. And right now, I am that guardian. If you want that to change, I guess you just have to tell Leslie that." No point in splitting hairs here. Sammie wasn't stupid. For all she knew he'd already told his counselor that she sucked as a parent and he wanted out.

"In the meantime, I'm the boss and I say you need to spend some time around men. You're so insistent that you are one and it's time you see how real men act so you can be one, too."

"I see men at school."

"They're at work then. You should get to know some men outside of work situations."

"These guys don't know me. They'll just be doing a job."

"You don't know them, Sammie, but they feel like they know you. Professor Whittier sat up with me all night on Friday. He didn't sleep from the time you left until the police brought you home. His father was in touch throughout that whole time, too. Lots of people we've never heard of were out looking for you and following the news to make certain you were okay."

Sammie had no idea how much trouble his little escapade had caused. But then, how could he? He saw the world through the eyes of a ten-year-old.

"Nuh-uh." The voice was muffled through the door, but closer to it. "I didn't see him here." The belligerence was still there, but it had softened some.

"Because he left while I was hugging the daylights out of you."

"It's you he likes, not me. Go ahead and date him. You don't need my approval."

Good heavens. Why had she ever thought she could raise a boy on her own? "I'm definitely *not* dating him, Samuel. He's got a girlfriend. She made lasagna for him just last night."

She took his silence as a good sign.

"Please come out, Sammie. Because if you don't I'm going to have to take the door off the hinges and I don't want to embarrass you that way."

"What if I don't like this guy?"

"As long as you've given him a fair shot, you tell me you don't like him and we politely thank him for his time and come back here and clean house."

The bathroom door opened.

CAL DIDN'T GET HIMSELF all wrapped up in other people's lives. He didn't allow relationships to form beyond the superficial. He had no expectations. So why in the hell had he been up at dawn replacing the basketball net on the old hoop attached to the garage?

Why had he offered to help at all? He knew better than to open Frank and himself up to the world.

What if George Lowen had *them* investigated?

The thought stopped him cold.

And what if he did? Ramsey Miller couldn't find anything to prove that Frank was guilty of wrongdoing. All of the cops before him hadn't found proof.

He and Frank had been living in the past for too long. Frank's reputation was no longer as important as it once was.

Cal had built his own reputation. He had a good job. He could support the both of them. He wasn't going to let his own paranoia and fear of George Lowen keep him from being Morgan's friend. He wasn't going to desert her in her moment of need.

And he wasn't going to keep running scared for Frank's sake. Feeding his father's fears. He'd just have to make sure his father remained unaware of any queries. That shouldn't be too difficult, since no one knew how to reach Frank directly unless they waited for him outside the Alzheimer's unit. Net fixed, Cal grabbed the box containing a new basketball and went into the house to seek out his old man.

"I did what you said, Dad, and talked to that girl. Morgan."

"How's her son?"

"There's some backlash. I'm bringing them over here to spend a little time with us this morning," he said, extracting the basketball from its packaging.

"Fine."

"You going to be around?"

"Aren't I always?"

"I mean, will you come out of your damn room and be a part of this?"

"If you want me to, fine."

Dressed in jeans and a T-shirt with a big orange *T,* for University of Tennessee Basketball, emblazoned across the front and new sneakers on his feet, Cal stood in the doorway of his father's room and stared.

"Really?"

It was that easy?

Just bring someone over and his father would join the world of the living?

"The girl obviously means something to you, Cal."

"She's a student."

"You've never visited a student at home before."

"Her son was missing. It reminded me of…you know what it reminded me of."

"At first, that's why you went. It's not why you stayed."

"I'm seeing someone, Dad. I told you that. I was

there Thursday night, remember? Her name's Kelsey.
She's an art professor and I like her a lot."

"Sure you do. Just like you like all the others."

"Yeah, so? What's your point?"

"I have no point to make, son. You started this."

Sometimes his father really pissed him off. Tossing
the new basketball into Frank's room, he walked out.

CHAPTER SEVENTEEN

MORGAN FOLLOWED Cal to his place, driving Sammie. She'd agreed to his request to meet Sammie on Sammie's turf, thinking the boy would be more comfortable with that. And Cal had said his place was kind of hard to find. But at the same time, she wanted to be free to keep her promise to Sammie and leave the second he said he was ready to go.

Or, if she got really lucky, to be able to slip out to the grocery alone while her son spent time with Cal and his father.

For the first ten minutes of the drive, her son had been engrossed in the handheld gaming device his grandmother had given him. Morgan was trying to decide if she was going to let him take it into Cal's house or not. On the one hand, she didn't want to incite an argument with Sammie by forcing him to leave the game in the car. On the other hand, she didn't want her son wasting two grown men's time by sitting in their home and ignoring them while he shot at martians.

Putting the unresolved issue aside for a moment, she wondered what Cal had thought of her son. Their meeting replayed itself in her mind. Her answering the door. Calling out to Sammie, who showed up dressed in respectable cotton shorts, a tank top she'd picked up for two dollars at a discount store and the basketball shoes with the hole in the toe. Cal looking her straight in the eye for a second, like he was as glad to see her as she was to see him, then turning his focus on Sammie and saying hello.

Sammie had answered back, politely enough. And then they'd split up into the two cars to make the trek out to Cal's place.

It had been completely uneventful. But she was obsessing about it anyway.

Had the UT basketball shirt he'd had on been for Sammie's benefit?

Could he tell she was sexually attracted to him?

Where in the hell had that thought come from?

Morgan glanced at her son. "Thanks for doing this, Sammie."

"Whatever." *It's not like I had a lot of choice,* her son's tone seemed to say.

"What did you think of Professor Whittier?"

"He says hello nice." Sammie's voice dripped with sarcasm.

Morgan took a deep breath. She loved her son more than life. If she had to go through pain and stress while raising him, then so be it. He was worth anything she might have to endure. *Anything.*

Cal's house was set back in some woods, down a curving driveway. The brick house was quite a bit larger than her duplex, but still not huge. The bungalow was well kept and had a newish-looking roof.

"New ropes," Sammie said. Following her son's gaze up to the garage roof line, Morgan saw the old rusty hoop hung with a fresh white basket and couldn't speak.

Not that she needed to. Her son had already opened the passenger's side door and was climbing out. It was only when the door slammed shut behind him that she saw the gaming device resting abandoned on his seat.

YOU'D THINK A MAN who made his living by teaching others would learn from his own lessons. Especially when he'd learned his lessons the hard way as Cal had.

You didn't bring anyone into your home. You didn't let anyone that close.

It was too personal.

It opened your life up to more than just casual curiosity and questions.

Morgan looked out of place sitting at the hand-carved wooden table Frank had bought from an Amish family fifteen years before. That, the file cabinet and the recliner in Frank's bedroom were the only pieces of furniture that had moved with them every place they went.

The intricate carvings on the table depicted a family, and each of the four chairs had the likeness of a mother, father, sister or brother on the wooden back.

Morgan perched on the edge of the mother chair at one end of the table. She looked ready to take flight.

"Where's your television?" Sammie asked, standing under the archway between the living room and kitchen.

"Over there." Cal pointed to a small flat screen

mounted on the back wall across from the couch. "The big screen is in Frank's room."

Sammie looked at the old man who sat in the father chair. In the ten minutes the Lowens had been there, Frank had slowly scooted his chair away from the table and into the far corner of the room. He hadn't said a word since his initial hello.

Cal had taken a chance bringing Sammie here. He'd known that. His father hadn't had one-on-one contact with a child other than Cal since they'd left Comfort Cove twenty-five years ago. Certainly not in their home.

He'd wanted no suspicion whatsoever that he had a thing for kids.

Sammie returned from an inspection of the television, looking around some more before stopping about six feet in front of Frank.

"You watch a lot of TV at night?" Sammie asked.

"Yes." That was it. No smile. Frank didn't even look Sammie in the eye. This from a man who had once been known for his charisma with kids.

Nodding, Sammie continued with his exploration of their small space.

"You guys don't have much stuff out," Sammie declared next. "No pictures or stuff on the walls."

Sitting up straight, Morgan said, "Sammie, that's not polite." She glanced at Cal. "I apologize. Now where are those curtains you wanted me to take a look at?"

"Those are the ones over there." He pointed to the window over the kitchen sink, and to a bay window farther down the wall. Morgan went over to look. She noted the type of rod, asked for a measuring tape and talked about finding something in yellow to brighten up the room. Then she offered to pick them up for him.

Silence fell on the room again. Cal felt like a tongue-tied schoolkid who'd invited the popular kids to a party that was a total flop. What about Morgan Lowen had prompted him to break his and his father's rules? Why had he suddenly opened up their lives to someone after twenty-five years of living in relative seclusion?

And then he remembered...

Retrieving a shopping bag from the closet, he held it out to the boy. "Sammie, this is for you," he said.

Sammie got up from the floor in front of the book-case where he'd been perusing their collection of DVDs, came over and took the sack. Holding the handles open he glanced inside.

"Cool! No way! Look, Mom!" He pulled out the shoebox the salesclerk at the sports store had placed in the bag the day before. "They're even the right size."

The boy's grin made every awkward second of the past half hour worth the agony.

And then Cal looked at Sammie's mom. She wasn't smiling.

"I got his shoe size from the description on the Amber Alert."

Sammie stilled, dropping the lid of the shoebox to the floor, but not touching the name brand basketball shoes inside. "I can have them, can't I, Mom?"

Frank stood, his six-foot frame appearing increasingly diminished each day as his weighted shoulders slumped more and more. "If you'll excuse me…"

Frank left the room. Cal heard the bathroom door click quietly closed a minute later. Cal wanted to go after him. His dad was acting more strangely than usual.

He shouldn't have pushed this.

"Mom? Can I have the shoes?"

"I can't afford them, Sammie." Morgan's words were softly spoken.

"Uh, I thought maybe Sammie could work them off," Cal said. "We've been overrun with weeds this summer and I could sure use some help digging them all up."

"Can I, Mom? Please?"

Morgan glanced at Cal, and the look in her eye, promising a long talk as soon as they were alone, gave him a weird thrill inside. But when she told her son he could keep the shoes if he worked them off, Cal allowed himself to be distracted by the boy's enthusiasm as he dug into the box.

"You going to stick around forever, Mom?" Sammie asked as he carefully laced up his new shoes.

Morgan glanced at Cal. He wasn't sure what to do. Or say.

"You said you wanted me to have some man time, Mom. We can't very well do that with you sitting there."

"Sammie, please be more careful with your word choices."

"Sorry." Sammie's big brown eyes lowered for

a second and then, with a curious glint in them, he glanced over at Cal. "Did you ask my mom to bring me here?"

"Yes."

"Because of her? Am I an excuse for you to spend time with her? I mean, the shoes are cool and all, and I'll still work them off, but if this is just so you can get closer to her I'd like to know."

He could see why Morgan had challenges with this kid. But he liked him. "No, this isn't so I can spend more time with your mom."

"You swear?" The kid's gaze hadn't wavered.

"Yes."

His father's bedroom door closed.

Morgan looked at Cal. And then down the hall where Frank had disappeared. "What would you like me to do?"

"How about you give us an hour?" he said to Morgan. "We can shoot some hoops and maybe get some ice cream." He'd get the kid out of the house, out of his father's space. He could deal with his father later. Cal pulled some bills out of his pocket. "Maybe you could pick up some curtains while you're out?"

Morgan stood, nodding, but didn't smile as she took his money. "Okay. Call me if you need anything...."

"Sammie, why don't you grab the ball over there and head out to warm up the hoop?"

With a serious face, Sammie nodded, looking from Cal to Morgan. "You're coming out, too, aren't you?" he asked Cal.

"Yes. I'll be right out."

With a glance toward the hall leading to the bedrooms, Sammie walked out the door.

"I'm really sorry about the shoes," Cal said the second the door shut behind Sammie.

"You should have asked me first."

"I figured if I did you'd just say no."

"So you manipulated me instead?" She didn't sound mad. Just bewildered.

"I guess I did." He looked right at her. "But not purposely. I remembered what you said about his shoes with the hole in the toe…"

"…to the point of remembering his correct shoe size," she added, her gaze soft and warm even when she was upset.

"I thought they'd be a good ice breaker with Dad and Sammie."

"It was nice of you," she said, and then asked softly, "What's up with your father? Is he angry that we're here?"

"No. He's just not used to being around people. Not anymore."

"You said he has a job."

"On an Alzheimer's unit, cleaning floors and fixing things that break, not working with the patients. Or even the staff, really."

Frank hadn't been around kids since Cal had grown out of being one. And Cal was giving away too much. The more he answered, the more questions she'd have. He had to stop this.

"Will he be okay?"

"He'll be fine," Cal assured himself as much as

her. Today's episode had been just one more failed attempt to bring his father out of himself and back into the living world.

Not that he blamed Frank. He thought of Ramsey. Of the suspicions that had followed them for twenty-five years. They weren't ever going away.

Which meant that his father would never be free.

MORGAN BOUGHT THE CURTAINS right away. She wanted to be able to get back, just in case she received a call that there was a problem.

She wasn't sure about his father. The man was more than just depressed. He was removed from the world.

He'd kind of given her the creeps. To the point that she'd considered not leaving Sammie, after all. But she trusted Cal.

And her son needed male companionship now. Before their court date in nine days. Stating that she'd applied to a mentoring program wasn't going to be good enough.

Not when she was up against her father.

Instead of going grocery shopping next, Morgan drove to the state park that was only a few miles from Cal's place. Pulling into a lot that overlooked the lake, she turned on the MP3 player hooked up to the car's stereo system, chose her country music playlist and turned up the volume. She lay back in the driver's seat to indulge herself for the last private half hour she'd have this weekend.

CHAPTER EIGHTEEN

SAMMIE TOOK THE BALL in and shot at the net. The leather spun off his little fingertips and swooshed through the hoop.

"Good one," Cal said, rebounding and taking the ball out for a three pointer.

He made the basket.

"You ever play on a team?" Sammie asked, going in for his next attempt. He performed a mock hook shot layup by jumping, launching the ball with one hand and using the backboard to propel the ball where his height couldn't take it.

"No," Cal answered, grabbing the ball as it came through the net. "My dad's the real basketball player around here. He used to coach."

"You're pretty good."

"We spent a lot of time playing one-on-one, or Around the World, when I was a kid," he said. "But I didn't play sports in school." He hadn't been at any one school long enough to make a team. Nor had he been able to take a chance that any newspaper clippings regarding local games might somehow trigger something for someone in connection to what happened in Comfort Cove, Massachusetts.

The boy double-dribbled and made another shot.

"Why don't you like my mom?"

Cal missed his answering lob. "What?"

"Don't you think she's pretty?"

"Of course!"

"She's worth a lot of money, someday, you know."

What was this? Was the kid selling his mother? Was it something he did a lot?

"I would hope no one likes her just because of that." He stole the ball from the boy and took it downcourt. Shot. Missed.

"Sure they do." Sammie rebounded, but tossed the ball back to Cal for another try. "That's why she doesn't date."

Holding the ball midair, Cal stared at the boy. "She told you that?"

"No, Grandma did. And she didn't really tell me. I heard her telling Grandpa."

It took a lot of willpower to keep Cal from asking what the older man had said. Because it would be wrong to use the kid that way.

"So why don't you like her?"

He was prepared to play ball and dig weeds. Not to have an intimate conversation. Boys didn't have those. Not in his family, anyway.

He made his next attempt at a basket. "I do like her."

"Then you want to date her?" Sammie rebounded, jumped and missed, rebounded and jumped again.

"I'm seeing someone."

"Yeah, that's what she said." The boy missed again and took the ball down the driveway to bring it back up for a fresh try. He made the basket from the foul line.

"She talked to you about dating me?"

"When I asked, sure. Mom talks to me about everything."

Probably not quite everything, but it was good that the boy thought so.

"If you weren't seeing anyone, would you date her?"

Cal had never known there were so many minefields on a basketball court.

"She's a student of mine in school." He made a right-handed hook shot, rebounded and went for the left. Which he missed.

"But she'll be out of school before my real school even starts again. She's graduating."

Cal knew that.

Sammie stood there, a four-foot-something wizard, bouncing the ball back and forth between his hands.

"What's with all the questions about your mom's love life?" Cal finally figured out that he had to take the offense here or lose all control of the conversation.

"I dunno." Shrugging, Sammie took another shot. They played a little one-on-one and then the boy said, "It's just that she never dates and I know it's because of me."

"How do you know that?"

"Grandpa said so."

"To your grandma?"

"Yeah."

"Did you ever think that maybe you shouldn't listen to people's private conversations?"

"No."

"Well, maybe you shouldn't."

"If she waits for me to grow up before she dates, she'll be too old."

Cal tossed the ball to the kid. "She'll never be too old for someone to love her," he said. He was flailing around in his mind for more to add, something meaningful and deep that would satisfy the boy.

And keep him from repeating his fears to his mother. That was all Morgan needed—to think she had to start dating to meet her son's needs.

Dating wasn't something Cal could help her with.

And he sure as hell didn't like the idea of her going out with someone else just to satisfy a need in her son's fragile psyche.

"Your mother will date when…"

Cal had no idea what he was going to say—was making it up as he went—and was thankfully interrupted by the back door opening.

And then he stood speechless for an entirely different reason.

Frank Whittier stood there, dressed in basketball shorts that hung to his knees, a T-shirt that left no doubt the old man still had the chest and shoulders to be an athlete and a pair of scuffed basketball shoes.

"You need some help with your footwork, son," he said. "Here, let me show you." Frank took the ball from Sammie's grasp, and for the next half hour he monopolized the boy's mind with the things he should be thinking about—the intricacies of good basketball.

MORGAN CLEANED LIKE a madwoman while Sammie was with her parents on Sunday. Saying goodbye to her son, telling him to have a good time and to tell her parents hello for her had been the second-hardest thing she'd done in her life. The first had been sitting up all the previous Friday night waiting to hear if Sammie was dead or alive. To know if he was ever coming home to her again.

She knew he'd be coming back Sunday night. She just didn't know if his return would be temporary.

And so she cleaned. Her closet. Sammie's closet. The kitchen cupboards and refrigerator. She cleaned out her desk drawers and the bathroom drawers. She did the usual dusting and vacuuming and scouring, too. And when her mother called to say that they were taking Sammie out to his favorite gourmet burger place for dinner and would be bringing him home late, Morgan didn't argue. Though, technically, she had the right to.

She baked chocolate-chip cookies instead. Sammie's favorite.

And then ate half a batch of them waiting for him to get home.

At which time, stuffed from his dinner out, he was too full to eat them. He took his gaming device, kissed her good-night and went to bed. Not even noticing that one of the things she'd cleaned out of his room was the baby monitor.

AFTER A NEARLY SLEEPLESS night, Morgan dragged herself into class Monday morning. Attendance made up a percentage of her grade and she wasn't going to put Professor Whittier in the awkward position of having to either grade her down or do her a favor. She didn't want any favors.

Several reasons accounted for her lack of sleep. No monitor. Too many cookies. And too little Sammie. She was panicked that their time together was coming to an end.

Cal looked great that morning. Wearing a white shirt, dark blue pants and tie, and maroon leather shoes, he could have walked out of one of her dad's boardrooms. Or off a film set.

He was giving an overview of their final paper. Morgan already had hers half-done. She'd chosen to write about Mark Twain's lifelong message and had way more to say than the word count would allow.

Bella didn't seem to have any grasp on her paper, based on the number of questions she had.

Cal tended to his adoring fans with the grace of a great movie star, exuding a sexiness that kept every woman in his sphere riveted.

It was embarrassing, really, the way her classmates flirted with him. Thinking that because he was male, all he would care was that they were sexy and blonde and available.

Morgan was sure he'd experienced his share of erotic sexual encounters. She bet he knew his way around a woman's body—every curve and nub and opening.

Grabbing her water bottle from her pack, Morgan took a long sip of water. Cal glanced her way, letting his gaze rest on her for an excruciatingly long second before he moved on, leaving her a bit warmer than before.

Another woman in her row—Lyla Something-or-Other—had his attention now. As he moved nearer to her, Morgan's own attention went to the rock-hard thighs encased in his expertly creased dress pants. Last night she'd dreamed about those thighs, dreamed they were wrapped around her.... Morgan silently cursed herself. Cal Whittier's private parts, or the size of them, were entirely not her business.

"I didn't realize English was so boring." Whittier was looking straight at her. And so was the rest of the class.

"You care to join us this morning, Ms. Lowen?" he asked, kindly enough. The class chuckled.

"Sorry, sir. Didn't get much sleep last night. Uh, you aren't boring, sir." As soon as the words were out of her mouth she realized what she'd said.

Floor, please, now. Swallow me up.

"He asked you if you had any questions about your paper," Bella whispered from across the aisle, loudly enough for everyone to hear.

"Oh, sorry. No, sir. I'm good."

Like hell she was.

She felt hot and horny and scared to death she was going to lose her son, and feeling more alone than she'd felt in her entire life.

What was a little embarrassment on top of all that?

MORGAN'S LACK OF ATTENTIVENESS in his class bothered him. And it bothered him that that bothered him.

Which was why, when his father's ringtone sounded ten minutes after class, he picked up with a slightly impatient, "What?" And then quickly tempered it with, "Is everything okay, Dad?"

"I was just called in to Dwayne's office."

Dwayne Summers, their landlord, and his father's boss. The fact that the other man was communicating with his father was not the least bit unusual. The fact that his father was calling him and telling him about it was.

"What did he want?"

"He thought I'd applied for a job elsewhere."

"Why would he think that?"

"Someone called. Asked questions about me."

Damn. Rubbing his head, Cal dropped down to the couch in his office. "What questions?"

"How long I've been here. What kind of work I do. Am I a good employee. Reliable. Timely."

"Who was it?"

"A Ramsey Miller. Guy just gave his name. Didn't say where he was calling from. Dwayne thought I'd applied somewhere and gave him as a reference."

The words running through his mind were good in any language. And just as useless, too. Obviously Miller had put a private investigator on Cal. And found Frank by default.

"You told him you're not leaving, I take it?"

"I told him."

"And?"

"He was glad to hear it."

"I'll check on this Ramsey Miller guy and get back

to you. Just hang tight, Dad. I'm sure it's nothing." He hoped to God he wouldn't be struck down for lying before he could get his father out of this.

Whatever it took.

CHAPTER NINETEEN

MILLER DIDN'T TAKE Cal's call. Not any of the times he tried to reach the Comfort Cove detective that day. And Cal didn't leave any messages. He'd talk to the guy on his time. His terms.

But Miller had better understand that he *would* talk to him.

In the meantime, Cal had another matter to tend to. Not as disturbing as the Miller issue, but one that was still niggling away at his brain.

He put it off until ten o'clock that night, telling himself that if he gave himself time, he'd just let it go.

In truth, as soon as Morgan Lowen answered the phone, he knew that nothing short of her voice had been going to soothe what was eating at him.

"Are you still planning for Sammie to come here tomorrow after school?"

They'd made the arrangement when she'd picked her son up on Saturday. Instead of going to the day care after school, as he sometimes did when Morgan was working, Sammie was going to be spending Tuesday and Thursday afternoons with Cal and Frank.

Unless his mother had changed her mind sometime between noon on Saturday and Monday morning when, for the first time in four years, she hadn't been paying attention in his class.

Every student had days when their minds wandered. He knew that. Expected it.

And she had a hell of a lot on her mind.

But…

"Yes. Unless you need me to make other plans."

"No." Sitting at the computer in his home office, Cal took a sip of whiskey and stared at the blinking cursor awaiting his attention. An autobiography of sorts, a compilation of researched facts and memories, should not take twenty years to complete.

And maybe it wouldn't have if he didn't keep going back over it, and every bit of research he'd done, searching for the answers that were missing. If he didn't keep delaying the process by finding more research to do.

"So you'll pick him up from school at three as planned?"

"Yes." Why was he taking her lack of attention personally? It wasn't as if he'd been lecturing. And even then…

"I let Julie know to release him to you." Morgan interrupted his mental discomfort. "Since she met you last week you won't need to show identification."

She told him how to find the principal's office where Sammie would be waiting with Julie. He took notes.

And when she was telling him thank-you and it sounded like goodbye was coming next, he said, "Everything else okay?"

"Yeah. Fine. The enrollment drive for the day care,

which I missed on Saturday, was successful and I have a lot of extra paperwork to do to get all the kids registered by the start of school in September."

Not quite what he'd been asking. But he was interested, just the same.

"I'm sorry for this morning, Cal." Her voice had dropped. Like she was speaking intimately.

Or maybe his body just reacted that way because he'd had a long day.

"What was going on?" he asked.

"I didn't sleep much last night. And my paper is already half-done. My mind just wandered."

He knew immediately that she wasn't telling him the whole story. But she didn't owe him anything.

"You're sure everything is okay?"

"Yeah."

"No repercussions with Sammie?"

"He's actually been nicer since he was at your house. I don't know how I'm ever going to thank you for all of this."

"You thank me every time I walk through the kitchen. I can't believe how much of a difference the new curtains make."

"Curtains are hardly comparable to my son's life," she said with a sleepy chuckle. Cal wondered if she was in her bedroom.

He took another sip of whiskey. It was already half-gone. He had to get back to his book.

"I'll see you tomorrow, then," he said, wincing at his abruptness. "When you come by to get Sammie after work."

"You're sure he's not a problem?"

"If things go as well as they ended up on Saturday, I'm going to be the one in debt here," he told her. "We might be helping a little bit with Sammie, but he could be giving my father back a piece of life."

So they were even. No one owed anyone anything. Except him. He owed Kelsey Barber dinner.

AFTER ANOTHER SLEEPLESS night, Morgan dropped Sammie off at class on Tuesday.

"Remember, Professor Whittier will be picking you up this afternoon."

"I know, Mom. I'm going straight to Julie's office to wait for him." The boy's tone was affable. Maybe even eager.

Could a lack of male companionship really have been their problem?

"I'll remember to be polite and you don't have to hurry to pick me up," he added quickly. As soon as the words were out of his mouth he turned to her, a frown between his brows. "You've got the four-year-olds today, and it's Tuesday so the twins' dad will be coming to get them. Don't worry if he's late, is all. I'll be fine."

Her little man. So maturely aware of her feelings, too. What would she do if she lost him?

What would he become under her father's chauvinistic rule?

With the kiss to his cheek that he still allowed her, Morgan sent him off and watched until he was inside the building. Then, still sitting outside his school, she opened her cell phone.

The number wasn't on speed dial. But she knew it by heart. And was slightly shocked when her father picked up. Until he spoke.

"So you've finally changed your mind? You ready to end this thing before you drag that boy into court?"

She almost hung up. "I want to talk to you, Daddy. I know it's late notice, but can you meet me for lunch today?" She had an hour.

"I've got the Lyle brothers coming in, and then Dennison." He paused. She heard a page turn. "I'll have Margaret call and bump them an hour." He told her to meet him at his favorite restaurant at noon.

He didn't ask about her schedule. Didn't consider her work. Or the fact that she had lunch from eleven-thirty to twelve-thirty.

But she wouldn't get angry. Anger would be counterproductive. It wouldn't help Sammie. And she could have someone cover her class if she didn't make it back right at twelve-thirty. She'd arranged for a dance instructor to come in that afternoon, anyway. All anyone would have to do for her was supervise.

"Thank you, Daddy."

For her own mental health she translated his harrumph into "you're welcome."

CAL ONLY HAD TWO classes during summer session. The upper-level literature class he had with Morgan, and another, individually regulated graduate-level English Lit Review class. The latter had eleven students, all working independently and meeting with him as their schedules coordinated with his. Each student had to pick ten pieces of English literature from a predetermined list and write twenty-page reviews, analyzing the works according to a series of set guidelines. Cal's job was to assist them, answer their questions, discuss their work and provide grades.

Messages from two students requesting meetings were waiting for him on his answering machine Tuesday morning. Along with a return call from Ramsey Miller.

Cal called the cop first.

"Leave my father alone, Detective." The demand was unequivocal. Harassment was against the law. Not that a detective following up on leads in a case was harassment, but there came a point…

"I am doing my job, Professor," the man shot back. "I have a crime to solve and I *will* do what it takes to solve it."

"My father has not been out of this city in several years. He couldn't possibly have taken your evidence."

"He could still easily be involved in its disappearance. Like I said, *Professor,* I will do what it takes."

Cal leaned one hand against the window frame in his office, looking out over the green expanse below, at the people scurrying to and fro, or basking in the sun on the quad. A couple of guys were throwing a Frisbee.

Standing there in his olive slacks, white shirt and striped tie, he couldn't remember a time when he'd been that carefree.

"Even if it kills an innocent sixty-two-year-old

man?" Cal's voice was no less steely for the drop in volume. "My father was a respected educator. A man with a whole list of kids he saved from making poor choices. A list that would have been much longer if your people hadn't branded him so completely that you made it impossible for him to get work. You had nothing to charge him with, but the Comfort Cove police made certain that every time he tried to get a job, someone just happened to get a phone call and somehow the hiring boards would know to look at the missing-child case in Comfort Cove.

"The only job he was ever able to take was his current job as a janitor in an Alzheimer's unit. And now you're poking around there.

"My father holds a double doctorate degree from Harvard, Detective," Cal continued without taking a breath, saying the things he'd said in his mind a million times over the years.

"He has degrees in both psychology and education. He had so much to offer this world and he's been relegated to hiding out in a rental home and cleaning toilets for a living. And relationships?"

The man hadn't interrupted and so Cal just kept right on. "How could my father even hope to have one of those? What woman is going to tie herself to a man who is not in jail, who has no sentence he can finish serving, but who will never be free? A man with no credit, who has to live his whole life under the radar? One whose life can be cast with suspicion anytime, anyplace? He's a good, giving, honest man who has become a recluse because of you people supposedly doing your job."

He paused, and turned around. Took a deep breath.

"I grieve for Claire Sanderson every single day, Miller. You didn't know her. I did. I knew her sister, Emma, too. I loved them both. I thought we were a family. Claire's abduction is an abomination. But killing an innocent man is one also. Taking my father's life does not give Claire hers back."

When Miller remained silent, Cal finished on a softer note. "You all have had twenty-five years to find something on my father. You haven't done it. Look someplace else. Please."

"We are not focusing solely on your father." Miller's tone was softer, too. "But we need to know where that box of evidence is and why it was taken. I am not at liberty to discuss the details of our investigation, but rest assured, Professor, I come to work every day because of the children in this country who are missing, and to hopefully protect those who are not from becoming another statistic. I am not out to get you or your father."

"So you've had your look at us. Now leave us alone."

"I don't have my answers yet."

Cal identified with the frustration he heard in Miller's voice. He'd matured over the years. And had learned that putting out fires benefited himself and his father more than fueling them did.

Back at the window, he said, "I might be able to help."

"Help how?" The detective asked with silk in his

voice, reminding Cal of a feline ready to pounce on its prey.

If the man thought he was going to deliver his father up, he had another think coming.

"Not like you're thinking," he bit out. And then found the control he needed to soften his tone. "I've written a book. It's not done, but it documents what I know about the case. Every memory I have of Claire, of our family, of that day…it's all there. And everything I've found out since is there, too. While working on this journal over the years, I've gathered information, not just about Claire Sanderson, but about every single child abduction I could find that took place that year and the following couple of years.

"I've been scouring the internet for years—reading old newspaper articles as they're added to internet archives. Each abduction is filed according to the place the child went missing, but I have charts that also file them according to the type of abduction, age of child, sex of child, number of parents in the home, number and age of siblings, nationality, even date and place of birth. I've grouped them in any and every way I could think of to look for similarities."

He didn't mention the teddy bear that rested on top of those files.

"I take it, since you're telling me about these files, that you're willing to share them with me?"

Everything inside of him said no. Out loud he said, "Yes."

CHAPTER TWENTY

MORGAN MADE IT to lunch with five minutes to spare. Because she'd planned on meeting her father, she'd worn a pair of beige pants, a matching silk blouse and pumps that her mother had purchased for her. Her blond hair was up in the chignon her father liked, though she'd just pulled it up in the parking lot.

"Hi, Glen, is my father here yet?"

"Yes, right this way, Miss Lowen." The maître d' had been with the family since George Lowen had decided that the only way to be assured the best seat in the house of his favorite fine dining restaurant was to buy the place. Morgan had been ten at the time. Glen had just graduated high school and had been a host, seating guests.

George, dressed in a gray suit with a red silk tie, was already seated with a two-inch-thick T-bone steak and stuffed baked potato in front of him. His highball was half-empty.

The table was set with only two places. The second place had an entrée-size salad and a bottle of sparkling water waiting.

And bread. At least he'd remembered that she liked the sourdough bread, Morgan told herself as she took her seat, the petit filet she'd been envisioning fading from her mind.

"Hi, Daddy, thank you for meeting me," she said, leaning over to kiss the air by his cheek as though they met for lunch every week instead of once every five years.

"I know you like ranch dressing but I ordered honey mustard for you," he said as she sat down. "It's home-made and quite good."

She wanted ranch dressing. And she wanted this meeting to go well. "Thank you," she said, spreading her napkin in her lap before Glen had a chance to do so.

George took another big bite of steak. In lieu of saying anything to Glen, he dismissed the man with a nod and a full mouth.

The restaurant was perched above one of Tennessee's many lakes, and while the place was full, their table was in a private alcove that George had had erected just for him and his family. They had a perfect view of the lake and no one had a view of them.

Morgan did what she knew her father expected and ate the salad she didn't want with the dressing she didn't care for before speaking. George detested discussing anything of importance over his meal, saying it gave him indigestion.

Pushing his empty plate away, he motioned for a second highball—one was usually his norm—wiped his mouth on the linen napkin and turned his piercing gaze on her. "I assume you're here to discuss

Samuel's custody agreement. Do you want to talk about the visitation schedule?"

She couldn't let him get to her. They'd just end up fighting and nothing would be accomplished.

"I want you to drop your suit, Daddy," she said as quietly as she could. He wouldn't yell at her. Not here. But the sudden redness in his face was about as bad. She could hear the words without his having to actually speak them. She'd heard them often enough.

"Surely you have not just wasted my time."

"Sammie and I have been meeting the friend of the court that was assigned to us after you filed for custody." She chose her words carefully so as not to sound insubordinate. "She agreed with you that Sammie needs male companionship."

"Of course she does. It's obvious what the boy is lacking."

"But she also seemed to think that, at least for now, Sammie needs me, too."

"Did she say that outright?"

She would not be distracted. She had to think of Sammie.

"The thing is, Daddy, Professor Whittier, my English professor who stayed at the house with us the night that Sammie was missing, has been spending time with Sammie. And Sammie's responding. The change in him, in just a few days, is remarkable."

"How many times has he seen this man?"

George's highball appeared on the table. Morgan barely saw the waiter who delivered it.

"Cal is picking Sammie up after school every Tuesday and Thursday and watching him until I get off work so Sammie doesn't have to hang out at the day care as much anymore."

"It's about time. A day care is no place for a boy to grow into a man."

Sammie was learning responsibility at the day care. He was learning how to care for others. He was great with the little kids. But now wasn't the time to argue with George Lowen.

"All I'm asking, Daddy, is that you give us a chance. Sammie really likes spending time with Cal." Seeing the frown taking over her father's face, she hurriedly added, "He likes spending time with you and Mom, as well, of course, and if you'll drop this case we can set up a more regular schedule where Sammie sleeps over at your house several times a month."

George emptied half of his glass in one sip and Morgan's stomach sank.

"Did Leslie Dinsmore tell you outright that she thought Sammie needed to live with you?" he asked in that voice that always made her feel sick.

And that's when she knew that he was getting reports from every single meeting she and Sammie had with the "friend" of the court. More like "friend of her father," Morgan realized, hating herself for having thought for one second that Leslie Dinsmore had been an impartial party who would be fair to her.

"No, Daddy, she did not."

George stood. "Do not waste my time again, daughter." He turned away and then turned back and said, "A word of warning. If you want me to trust you with un-supervised visitations once the boy is settled in where he belongs, then you'd better not try to go against my wishes again. Do not resist me, Morgan. You will lose."

Morgan cried all the way back to the day care, but she made it in time to greet the dance instructor with a smile and introduce her to the children in her care.

PLAYING A HUNCH, Cal didn't stay outside for basketball practice. He shot hoops with Sammie until his father came out to join them, and then, as soon as Frank appeared, he remembered a phone call he had to make and excused himself to his home office.

When Morgan arrived to collect her son, Frank was on the driveway next to Sammie, helping the boy with ball handling and foot positioning. Cal headed out to greet his student, but by the time he made it outside she was already pulling away.

"I told her you were on a business call," Frank said when Cal appeared.

In spite of spending the past hour and a half in the Tennessee heat dribbling a basketball, his father wasn't even sweating.

And if the old man knew that Cal had made up the excuse of the call—what call would a college professor need to take that lasted an hour and a half?—he was playing a game of tit for tat. Or calling Cal's bluff.

Either way, Cal didn't like it. So he pretended not to notice. If he gave his father that satisfaction, there was no telling what conclusions the man would draw. And no telling what hell Cal would pay for them.

"I made spaghetti," he said instead, and followed Frank into the house.

"That call you got at work," Cal said lightly, while the two of them sat watching a rerun of a college basketball scrimmage on a satellite sports channel, eating the supper Cal had prepared. "Don't worry about it. It's all taken care of."

Fork resting on his plate, Frank didn't look up, didn't move except to say, "You talked to Ramsey Miller?"

"Yep. He won't be bothering you anymore."

With a slight nod, Frank took another bite of dinner. And a couple of seconds later, his gaze rose to the game once more. His father didn't ask how he'd found Miller. Or what was said.

Cal wasn't sure if that was good or bad. But because he wanted his father to let it go, he did, too.

"The boy has a problem," Frank said, halfway through his plate of food.

"Sammie? What problem?" Cal asked, juggling his plate with the remote as he muted their regular dinner companion.

"Seems he got invited to try out for the junior high basketball team."

"Junior high? Sammie's ten."

"Going into the fifth grade." Frank nodded. "Junior high is sixth through ninth here. He'd be playing one year early."

"Who invited him?"

"The coach came by his school. Knows someone named Julie."

"And does Julie know about the invitation?"

"Not as far as Sammie knows. He asked the coach not to say anything to anyone."

Cal didn't like the sound of this. Sammie's face had been planted all over the news the week before. Every creep in the city would know who he was.

And who his grandfather was.

"How do we know this guy's really a coach of anything?"

"Sammie knows who he is. He meets with boys in gym class starting in the fourth grade."

"So why not tell anyone?"

"The school district is pay-to-play and he knows his mom can't afford it. And practices are after school every day at the junior high. He'd need a ride and his mom has to work."

Cal was beginning to see the problem. He just wasn't sure what the solution would be. Was the boy angling to live with his grandfather so he could play basketball?

"What was he hoping to accomplish by telling you?" he asked, no longer hungry.

Frank, for once, didn't seem to have any lack of appetite.

"Truth is, I think he was trying to impress me with the idea that the coach thought he was good enough."

"Did he say anything to you about living with his grandfather?"

Frank frowned. "Not a word. But I got the feeling that if I offered to take him to practice, he'd be willing to work off the pay-to-play fee just like he's going to work off those new shoes of his. He asked if we needed the fence painted before winter. And wondered if we ever cleaned our windows, too."

Relaxing, Cal's mind raced with jobs, with solutions, with ways he could continue to help Morgan.

And then he stopped and stared.

His father, eyes trained on the television set in front of them, was grinning.

MORGAN WAS NOT WATCHING the clock. She just happened to notice when it was eight o'clock because that meant Sammie had an hour before his nine o'clock school-night bedtime. Eight-thirty was a checkpoint because that meant if Sammie was going to have a bedtime snack he had to be eating it. And eight forty-five was time to brush teeth, wash and change into pajamas. Nine o'clock was a given. Prayers and kisses good-night.

Nine-fifteen. She noticed just so she could check that Sammie had turned off his light as promised. Nine-thirty, make sure her son was asleep. Nine thirty-five was to check on the battery in the clock on the living room wall. It seemed to be running a minute or two slow. Ditto, nine forty-five and she was happy to note that the clock was keeping time just fine.

By nine-fifty she told herself to find something to do. There was no point in having a jittery stomach. She should make a cup of chamomile tea and take a hot bath.

At ten o'clock she poured the tea. And ran the bath.

At five minutes past ten she swallowed disappointment and started to undress.

Just because he'd been on the phone when she'd picked up Sammie that evening was no reason for Cal to make one of his ten o'clock calls. They had nothing to discuss. Nothing that needed to be said to each other, which was the usual point in a phone call.

He probably had a date with Kelsey tonight. Maybe at her place. Another dinner. Italian. With wine and... maybe even a bedcap.

Stripped to her panties, Morgan glanced at herself in the mirror. Her breasts weren't overly large, but they were sizable enough to get noticed. And give her some cleavage.

There'd been a day, before Sammie came along, that she'd despaired over ever having cleavage. In those days she'd been certain that if cleavage ever arrived, she'd live happily ever after.

Tonight she was just glad that her breasts weren't sagging yet.

She touched her nipples. They were okay. They hardened under her touch and she let them go. It had been so long...

And it would be longer, she admonished herself, slipping her panties down her thighs. She'd get in the bath. Drink her tea. And when she was relaxed enough to sleep she'd...

Her cell phone rang. She'd turned the volume down so it wouldn't wake Sammie and she'd brought it into the bathroom with her.

Pulling her panties back up, she grabbed the thing before it could vibrate off the counter.

"Hello?"

"Were you asleep?"

He always asked. Kind of silly. But she liked that he did. "Of course not."

"You busy?"

She stared at herself in the mirror. "No."

"Good. Do you mind if we talk a minute?" There was a new note in his voice. Something more personal than she'd heard before.

Her nipples were hard again. And she hadn't touched them this time.

She turned her back to the mirror and grabbed her robe with her free hand, holding it up to her chest. "No, I don't mind. What's up?"

"How was your day?"

"Fine." Minus the bit with her father. But he hadn't called to hear about that. He hadn't known she was meeting with her dad. "How about you? Your father said you were on a business call."

"I had some calls to make. Mostly I just wanted to give Dad some time alone with Sammie. It seems to have paid off."

"The way Sammie ran his mouth tonight, I'd agree," she said. "Every word out of his mouth was either *basketball* or *Frank*. He said your dad told him to call him Frank."

"It's his name."

"I would have preferred Mr. Whittier."

"Yeah, well, I'm guessing Dad was going for something a kid would feel more comfortable with. I can tell him to cut the Frank and go back to Mr. Whittier if you'd like."

Morgan smiled. "No, Frank's fine. I'm just glad it's working out so well. The man time with Sammie."

Not that it was going to help her with her case. Which she needed to tell Cal before his father got too attached to Sammie. "Maybe too well," Cal said.

Sliding down to the fluffy bath mat, Morgan leaned back against the tub, watching the shadows from the candle she'd lit flicker on the ceiling. "What's up?" she asked.

It hadn't occurred to her until that second that Cal had called to bail out on their plan. But that would save her from having to tell him that their plan wasn't going to have a chance. She'd just hoped that Sammie would have at least one more day like today before she was forced to pull the rug out from underneath him again.

"I have something to discuss with you, but I'm going to ask you not to discuss our conversation with Sammie."

"Okay." What else could she say? She had to know what was going on. "If, after hearing what you have to say, I change my mind about that, I'll let you know before I talk to him."

"Fair enough."

"So what's up?" Her tea was growing cold. Her bathwater was growing cold. She was getting cold, too.

Morgan listened, without saying a word, while Cal told her about the honor her son had shared with his father. An honor he hadn't told her about because he knew she didn't have the means to help him.

Her father was going to use all of his power to win his fight. And if she didn't have Sammie on her side, because she couldn't give him what he wanted and needed, she didn't have a hope in hell of keeping her son.

"...so here's what I propose," Cal was saying. "After just two visits, it's safe to say that my father needs Sammie as much or more than Sammie needs Dad. My father would very much like to pay for any fees and expenses involved if Sammie makes the team. And he'd like to be able to pick Sammie up after school and take him to practice. Dad doesn't drive, but they could take the bus. Dad's already checked and there's a route between the nursing home and Sammie's school and, with one transfer, they could be at the junior high in time for practice. After practice, either you or I could pick the two of them up and drop them off at home. That's saying Sammie makes the team at all. First he'd have to make it through tryouts, which start next week."

For the second time that day Morgan was choked up. This time the tears didn't fall. She could hardly believe that life could be so horrible and so wonderful all in the same day.

"So what do you say?"

What could she say? She had to think of Sammie. Of what was best for her son. Sammie knew that her father wanted him to live at the mansion. He didn't know that George was taking them to court to win custody away from Morgan.

"What if my father wins the court case?"

"What if a tornado hits one of our houses tonight?"

Her father intimidated the hell out of her. He scared her until she couldn't think straight.

But she didn't waver in her belief that Sammie was better off with her.

There was still a chance that Leslie would be fair.

And that Frank's offer would help keep Sammie home.

"With your permission, my father would like to make his offer to Sammie on Thursday, telling him that he has to discuss the offer with you before accepting."

"You have my permission under one condition."

"What's that?"

"I'd like to hear your father speak for himself."

Several minutes later, all was quiet in Morgan's house as she lay in her newly warmed bath, with a newly heated cup of tea, smiling at the shadows that danced on her ceiling.

CHAPTER TWENTY-ONE

ON THURSDAY, FIVE DAYS before their custody hearing, Leslie Dinsmore followed Sammie from her office after their meeting.

"Can I speak with you?" The words were no less threatening to Morgan in spite of the woman's kind smile. "Sammie can wait with Molly." She motioned to the receptionist inside the security screening area of the court offices building. Leslie had been to their house the day before, as had a man from child services, in two separate visits.

Just as Julie's attorney friend had predicted, she was on trial as surely as if she'd committed a crime. Had they found something wrong with her home? Something that made her an unfit parent?

Leslie's office, a room she shared with other attorneys and volunteers, was completely decorated in bright colors, from the tile on the floor to the artwork on the walls. It reminded Morgan of the day care.

"Is there a problem?" she asked, acutely aware of the big cherry stain on the sleeve of her shirt. There'd been an accident during snack time at work and the tray of drinks Morgan had been delivering to the three-year-olds had ended up on the floor by way of her arm.

"No, I just have some questions." The woman's

flat sandals made soft sounds as she headed to the couch. Leslie Dinsmore always looked professional and today's light cotton navy slacks and clean white blouse were no exception. She was perfectly coiffed and clean, and wearing clothes that fit her slender body as though they'd been tailored just for her.

Morgan resisted the urge to ask if anyone had noticed the tailored clothes in her closet when they'd inspected her home—all gifts from her mother.

She resisted the urge to blurt out how much she loved her son. And that expensive clothes and shoes were not as important as quality time spent together.

Keeping her mouth quiet, Morgan took a seat in an orange-colored armchair across from the blue couch.

"Every other word out of Sammie's mouth today was *Frank*," the woman said, easily enough. Her pen and papers sat on the table beside her as she turned her full attention on Morgan.

"Frank Whittier," Morgan said. "He's the father of Dr. Caleb Whittier, head of the English department at Wallace," Morgan explained, the words she'd already worked out in her mind for court on Tuesday coming to her aid. "I've known Dr. Whittier for four years. He's my undergrad adviser and I've had several classes with him. I was in his class the day that Sammie went missing, and he was kind enough to stay with my parents and Detective Warner and me that night. He kept the coffee coming, made sure we all ate and generally maintained a level of calm in the midst of all the panic."

"So that's the Cal that Sammie mentioned."

"Right." She quickly added, "Dr. Whittier and I aren't dating or anything. My focus is fully on Sammie. But I mentioned to Dr. Whittier that you'd said that Sammie was lacking male attention and he knew about Sammie's obsession with basketball. His father, who is retired and lives with him, used to be a basketball coach. They offered to have Sammie come over to shoot hoops on the afternoons when he used to hang out at the day care and wait for me to finish work."

Leslie nodded, her short brown hair bobbing. And she smiled. "Sammie's obviously thrilled with the arrangement."

"Yes, he is."

"He tells me that Frank is training him for tryouts for the junior high basketball team."

"That's right. He was invited to try out even though he's only going into fifth grade in the fall. The coach is a college friend of the secretary at Sammie's school. Julie talked to him about Sammie after the... campout...and he said he'd take a look at him."

The campout. She couldn't say Sammie ran away. It sounded so awful. And her son hadn't really run away. He'd just gone camping overnight without permission. He'd planned all along to come home.

"Julie said that the coach has made it a practice to look at the upcoming fifth graders and that he occasionally invites boys to try out for the team a year early. They don't play much, but they get to be a part of the team and to participate fully in all practices. He's a firm believer in engaging kids in healthy activities at a young age so they will hopefully keep them up as they get older."

Morgan had spoken with Coach Safford personally after she'd received a phone call from Frank, assuring her that he was committed to helping Sammie should he make the team.

"I'm glad to hear this," Leslie said. "Sammie's so excited and I wanted to make sure that he wasn't reading more into something than was there."

Morgan nodded. "It's for real," she said. *Please, please tell the courts I'm a good mother and that my son belongs with me.*

Leslie smiled. "This sounds good, then."

"So that's it? That's what you wanted to speak with me about?" No bad news from her father's side of the fence?

"That's it." Leslie stood. "Unless there's anything else you'd like to discuss with me."

Morgan stood. "Nope. All is well."

"I gather Sammie has enjoyed his visits with your parents, as well," Leslie said as they slowly crossed the room together.

"Yeah, he usually does. My mom spoils him." Did Leslie know that Sammie's visits to her parents' home were not a new occurrence? That the only change was her father's participation?

She dismissed the idea of telling the woman herself. Leslie was Sammie's "friend," a supposedly impartial third party, and Morgan didn't want to be accused of trying to sway the woman.

"I see that you're representing yourself in court on

Tuesday," the woman said, stopping just before they reached the door.

"Yeah," Morgan said, stopping, too. Leslie Dinsmore seemed sincere. As if she really just had Sammie's best interests at stake and wasn't being influenced in any way by her father.

"I spoke with an attorney." She took a chance with the truth. "She told me that in this case, in her opinion, I'd be more effective speaking for myself. This isn't a matter of law, it's a matter of Sammie's well-being and happiness. She said that my father is basically putting me on trial and all she'd do as my attorney is call me to the stand to refute or reframe his claims. She said I'd be better off saving the fifteen-hundred-dollar retainer fee for Sammie's school clothes."

Which was good because she'd have had to borrow the money to cover the legal costs.

"Your attorney might be right," Leslie said. "And one other thing, just so you know, it wouldn't be a negative if you *were* dating your Dr. Whittier. Aside from any complications that might present for you two at school, that is. A man in your life could be good for your son. Having a bit of your focus and attention on someone other than him might actually be a good thing for Sammie."

Morgan's chest tightened. Had Leslie read her mind? Was she trained enough to see that Morgan had a thing for her college professor?

Either way, there was no way she could ask Cal out....

"I'm not saying you need to go and purposely find

a man to date," Leslie added. "Quite the opposite. I'm just saying that if someone comes along that interests you, don't feel you have to deny yourself a normal life to be a good mom."

On that note, Morgan made her escape.

MORGAN DIDN'T STICK around after class on Monday. Cal stopped her on her way out the door to wish her luck in court the next day. And to confirm that he was still supposed to collect Sammie from school Tuesday afternoon.

"If you don't mind," she said. "The judge said Sammie doesn't have to be in court. He just wants to hear from my father and me and Leslie Dinsmore this time. It's a preliminary hearing, I guess. No witnesses."

"So he won't be making his determination?" Cal asked, standing with her just inside the doorway of the classroom, his soft-sided briefcase tucked under his arm.

"I don't know."

She wasn't meeting his gaze and seemed in a hurry to leave.

So Cal let her go.

HE HAD TWO CALLS waiting for him when he got back to his office. He returned Kelsey's first and accepted her invitation to grill steaks at her place that evening.

"We can swim in my pool after, if you'd like," she'd said.

"I'd have to swing by my place for my suit," he told

her, thinking a night by the pool with a beautiful and engaging woman was just what he needed.

"Or...you could swim without one."

Thinking that sounded even better, Cal told Kelsey he'd pick up a bottle of wine and then called his father to let him know he'd be on his own for dinner.

Frank thanked him for calling, and that was it. His father rarely asked where Cal went, or with whom. Never expressed pleasure or disapproval, or even curiosity. And somewhere along the way, Cal had ceased sharing the details of his life with his father.

Except for Morgan Lowen. They both talked about her.

With thoughts of an evening with Kelsey to shore him up, Cal returned his second call. Ramsey Miller picked up on the first ring.

"You're right, there are some interesting similarities among the abductions in your files," the detective said without any pleasantries. "You had some things I didn't, a couple of reported abductions that I didn't know about, and I spend my days going through cold case abductions. But after spending two full days cross-checking, I'm still nowhere. There's not enough solid evidence to tie any of it to Claire Sanderson's disappearance."

Cal could have told him that. If he'd have found something, he'd have done something about it.

"I have to wonder if you were wasting my time, Professor. Sending me in one direction so I don't go in another. I need that missing evidence."

"I want Claire Sanderson found just as badly as

you do." Probably more so, but it wasn't a point worth arguing.

"You want me to leave your father alone."

Cal tapped a pencil against the edge of his desk as he heard the thinly veiled threat. "What do you want from me?"

"Your book."

"It's not really a book. More of a journal, with some prose mixed in. It's not finished." And it wasn't for anyone's eyes but his.

"You got something written there that would implicate your father in the disappearance of Claire Sanderson?"

"No."

"Prove it."

"You got a warrant?"

"No, but I can get one."

Cal wasn't so sure about that. He also didn't want the man anywhere near his father.

"If I cooperate, do I have your word you'll stay away from my father?"

"That is not a promise I can make. Let's be clear, Professor. I believe your father knows something about what happened to that little girl. If I find any new evidence to support that theory, I will follow up on it. And let's be equally clear on this. You need to send me the manuscript willingly and in its original form—since we have the software to track any changes or deletions. If you don't, I will be forced to come to Tennessee to collect it. At that time I will also make the best use of the state of Massachusetts' money and stop in for a visit with your father."

Cal broke the pencil with one hand. "I assume you have email?"

No one at the day care knew that Morgan might lose her son. No one in her life, besides Cal, knew about her pending court date. Except for Julie.

If it got to the point where she could call witnesses on her behalf, she'd let her boss know what was going on. And ask Cal and Frank Whittier to testify on her behalf, too. But for now, she had to rely on herself.

Monday evening, Julie phoned Morgan.

"How are you doing?"

It was five after nine. She'd sent Sammie to bed half an hour before. "I don't know," she said. "I want to be fine. I want to believe that I'm going to walk into court tomorrow, be myself, tell the truth and walk out with full custody of my son. It's possible the judge won't even make a determination tomorrow, but he can if he decides it's in Sammie's best interests. If he's convinced Sammie isn't safe with me."

"So you're ready?" Julie asked softly, her voice filled with compassion.

Morgan looked at the massive array of "evidence" she'd gathered to support her fitness as a mother. Would the judge really be swayed by the scrapbooks she'd made? "Does it matter that I've got every single thing Sammie ever created or wrote?" she asked.

Turning a page in one of the leather-clad volumes, she looked at the scrap of notepaper with a couple of inked squiggly lines on it. Sammie's first attempt with a pen. He'd been less than a year old. She'd been studying for a freshman psych class that she'd later had to drop because she couldn't work, raise her baby and get enough sleep to allow her to stay awake in class. She'd waited until Sammie was a little older, and she was a little more experienced at motherhood, before she'd enrolled in college again.

"Of course it matters," Julie said.

"You think I should bring the scrapbooks, then?"

"I think you should bring anything you want to bring."

"Even his first baseball glove?" It was tiny enough to fit two-year-old fingers. Plastic and ripped.

"Okay, probably not that." Julie chuckled. "Seriously, Morgan, report cards, inoculation records, his scouting achievement awards, that Great Reader certificate he got from the summer library program—those are the kinds of things you could have with you, just to show, if you need to, that Sammie is doing fine."

"He achieves," Morgan said, finding each of the items Julie mentioned among the menagerie on the table. "But none of that means he's emotionally healthy or mentally well adjusted."

"And if he's not, it doesn't mean you aren't a good mother. It only means he needs help. We have a lot of kids in school that come from well-rounded two-parent families and still struggle. Sometimes because of disorders like ADHD, but other times the behavioral problems aren't easily defined or explained. I've seen it more than once where you'll have a couple of siblings from a family turn out fine and have a third that's a problem."

Morgan listened intently. Taking heart. Allowing Julie's words to soothe the panic rising inside of her.

"Thank you."

"I want to come with you tomorrow."

"You don't have to do that. It's a closed hearing so you'd have to wait out in the hall, anyway."

"So I'll sit in the hall. I'd already requested a half-day vacation in case you needed me to testify."

"So treat yourself to a rare morning off with no kids."

Julie's girls were at day camp all summer while she worked.

"Look, you don't have to do this on your own."

Lord knew, for once she wasn't sure she could.

"What if the judge takes him away from me, Jules? What if tonight is the last night I have my boy sleeping here at home with me?"

"Don't, Morgan. Don't do that to yourself. You have to believe everything is going to be fine."

"I want to believe that." She had to hang on to hope. "I can't imagine mornings without his little face frowning at me for one reason or another. Or his kissing me goodbye each day…" She choked up. Morgan swallowed and then said, "He still kisses me every single morning."

"I'm not surprised. He loves you."

"Not tonight he doesn't. It's probably a good thing he's not going to be there tomorrow. I'm afraid he'd tell the judge that he didn't want to live with me."

"Why would you say that?"

"Oh, I've been irritable all night. I snapped at him for chewing with his mouth open, and again when he put his glass down with too much force and splashed milk on the table. And he had the television turned up too loud. The poor little guy couldn't get anything right."

"You're human, Morgan. And on edge. No one expects you to be perfect."

Her father did. And tomorrow she had to be up to his standards.

"I sent Sammie to bed early. He threw a fit. Started in on the whole 'babying him too much' thing. He wouldn't say his prayers in front of me." Her eyes blurred with tears.

"And this time tomorrow everything will be better. Keep your chin up."

"I'm trying." But there was a very real possibility that things would not be better.

"Sammie needs that from you."

And if Sammie needed it, she'd find a way. She always had.

"What time do you have to be in court?"

"Nine."

"I'll be ready at eight."

She wanted to be strong enough to show up alone. To show them she could. To let her father know that he didn't scare her. "Okay."

"You got any wine in the house?"

"Yeah."

"Drink some. And then lie down and get some rest."

Morgan poured herself half a glass of wine. She took a few sips, staring at the dining room table. She'd expected her mother to call. To care enough to touch base, if only to beg Morgan to do as her father wanted.

The phone didn't ring.

Dumping the rest of the wine down the sink, Morgan took Julie's advice and went to lie down.

On the floor of Sammie's room.

CHAPTER TWENTY-TWO

THE WINE WAS GOOD. So was the company. Cal grilled the steaks. He talked to Kelsey about France. He'd been there once, during college. She'd studied in Paris for a couple of years. They'd frequented the same quaint little coffeehouse on a street just off the Champs-Élysées.

He wondered how Morgan was holding up, the night before court. If she'd given him any encouragement at all that morning, he'd have called her to find out. As it was, the barriers she'd erected had been very clear and he had to honor them. She had to handle things in her own way.

"See, we're kindred spirits." Kelsey smiled at him over the wrought iron table by the pool in her very private backyard. Her red hair was down and flowing wildly around her shoulders, the curls as sexy and bold as the woman herself. "With all of the places to drink coffee in a two-mile radius, we both chose the same one."

"Either that or we share an uncanny ability to find the best coffee around." He smiled back at her. Her eyes were a cross between green and blue and sparkling with pleasure. Life. He could almost feel the energy she exuded. "And enough of an addiction to have to go back once we find it."

"I think we share more than that," she told him. Their plates were empty. Her wineglass was not.

"You do, huh?" His smile was slow, telling her about the kind of warmth he'd like to share with her.

"I think we share a need for independence while recognizing and appreciating our deeply sensual natures."

She got all that from a staff meeting and a few dates? He chased the thought away with another— she was probably going to be his next relationship. Yet oddly, he wasn't all that thrilled with the prospect.

"You're a passionate guy, Cal. You're always looking for deeper meaning, in literature and in life. I like that."

She wasn't wrong about that.

"And I study art for the same reasons. To find the heart of people. To understand the communication that is too deep for words."

Cal moved in his seat. Adjusting his weight. Repositioning his backside. Hearts weren't something he discussed. Mostly because to discuss others' hearts would mean he'd have to discuss his own and he didn't do that. Even with himself.

She took a sip of wine, studying him, as though she knew what he was thinking. And then she stood.

"What do you say we go swimming?" She reached for his hand and he allowed her to pull him to his feet. This was what he wanted.

"I study romance in literature," he told her, because

he felt he had to. He still had a hold of her hand. "But I don't do romance."

"No hurt feelings or expectations," she said, as though she'd read his mind. Or his life.

"Right."

"I know." She nodded and the glow in her eyes didn't change at all. "Me, neither. So, you want to swim?"

He did. His body had been humming with need for days. And he found her immensely attractive. More so now that they'd established their relationship would only go as deep as six feet of chlorinated water.

"The water's lovely," she said. "I swim every night." She unfastened her top, revealing bare shoulders and cleavage. She wasn't wearing a bra and didn't appear the least bit shy showing him that fact. Her blouse landed on the cool decking.

"Naked?" he asked her, liking this conversation a whole lot better. He was at home here. Knew exactly what to say. What to do.

"Of course. You ever swim naked, Professor?" She reached for his belt buckle.

"Every chance I get," he answered, looking her straight in the eye. He could feel her fingers slide his belt out of the loop, and then the slight tug as the leather unfastened from the hinge. He looked down at her breasts. Thought of the water lapping against their bodies.

And when her hand reached for the button at the waistband of his pants, he covered her fingers with his own.

Her question was wordless, but plain as she met his gaze.

"I'm sorry." He couldn't believe he'd said the words. "I don't think this is going to work."

He couldn't go through with it. He wanted to. He should. But he couldn't. Morgan's features kept appearing in his mind's eye. As he'd seen her in class—vibrant, engaged. And at home—eyes shadowed with worry and fear. She'd be afraid tonight. The night before her first day of court.

Classy woman that she was, Kelsey didn't pressure him for answers. "Then I'm sorry, too," she said softly. "You're welcome to stay. Pour a second glass of wine. Or you're welcome to show yourself out." She didn't wait for his decision. Turning, she stripped out of her skirt, slid her panties down perfect, long, tanned legs, left them in a puddle by her blouse and dove into the pool.

Cal let himself out.

SOMETHING WAS WRONG with him. Deeply wrong with him. No woman had ever infiltrated his mind as Morgan Lowen had. Cal fretted all the way home and then, without stopping for a glass of whiskey, went straight into his office. His father's door was shut, but it wouldn't have mattered either way. He needed time alone, time to focus on real life.

Cal opened his book, started at Chapter One and began to read.

Miller had the pages in his possession. Cal had to take a new look at them, from the perspective of a police detective rabid to take his father down. For the next couple of hours he refused to let his mind wander.

"YOUR HONOR, I AM NOT a heartless man. To the contrary, I stand before you with a very full heart this morning as I do one of the most difficult things I've ever done in my life. I am here today as a parent, doing what is best for my child and my grandchild in spite of the fact that in order to do what's best I must hurt those who I am trying to help."

Morgan almost broke her promise to herself and turned her head to look at the man who was seated with her mother and their attorney at the table across the aisle from her. She'd been in the courthouse for half an hour and didn't even know what her parents were wearing.

Her father, as the plaintiff, had been given the opportunity to be heard first. Morgan was shocked that he was speaking for himself.

But then maybe, like her, he'd been counseled that he'd be better suited to speak his heart to the judge rather than rely on legalities put forth by a paid professional.

He'd also obviously been thoroughly coached on how to present himself and what to say. Because her father would never have admitted out loud that he had a full heart. It just wasn't his way.

Dressed in a navy linen suit with matching leather pumps, she sat alone at her table. Julie, the only member of the audience in the otherwise closed court room, sat right behind her. She wasn't allowed to speak, but when her father had offered no objections, the judge had allowed Julie in the room.

Leslie was not there. She'd sent her report in electronically.

"Your Honor, I have two serious issues to bring for your consideration in my request to grant my wife and me full custody of our grandson, Samuel Elias Lowen. I will speak to the most recent tragedy, Samuel's disappearance, first, as it is what brought my grandson to the court's attention.

"Samuel is searching for his place as a man in this world. His mother gives him neither the responsibility nor the freedom to know what he needs. Samuel has tried repeatedly to discuss this situation with his mother, but she cannot see him as anything other than her little boy. The boy had been growing increasingly angry. He was afraid of the negative feelings he was having toward his mother. And so, in desperation, he ran away to show her he needed to be given the chance to grow up."

Morgan could hardly bear to listen. But she hung on to every word. Had her father really talked to Sammie? Had her son confided in him?

She didn't believe it. And yet, George sounded so convincing. The judge certainly looked like he was believing every word.

Part of what her father said was right; she hadn't been able to hear what Sammie was telling her. She'd let him down.

And he'd run away to teach her a lesson.

And then she'd made things worse with that stupid

monitor. Had Sammie told her mother about that? Had her mother told her dad? Was her poor judgment, her bad choice, in Leslie's report, as well?

Staring straight ahead, Morgan felt a cold calm come over her. She would get through this hearing.

Julie cleared her throat. Morgan reached out a mental hand to clasp the one she knew Julie would be holding out to her if she could.

"The day my grandson was born, life changed for me, Your Honor. I think of him all the time as I make everyday decisions that could someday affect him. He is heir to everything I build. He will have to live with the legacy I leave. To that end, I watch every step I take, every single word I say, so that I do not, in any way, leave my grandson to face hardship or shame."

Even Morgan heard the truth in this part of her father's testimony. He wasn't an evil man. Just a calculating one. He analyzed and added up every move that was made. By himself, and others.

And only a man with George's ego would live every moment of the day based on the legacy he would leave behind. Most people wouldn't think themselves so important as to believe that every move they made would influence those around them.

The courtroom was deathly quiet as her father's voice finally faded away. Morgan wondered if she'd even get a chance to speak. She didn't know what she could add that would in any way mean anything to Judge Marks.

And then she heard her father's voice again. "As with everything else I do, I did not take this step lightly, Your Honor, but, rather, after much introspection and many deep conversations with my wife. We have met with professionals, spoken with our daughter and grandson and sought counsel on the decision to appear before you today. After our scare of two weeks ago, our fear for Samuel's welfare has grown to the point where we feel we have no choice but to protect him in this way."

Was her father speaking for her mother because that was what he did, or was her mother really in on this? Had they really had deep conversations about it? Conversations that went beyond her father telling her mother what had to happen and why?

Certainly they'd had no family conversations as his words implied. No family counseling, either. Her father wouldn't hear of that. Morgan knew that firsthand, too, because she'd asked for them to go to counseling before she'd married Todd.

"The second issue I bring for your consideration, Your Honor, is longer reaching. My daughter, Morgan Elise Lowen, is a woman who bets on the underdog every single time. She sees the best in people, Your Honor, and while that is an admirable trait, it is also a very dangerous one. My daughter trusts unconditionally—and in so doing, she puts herself, and consequently her son, in precarious positions."

He was really doing it. As much as Morgan had known that her father would win at all costs, she'd still held out hope. He was her father. Privy to her most private failures. The man who was supposed to protect her. And he was crucifying her.

Her father had always been hard on her. But he'd never stabbed her in the back before.

"My daughter has refused the help of our security team," her father continued. "She believes that she and Samuel can live what she calls 'normal' lives. Without security supervision, Samuel was able to walk out of his school, board a public bus and walk for miles, and all of that time he was exposed to any number of people in this city who would not find it unpalatable to kidnap or kill him for a piece of my fortune. Samuel is not an ordinary child. He is heir to the Lowen fortune, Your Honor, which makes him prey to a lot of immoral people. And yet his mother refuses to protect him from them."

Her father's voice was as stern as always and Morgan couldn't help but steal a glance at him. He was dressed impeccably, his gray suit and white shirt expensive and crisp, and his expression bore the calm and the control she knew.

Morgan looked away. But not before she saw her mother, dressed in a pink linen suit Morgan had never seen before, sitting at the table next to George Lowen with a look of compassionate support turned on her husband.

Because George spoke the complete truth.

In Morgan's determination not to expose her son to the emotionally cold and removed life that she'd known as a child, in order to preserve his freedom to be whomever he wanted to be when he grew up, not just his grandfather's clone, she'd put her son's life in danger. Sammie was a Lowen, no matter where or how they lived. And, as had dawned on her the night of Sammie's disappearance when she'd had to take those horrible phone calls, Sammie was possibly prey to creeps who wanted to hurt her father.

There was no sound from behind her, as though Julie were as frozen as Morgan felt.

Filled with stark cold fear, Morgan barely heard her father take his seat. She knew the judge thanked him before asking if her mother had anything to say, but because she expected the negative response, she didn't even know her mother had replied in the affirmative until she heard her begin to speak.

Grace's first words struck at the ice around Morgan's whole being, thawing just enough of her to allow her to feel. Grace told the court what a good daughter Morgan had been and was to her, and what a good daughter she'd tried to be to her father.

Listening intently, Morgan waited, hoping that her mother was finally going to do what Morgan had been begging her to do her entire life—stand up for her. Tell the world, or at least her father, that he was cold and heartless and unbending where Morgan was concerned. Let him know that she was a person in her own right, with enough sense to make her own life decisions.

Or, at least, enough sense to be listened to instead of merely brushed aside like a wayward ant at his picnic.

"I love my daughter as only a mother can love a child, which makes what I have to do the most painful thing I've ever done, and I hope and pray, Morgan, that some day you will understand and forgive me."

Her mother's voice cracked. And then she started to speak again. When Morgan heard the woman who had given birth to her, who had given her the only emotional nurturing she'd known during the first years of her life, giving the judge intimate details of her life, chronologically exposing her deepest shames, the foolish mistakes she'd made, when she heard her mother speak of her inability, even now, to see the bad in people, she wanted to lay her head on the table before her and die.

CHAPTER TWENTY-THREE

"THANK YOU, DR. WHITTIER. I can't believe it, but it looks like I'm really going to graduate."

Rising from the chair in front of Cal's desk, Shane offered his hand.

Standing to shake hands, Cal smiled at Shane Arnett, a young man in his mid-twenties who'd been in and out of his classes for more than six years. "It's been a long haul, Shane, but you had it in you." As soon as Shane completed one more paper in Cal's English Lit Review class his graduation application would be approved. "Do you need any help with your job search? I know some people. I can put in a good word for you."

Shane shook his head. "No, sir. I know it's hard to believe but I'm ahead of the game on this one. I put in applications last spring, did all my interviews and just this week was offered a one-year teaching position at Silmore Junior High, contingent on obtaining my degree."

"Congratulations!" It was that rush of having helped someone accomplish something worthy that got Cal up every single morning of his life. "If you ever need anything, or there's anything I can do to help, you have my number."

"Yes, sir. Thank you." At the door, Shane turned. "You know, a lot of teachers offer to be there for you, to give you all the help you need, but you're the only one I've ever had who really has supported me every step of the way. As many of your classes as I dropped, you never gave up on me."

"Because you never gave up on yourself," Cal said. The point was critical. He'd done nothing more than support the decisions Shane had made. The effort had come from him. "If you were willing to give yourself another chance, who was I to tell you you couldn't?"

Shane chuckled. "Another chance?" he said. "Try seven of them. Hell, even my own dad gave up on me."

Shrugging, Cal said, "Some of us need to try more times to succeed, but the ultimate success is no less valuable. Book learning is important, but you graduate with an understanding far more valuable to you in life. You know now that the important things are to not give up on yourself and to keep trying."

Cal's words rang in his ears after the young man left. He'd had another student on his mind all morning. And for most of the night before, too.

Morgan had been scheduled in court two hours ago. Surely the hearing wasn't still going on. But she hadn't called.

Surely, if she'd won, she'd have called.

And if she hadn't, she had to believe in herself as Sammie's parent and keep trying. Money might be able to buy a judge, but it couldn't buy love.

Why hadn't she called?

Rather than waste more time asking questions for

which he had no answers, Cal pulled his cell phone out of the pouch on his belt and pushed the speed dial number he'd programmed a week or two before.

The phone rang. And rang some more. After eight long rings, his call was diverted to voice mail.

"Morgan? It's Cal. Just wanting to know how things went this morning. I'll have my phone on all day. Call when you can."

With a frown on his face, he hung up.

CAL WAS STILL FROWNING when he left Wallace just after three that afternoon, wondering what he'd find when he got to the elementary school. Would Sammie still be there waiting for him? He hadn't been told otherwise.

Morgan hadn't called at all. And when he'd tried her a second time, he was sent straight to voice mail.

Was she purposely avoiding him? Had she taken the whole day off or just the morning?

Had her phone's battery died?

No, she had a backup battery. And a car charger, and a wall charger in her purse, too, so she never had to worry about being disconnected from Sammie. Had she told the court that this morning? Told them how Sammie factored in to every single move that she made every single day? Hell, according to Sammie, she hadn't dated in years because she wasn't going to risk a negative fallout for Sammie.

Parking in the lot outside Sammie's school, he strode down the walk like he belonged there. Headed toward Julie's office the same way. A swell of relief at the sight of the boy told him how much he was wrapped up in Morgan and her son. That was something he'd have to take care of later. At that moment, Julie was approaching him. With a motion of her head, she showed him into a private office.

"Sammie? Could you give me just a second alone with Dr. Whittier?"

She knew something. And by the look on her face it wasn't good.

"Jeez, Ms. Wallace. I want to know about court, too."

Julie's gaze faltered and Cal said, "Just for a second, Sammie, okay? Your mom probably wants to tell you about it herself."

"Okay." Sammie didn't sound happy, but he didn't dawdle as he walked over to where the school nurse sat ready to engage him in conversation.

"Have you heard from her?" Cal asked immediately. Morgan's reasons for today's silence ceased to matter.

Julie shook her head. "I was there for most of it," she said. "For all of her parents' testimonies and some of Morgan's. Then, in the middle of hers, the judge called a recess and I had to leave to get back here. I just took the morning off."

"How did it look from what you saw?"

"Not good, Cal." The woman looked like she might cry. "The judge's decision aside, just having to sit there and hear your parents talk about you like that... it couldn't be easy."

He wanted to know every word that was said. And had to get to the facts and back out to the young man who was waiting for him, who also had a stake in what went on that day.

"Do you think they swayed the judge?"

"I have no idea. He seemed nice enough. And her father's testimony was definitely skewed. The man's dangerous, the way he can take a bit of truth and put it out there in a way that doesn't resemble the truth at all. I wish I could have stayed to hear all of Morgan's testimony. She was doing a good job, but she wasn't visibly upset."

He thought of Shane Arnett, of the man's ability to continue to believe in himself when even his parents had given up on him, and knew he had to get to Morgan.

"She didn't call you afterward? Didn't let you know how things went?"

"She called to tell me that it was over and that she'd talk to me later about it. That she couldn't go through it right then. She said she needed a little time alone to pull herself together before she had to pick up Sammie. She asked me to call immediately if Sammie had a problem, but she wouldn't tell me where she was or what she was doing. She did say that you'd still be coming by to pick up Sammie as usual."

"It doesn't sound promising," Cal said, studying Julie's concerned expression, searching for some sign of encouragement. "But worst case scenario, if the judge made his decision on the spot and awarded full custody to her parents, then wouldn't they have come to pick up Sammie?"

"Unless they're allowing her to tell him herself, and

to help him pack and then bring him to their house. They've said all along that they want her to have un-supervised visits. It's not like they think she's a flight risk or unsafe for Sammie to be around."

"What if she were married?" The question was logical. But moot, since there was no one in her life to marry and everyone who knew her knew that.

"The question never came up," Julie said, her eyes narrowing. "Since she hasn't had a date in years, I don't think anyone sees marriage as a consideration. I also don't see how the guy could have made a decision so…so life-altering in the span of a few hours. There's evidence for him to consider in addition to today's testimony."

The door opened and Sammie peeked his head in. "Come on, Cal, can we go? Mom's going to be coming and I won't have much time to practice."

Getting his mind back to what mattered—the ten-year-old boy whose future was at stake—Cal told Julie goodbye and focused solely on Sammie during the drive home.

THERE WAS THIS LITTLE glen, a natural clearing in the midst of trees where the stream that flowed through her father's property slowed down to a trickle, that Morgan had discovered when she was about five or six years old. She'd run away from home because her father had told her that she couldn't play Little League baseball because she was a girl.

She hadn't known back then, of course, but the only reason she'd been allowed to run anywhere was because she'd wisely chosen to stay on her father's property. Had she left the grounds, she'd have been picked up immediately and brought safely back home.

She also hadn't known then that she'd been watched every single second she'd thought she was trekking out on her own. She'd had her own personal bodyguard from the day she was born, though she hadn't realized that until she was about twelve.

One thing she'd give her father, his control of her was discreet.

She'd brought Sammie to the glen for a picnic once. He'd preferred the woods on the other side of the property, which was where he'd run when he'd had to get away from her.

But when Morgan needed comfort, she found it in the glen. If she needed strength, the glen gave it to her.

Morgan hadn't counted on having life hurt so much that she couldn't bear to go on. She hadn't counted on losing Sammie.

Lying flat on her back along the stream in her private glen on Tuesday, the summer sun caressing her skin with the warmth the morning had stolen from her, Morgan felt like dying. She'd parked in a public parking lot and then taken a shortcut through some woods to the back side of the unsecured portion of her father's property and headed straight for her glen.

It had been waiting for her, as always. She'd cried for the first while. Sometimes out loud. And then she'd just lain there, spent. Eventually, with the glen holding her troubles for a while, she'd slept. She hadn't rested well in weeks and, as though her glen knew that, the land soothed her to sleep.

It was there to cushion her when, upon regaining consciousness, she crashed back to an awareness of the earthly trials awaiting her.

Trials.

The custody hearing wasn't done yet.

But Morgan was fairly certain that she was done with it.

When the air started to cool just a bit and the sun began its slow descent, Morgan rose and made her way back out to the road and up to her car. She drove into Tyler with calm and confidence. She had a job to do. A son who needed her. And as long as there was anything he could take from her that would benefit him, she would be there to provide it to him. No matter the cost to her.

She had no doubt whatsoever about her ability to give to those who needed her.

Pulling to the edge of Professor Whittier's driveway so as not to disrupt the one-on-one basketball game currently in progress, Morgan put the car in Neutral, unlocked the doors and waited. Cal had called a couple of times. She'd listened to his messages. She hadn't returned his calls.

Maybe tomorrow she'd be ready to have friends again. Tonight she was a mother. And she had to tend to her son.

With that sole thought in mind, she put the car in gear the second Sammie came running down the drive.

He was wearing new basketball shorts that matched

his new shoes. Shorts she hadn't purchased. Tonight, those shorts were another sign to her of what she must do.

"You coming in, Mom?"

"Not tonight, sweetie. Tell Frank thank-you and jump in. I've already called in our pizza order and it's going to be ready in five. Traffic was kind of bad so it took me a while to get here."

With a grin and a nod, her son did as she bid.

CHAPTER TWENTY-FOUR

TUESDAY NIGHT CAL FOUGHT a good fight. But he came out of it uncertain whether he'd won or lost. Since he was fighting with himself, either way he came up a winner. And a loser, too.

At five, when Morgan drove off with Sammie without so much as a hello, let alone a rundown of what had happened in court, he was peeved. How dare she involve him in her crisis and then just leave him hanging like he didn't deserve to know the outcome?

By six he remembered that she hadn't involved him. He'd involved himself. On more than one occasion. He was the one who'd pushed. Not Morgan. She'd never once called him. Never come to him at all.

And he wanted her to.

With that realization he took himself out for a beer, leaving his father to fend for himself for dinner—something that Frank seemed better able to do now that he had a reason to need his strength. After one beer, he went to his monthly junior arts league meeting, listened to the items on the agenda, voted and left without taking the time to socialize with anyone. Tonight he only had the wherewithal to find out how Morgan Lowen was doing.

Tonight, for the first time in his adult life, he wanted to be needed by a woman.

Pulling into a bar not far from the arts center, he determined that one more beer would wash away the unfamiliar desires that were trying to hijack his life and then he'd head home to bed. An early night wouldn't be remiss.

He missed the parking spot he'd claimed as his. And missed his turnaround to take a second shot at it. He was out on the road again instead, heading toward Morgan's duplex. It wasn't far.

He considered making a ten o'clock call. They'd kind of established a pattern. He'd just see if her lights were still on and then call her from the car.

One light was on. The small one in the living room, on the end table at the far end of the couch. The end by the archway that led into her dining room. The shades were drawn, but he could tell by the glow of the light, and by its placement on the curtains, which lamp she'd left burning.

Pulling his phone out of its pouch, he held it up. Looked at it and then at the house.

If she wanted to speak with him, she knew how to reach him.

He was her professor. Maybe she didn't feel right coming to him with personal problems. Maybe that was why she always left the pursuit up to him.

Not sure how clear his thinking was at that point, Cal didn't analyze any further. He'd found a valid reason to call.

She'd failed to pick up two other calls from him that

day. He looked away from the window, not wanting to see if her shadow appeared on the other side of the shade. If she was even in the living room.

Or home at all.

"Hello?"

He slid down in the seat to a more comfortable position. "Hi." He gave her a chance to take control of the conversation. To tell him why she hadn't answered his calls. Or returned them. To tell him she couldn't talk. To give him any indication of what was going on with her. Silence hung on the line.

"How are you?"

"Okay." And then, "Fine."

"How did it go today?"

"Good. I guess. The judge took the matter under advisement. He set another hearing two weeks from today, at which time he might or might not call on further testimony and he might or might not render his decision."

"At least you have a fighting chance."

"Yeah."

Mind racing for something to give her, Cal said, "You think he could have been giving you all time to work this out on your own?"

"I don't know. Maybe. He didn't say so. I just don't think he was ready to make such a serious decision in an hour's time. I figure he needs to think about ramifications or possible solutions he might be able to offer."

"So you definitely have hope that you could win?"

"I don't know."

His air conditioner was running hard. Cal turned

it off. "You sound different." She was concerning the hell out of him.

"I think I am different," she said. "I have a new perspective, I guess. Anyway, I don't think I'm going back to court."

"What?" Surely she wasn't thinking about taking Sammie and running. He dismissed the thought almost as soon as it formed. Morgan wouldn't run from trouble.

"I think my folks are right." Her words shocked the feeling right out of him. "Hearing them in court this morning, listening to them as I imagine the judge would hear them…I think if I were in his position I'd grant them full custody. And if I really think that, and I really love my son, and I really mean it when I say I will do anything for him, then I have to turn him over to them."

"You don't mean that."

"I think I do. I've spent this day looking back over my life, over my choices, and I can't honestly tell you whether I went into court today to fight for myself or fight for my son. I couldn't bear to lose Sammie. I was so certain I was right, I wasn't really listening to Sammie. Or anyone else. I was just like my father.

"And what kind of life am I giving my son? He ran away that Friday, but he could just as easily have been kidnapped. There was one man out there ready to take advantage of an opportunity to hurt my father. I'm sure there are more. And how do we know when any of them might see an opportunity and act on it? Beyond that, Sammie could be living with every opportunity at his disposal and I'm depriving him because I don't get along with my father. Daddy's a chauvinist. He'll be different with Sammie than he was with me. Value him more because he's his heir."

"Sammie's been around ten years. Your father has had the opportunity to spend as much time with him as he wanted, right?"

"Yeah."

"How much time has he spent with him?"

Morgan didn't reply and Cal thought maybe he was getting through to her until she said, "Anyway, I can tell you tonight that from now on all of my fight will be for Sammie, and only Sammie."

He wanted to tell her that it always had been, but figured she wouldn't believe him. She'd had a rough day. Hearing your own parents discredit you in court was enough to get anyone down.

There had to be a solution here. He racked his brain and couldn't find it. "Have you told your folks yet?"

"No. I called them but they didn't pick up. They have season tickets to Little Broadway and I think there was a show tonight. Anyway, I left a message on Mom's cell telling her I wanted to speak with them."

Thank God. They had time.

"I plan to call them in the morning."

"Wait."

"There's really no point, Cal. I have to do what's best for Sammie. I won't be able to live with myself if I don't."

"Do you think spending time with Frank is best for Sammie? The training? The tryouts?"

"Of course."

"And do you think your parents will facilitate that?" Her pause was answer enough. "I can ask them."

"But what if you do and they say no? If you've given over Sammie's care to them, you won't be able to do anything to help him with that."

It wasn't about his father. Or basketball. But he used them because he knew that she'd been so pleased with the change in Sammie since he'd been introduced to Frank.

"You're right. It would kill Sammie to stop now. He's finally feeling happy about something in his life. In control."

"I want to see you," Cal said then, quickly, before she could close the small chink he'd made in her stoicism. In her certainty.

"It's… Cal… I mean, Sammie's in bed asleep. I can't go out. And we have class in the morning. And it's late and…"

She hadn't said no. That was all the encouragement he needed.

"I'm parked outside your house," he told her. "If I come to the door will you let me in?"

"Well, yes, but…"

He was out of his car and at the door before she could complete whatever objection she'd been trying to make.

MORGAN WASN'T DRESSED for company. Cal was tapping lightly on her door before she had a chance to tell him so. She'd pulled her hair up into a ponytail, thinking that she'd soak in a bubble bath, with a cup of chamomile tea in an attempt to relax enough to sleep.

She'd made no effort whatsoever to make the hairstyle look good, as evidenced by the bulges and loose tendrils that had escaped the elastic band. She was dressed in old cutoff sweat shorts and a tank top left over from her pregnancy days. And she'd cried off all her makeup in the glen.

"Sorry, I wasn't expecting anyone," she said, with a brief glance down at her bare feet as she pulled open the door.

Cal, on the other hand, looked perfect. The knot in his tie was, even this late at night, still nicely in place.

And his feet, she noted, were properly encased in freshly shined shoes.

Things got weird the second she looked him in the eye. His gaze was naked, exposing an emotion that was completely unfamiliar to her.

"I had to see you," he said.

She stood back, letting him into her home, into her pain. And she waited.

He opened his arms. She walked into them. And settled against the rock-hard solidity of his body as though she'd been there before. And belonged. This was nothing like her fantasies about Cal Whittier. All she needed at the moment was comfort, a sense that she was not alone. That she could stand and survive.

Unaware of time passing, Morgan held on to Cal until she felt more like herself. And then, she led him silently to her living room and sat on the couch.

Cal took the seat next to her. Close, but leaving enough space.

"First, let me be clear about one thing. I'm here tonight as your friend, Morgan. What happens tomorrow in class is completely separate and apart from tonight."

She already knew that, but nodded because he seemed to need her agreement.

"I just don't want you to feel like you have to accept my presence or my questions or anything else because I'm your teacher."

"If I felt that way, I'd report you to the university board," she said. Morgan had no problem with sticking up for herself. Her problem lay in knowing when she needed to do so.

His grin was kind of disarming. "Okay, good. You sound more like the Morgan I know."

She felt more like her, too, which was nice even if it served no purpose. How she felt didn't change facts.

"Please tell me what your parents said today."

Uh-uh.

"I can't help if I don't know what we're up against."

It was the "we" that did it. It took all of her strength not to cry when she heard that "we." "It wasn't good," she told him. But there was no sense in hiding the truth from him, either. She was who she was. Or had been who she'd been.

She was a Lowen and that made her child vulnerable to crazy people. She had neither the resources nor the inherent mistrust in humanity necessary to keep him safe.

She tended to trust people. Naturally. Without conscious thought. She looked for the bad—her parents were wrong to think she didn't—but she didn't always see the bad.

If Cal was her friend, he'd still sit there when she was done spewing all of the words that kept playing like a cruel rerun through her mind. And if he wasn't, then his opinion didn't matter, anyway.

And so she told him, almost verbatim, the things her parents had told the judge that morning.

"It wasn't easy for my mother, Cal. And I know it wasn't a walk in the park for my father, either. He hated to put our private business out there. And, I'm sure, to give up control of his family to an impartial third party. He's doing this because he really believes it's for the best. My dad's cold and sometimes heartless, but he doesn't ever set out to hurt people for the sake of hurting them. He doesn't go out of his way to hurt them. He just doesn't seem to have any compunction about squashing people in the process of doing what he believes is best."

As she fell silent, Cal watched her. She knew he was thinking. A lot. But he didn't share any of his thoughts with her. He was still there, though.

"What did you tell the judge in rebuttal?" he asked.

"That every single incident my mother relayed happened, pretty much as she told it. And I told him that with the exception of one major incident, they all took place prior to Sammie's birth.

"I told him that I did have a tendency to trust the good in people and admitted to a situation that recently happened at the day care. It was for that open house I told you about that took place the Saturday that Sammie came home. A woman had assured me she was handling all of the decorations and so I didn't follow up with her. I trusted her to have them done and ended up staying up all night the night before Sammie went missing to get them done. As a consequence, I didn't listen as well as I should have that Thursday night when Sammie tried one more time to get me to give him more freedom.

"But the truth is, Cal, even if I'd heard Sammie that night, I still wouldn't have given him what he wanted. He's ten years old. He shouldn't be on the internet by himself, or determining what and when he's going to eat, or deciding his own bedtime. He has to do his homework whether he wants to or not, and I think he's too young to have a dirt bike. I also won't leave him home alone. Childhood only comes once in a lifetime. And it's the only time when you have someone there to know what to do if a pot catches on fire, and to take care of it for you.

"Sammie's already had to grow up so fast because it's just the two of us and we don't have a lot of money."

Once she'd started, she couldn't stop, and when she'd finally finished, his reply wasn't what she'd expected. "So you ran the bus over yourself," he said, a steely but kind glint in his eye. "But did you also tell the judge about the fact that because you believed you had a history of making poor choices where men are concerned, you have chosen not to date while Sammie is still young and dependent upon you?"

She didn't think about dating, except in her fantasies. "No."

"The bodyguard situation is serious," he continued. "I grant you that. But just because Sammie's grandfather has money is no reason for him to have to have custody of your son. Think about it, that would mean every offspring with a rich parent would either have to be rich enough in his own right to afford a bodyguard for his own children, or lose custody of them."

Which, of course was ludicrous. But... "My father's point was that I didn't have enough good judgment to accept his offer of security protection for Sammie."

"Because you said his offer came with the caveat that you live in his house and follow his rules."

"Right. My father is manipulative. He has ways of getting what he wants and he'll hold out until the world ends if that's what it takes to get things done his way. Bottom line is, Sammie is the boy my father didn't have. He's the Lowen heir and he wants him home."

"Did you point that out to the judge?"

"No. The attorney I saw told me not to make this a fight against my father, but to keep the focus on Sammie. And the point is that while my father might be wrong to put stipulations on his help, I was wrong to deny my son protection simply because I didn't want to do as my father asked. It's like the attorney said—it's a fight between my father's will and my own and Sammie got caught in the middle."

"His stipulations were unfair, Morgan. The judge would see that. You weren't just continuing the ongoing fight between you and your father, you were trying to protect your son from suffering from the same manipulation that kept you down all those years. You might need to reconsider having some protection for Sammie, and probably yourself, but I would think that since Sammie's safety hasn't been compromised due to your father's money up to this point, you've done a pretty good job of watching over him and keeping him protected. You might not have bodyguards, but, as you said, you don't leave him home alone. You don't let him walk to school alone. You don't let him on the internet where someone could lure him into an unsafe situation. Frankly, it seems to me that you've been your son's bodyguard."

For the first time since she'd heard her father speak that morning, Morgan knew a moment of sheer relief. She'd been looking and looking for the other side of the story her father had painted.

And hadn't found one. Cal had given her something to think about.

CHAPTER TWENTY-FIVE

"I'M GOING OUT on a limb here, but I'd guess that part of the reason you are so careful with your son, so unbending on the issues that he'd been pushing you on, is because you grew up as the child of a very rich man. The dangers, and what it takes to avoid them, are ingrained in you."

Could he be right? Could he possibly be right? Morgan blinked back tears. She'd cried enough.

"Julie told me that you'd brought report cards and records of achievements and proof of activities to show the judge. You didn't say anything about that. Did you show them to him?"

"No. Sammie's grades and activities weren't the issue."

"But they are proof of your parenting skills, Morgan. And of your involvement in your son's life. Sammie wants to surf basketball sites on the internet, so you sit back and give him the time to do so. He wants to train to try out for a team, and you allow him to do it. You hear he needs male companionship, you provide it for him."

No. She shook her head and more hair came tumbling out of her ponytail. "You provided that, Cal, not me."

"You live your life in such a way that I was there and willing to provide it when the need arose. Sammie didn't even know me."

How did he do that? How did he turn things around and make her feel okay?

"Beyond all of that, I have to tell you what's on my mind, Morgan."

She tensed. "Okay."

"Two things. First, you have to believe in yourself. The judge can't believe in you if you don't believe in yourself."

He told her about a student of his, without naming names. Morgan didn't even know if the boy who'd dropped out of school six times was a current student or a former one. But she knew that he'd finally earned a degree. Long after his parents had given up on him.

"This is so much bigger than a college degree," she said. But she wanted to be the boy in the story.

"I'm not arguing that, only saying that in everything in life you have a much better shot at being the best you can be if you believe in yourself. It sounded like you weren't giving the judge the best of you today, but rather giving him the same you your parents see."

He had a point. One that mattered. "You said you had two things on your mind."

Nodding, he glanced down at his hands and then said, "I agree that all boys should have a positive male influence in their lives. But I am equally sure that a young man desperately needs his mother. Sammie desperately needs you."

"I—"

"No." He held up a hand. "Let me finish because I have a feeling what I'm about to say will never be spoken aloud again as long as I live."

She stared at him, completely open to whatever was coming.

"A mother shows a young man how to love, Morgan." He spoke so softly she barely heard him. His throat sounded dry. Choked. And she sat still, as if to move would break something that was priceless.

"My father was the best dad I've ever known or seen. His unconditional and selfless love for me, his sacrifice, can never be matched and I owe him my life. But even with all of that, I'm not sure I ever learned how to love."

"You obviously love your father."

"Of course I do. I'm talking about intimate love. Man-woman type of love."

Confused, Morgan chose her words carefully. Was he telling her he was gay? Because he was raised in an all-male world? She'd never believe it.

"What about Kelsey Barber?" she asked. And there'd been women before her. Morgan had heard the rumors.

"I don't lack female companionship," he told her, and somehow coming from him it didn't sound like bragging at all. "I enjoy women. I sleep with them—one relationship at a time. But I don't love them. I choose women who are willing to date monogamously without long-term commitment. Women who value their independence and freedom more than they value me."

"That sounds horrible."

"Up until recently, I thought it sounded perfect."

"And now?"

He looked away and she thought he wasn't going to answer her. She didn't blame him. They'd somehow gone from her parenting skills to a place they shouldn't be. She wasn't even sure how they got there.

"Looking back, I realize there was always something missing in my relationships."

"What brought about the change?"

"I have no idea," he said, gazing back at her. That lost look in his eyes reminded her of Sammie, when he was trying so hard to understand why he couldn't have his way. "I just know that the other night, with Kelsey…" He shook his head. "Anyway, I broke things off with her."

Morgan's heart started to pound.

"You broke up with her and you don't even know why?"

He shrugged. "Sounds crazy, huh? But yeah, that's about how it went."

"I'll bet she had something to say about that." Morgan felt a little bit like smiling, but she felt sorry for the woman, too.

"Not really." Cal slid down until his neck rested against the back of her couch, his feet out in front of him, his hands on his stomach. "She told me I could stay or go and then went for her nightly swim."

She had to ask. "What did you do?"

"I left."

"You want a glass of wine?" She had a sudden need for one.

"You plan to join me?"

"I think so, yes."

"Then thank you. I'll have one glass of wine before I head home to bed."

Bed.

The word held the world right then. Promise and danger. Hope and fear. And something delicious that was as forbidden as it was compelling.

CAL FOLLOWED HER OUT to the kitchen. As much time as they'd spent together in her home that dreadful night Sammie had disappeared, they'd never been in the kitchen together. He filled the place and then some.

And she felt next to naked in her old sweat shorts and tank top. She wasn't even wearing a bra.

"Let me get that," he said, reaching for the bottle of pinot grigio that she'd pulled out of the refrigerator. Her father would turn his back as soon as he saw the exclusive wine come from a refrigerator rack instead of a properly chilled wine cooler.

"It was a Christmas gift from my mother. Part of my father's private stock."

Cal opened the bottle. She got glasses down. He poured. And she wondered if he was regretting the intimacy of their recent conversation.

Self-conscious, she pulled the elastic out of her hair, letting her hair fall loose around her shoulders.

He held up his glass. "To good friends."

"To good friends." The glasses clinked. She sipped. And resisted the urge to sip again. Rapidly.

"And good wine," he said, with a questioning tilt of his head.

"When I was growing up we always had a glass of wine at dinner."

"When you were growing up?"

"Yeah. I switched from milk to wine on my thirteenth birthday. Which sounds terrible, I guess." She leaned back against the counter, facing him, the arm holding her wineglass propped up on the arm around her stomach. "But I'm not so sure it was. My father taught me to appreciate and respect fine wine. Alcohol was never a mystery to me. I think partially because of that, I never went out drinking with friends. Even in my most rebellious high school days. I never saw the thrill, or the benefit that was worth the risk of getting caught and being in trouble."

"Speaking from experience, there was no benefit worth the trouble. Or thrill that was worth the hangover." Cal leaned against the counter opposite her in the galley-style kitchen, one ankle crossed over the other. She was sink side, he was stove side. And he was grinning.

"You indulged, huh?"

"A time or two."

"Any serious repercussions?"

"Got suspended from school once. No DUIs or court appearances. Truthfully, the worst consequence, as far as I was concerned, was the disappointment in my father's eyes."

Morgan had had the hots for this man for four years. The more she got to know him, the worse it got, because the more she knew about him, the more there was to like.

But she didn't date.

They were only a couple of years apart in age.

But he was her college professor.

"I love hearing about you and your dad," she said, opening up to him in spite of herself. "Frank is so completely different from my father."

"My dad has always had a way with kids," Cal told her. "He relates to them, understands them."

"He genuinely likes them."

"He should have had a houseful of them." His voice took on a hint of bitterness that wasn't usual for him.

"Why didn't he ever remarry after your mother died?"

Cal shrugged. Took a sip of wine and stared into his glass. "It's not something we ever talk about, but I suspect that he never found a woman who could fill the void she left."

Morgan wasn't sure he was being completely honest with her. A first with him.

She sipped. And put his reticence down to too much intimate conversation for one night. Cal had a right to preserve his father's privacy.

"I think we need to talk," he said, and when she glanced up, he was studying her intently.

Gulping, Morgan felt like a schoolkid all of a sudden. One who'd been called to the principal's office.

"Okay." The way he was looking at her, all personal and close, she knew that they were about to address the conversation they'd had in the living room.

Bracing herself, she waited for him to say what was on his mind.

Backtracking would be fine. A bit of a letdown, but probably for the best.

"I'm finding myself drawn to you."

She waited to find out where he was going.

"I don't think I'm alone here."

Morgan wanted a sip of her wine in the worst way. And was afraid to move.

"Am I?" It was the hint of insecurity that got to her. Caleb Whittier was the most self-possessed man she'd ever met.

"N—" She coughed. Took a sip of wine, looked him in the eye, and tried again. "No."

He drank. Nodded. His gaze was focused exclusively on her. And intense. "You want to help me out here?"

"I'm not sure where you're going with this."

"So take it where you want to go with it."

The conversation? Or the friendship?

"You're my professor. I'm your student."

"Not here, I'm not. And you're not. We're in your home, Morgan. Two consenting adults. Equals. Tell me what you want from me."

Liquid heat spread through her skin and up to her face. She couldn't believe she was blushing. "I can't do that." She absolutely could not tell the man he was the sole star of every single one of her fantasies. Let's see, how would that go? *Well, last night, in my dreams...* Or how about, *Last week, in class, when you were... I was...*

"Why not? Because of class? It's over in a couple of weeks."

She was in way over her head. "By your own admission, you've had a lot of…female companions.…"

"Lovers, you mean."

"Yes. Right. Okay."

"I've had my share."

And then some, she was sure. Cal was thirty-two and every woman's dream man. At least every woman at Wallace University that she'd ever heard speak about him.

"I haven't," she blurted. "I mean, I've probably had my share, but I've only slept with two men in my life. My husband and the one man from Daddy's company that I dated shortly after Sammie was born."

He smiled. "I'm not sorry to hear that."

"Well, since you've got more experience, and since you started this conversation, you should say what's on your mind."

There was a glint in his eye as he peered over at her. Her private parts responded.

"I believe we are about to become more than friends."

Oh, God. She started to shake, little tremors that rushed through the blood in her veins. Her fantasies were coming to life and she had no idea what to do.

"Do you disagree?"

She shook her head.

"I've never wanted a woman like I want you."

All her fantasies, dreams, faded, far surpassed by real life careening out of control.

"Do you want me, too?"

Trying desperately to get a grip, to hold on to her self-control, Morgan nodded.

Cal frowned. "You sure about that?" He leaned back against the counter again. Took another sip of wine. "You don't have to pretend something you don't feel just because I'm your teacher, Morgan. Surely you know that I would never, ever let personal life interfere with a grade. Either way."

"Of course I know that." Thank God, she could talk again. "And I'd never, ever pretend to feel something for anyone," she added. And then, even as she cringed at what she was saying, she didn't stop. "I am absolutely certain that I'm attracted to you, Caleb Whittier. I've got four years' worth of fantasies to back me up on that fact."

His grin was instant. And huge. He took the couple of steps between the counters, stopping with half an inch between their bodies. "Four years?"

"Yes." She'd put it right out there. No point in acting like she hadn't.

"What kind of fantasies?"

"Uh-uh. You have to do some time before you get to share my fantasies," she told him, smiling in spite of the fire raging through her. In spite of the confusion.

"I've got time."

"Good, because I have to wait until I finish your class before I can go any further here."

"Agreed."

And I don't date, she wanted to add. But it was too

late. And Leslie had told her that if she ever had the opportunity to, she didn't have to say no for Sammie's sake.

But then Leslie hadn't heard about Morgan's other two disastrous attempts at having a relationship with a man.

Judge Marks had.

CHAPTER TWENTY-SIX

MORGAN FELT AS THOUGH she'd been made love to. She hadn't been touched. Not even a brief kiss good-night, or a friendly hug.

And yet she was in a committed relationship as surely as if she was wearing a ring.

Just one that hadn't started yet. Or wasn't physical yet. Or…something.

"Why are you smiling?" Sammie asked as she drove him to school Wednesday morning.

"Because the sun is shining and I'm glad you're here with me and we're healthy and—"

"Last night when you took me to see Leslie after you picked me up from Frank's, I told her that the judge hadn't decided yet where I'm going to live."

"What did she say?"

"Nothing. She doesn't usually say nothing about anything."

"Anything," she corrected automatically. Then had a momentary pang of regret, thinking she should apologize, and then decided to let the correction stand.

"'Anything.' And I told her that I wanted to live with you, Mom."

Putting the car carefully into Park as she pulled up

in front of Sammie's school, Morgan turned toward her son. "You did?"

He nodded. "I just wanted you to know."

Tears would upset him. She knew that. So Morgan smiled, kissed her son goodbye, told him she loved him as best she could with a lump in her throat and then let the tears well as she watched him trudge into the building.

With a heart filled to capacity she drove to the university and, getting there fifteen minutes early, sat in her car, picked up her phone and called her mother.

"Morgan? Good morning, dear. I'm so sorry I missed your call last night. I tried to call you all afternoon and you never picked up."

She concentrated on her fellow students walking across the campus, on their way to wherever they were headed. "I needed time to think."

"I understand, sweetie. You have no idea how horrible I felt all day. I didn't sleep at all last night. I love you, baby. You know that."

"I know, Mom." She wasn't surprised that Grace regretted her actions the day before. Her mother was firmly under George's control. She loved the man. Morgan didn't understand it, but she accepted it.

"I didn't see that you'd called until this morning. My phone had gone dead after trying you all afternoon...."

And talking to George, too, Morgan was sure. Her father would have kept in particularly close contact with his wife yesterday afternoon. He'd have known Grace's state of mind and would make sure that she stayed solidly certain that she'd done the right thing.

"I forgot last night was theater night."

"Oh, we didn't go to the theater, honey. Your father gave those tickets away. Neither one of us felt like socializing. We just stayed here at home. Had a quiet dinner. And talked."

Dare she hope? "What did you talk about?"

"How our lives were going to change when Sammie came to live with us. Redoing his room. Where he's going to go to school. Your father called the Hayward Academy this morning and was lucky enough to get a spot, even at this late notice."

Hayward Academy. A very elite school for boys. Where they wore uniforms. One that was academically focused and had only intramural sports teams.

Sammie told Leslie he wanted to live with Morgan. Cal supported her. Julie supported her. "I wanted to speak with you about that, Mom."

"Oh, yes, dear, I'm sorry. We should have talked to you, as well. We'll have to work on that. To be sure and include you in all of the decisions regarding Sammie's life…."

"No, Mom, I want to talk to you about the whole custody suit."

"Okay." Her mother sounded hopeful. And, strangely enough, that strengthened Morgan's resolve.

"I want you to talk to Daddy about the possibility of a compromise," she said, both hands on her steering wheel. "I'd talk to him myself, but I make him angry and then he doesn't hear what I have to say."

"What kind of compromise, Morgan?" Doubt entered her mother's voice.

"I'll agree to change some things, agree to twenty-four-hour security, extended visits with you all, to include you in any major decisions I make to get your opinion in case I miss something, and in exchange, Daddy drops his case."

Silence hung on the line.

"Sammie is my son, Mom. He belongs with me." She stopped short of telling her mother that Sammie *wanted* her, that her son had officially chosen her. She wouldn't put Sammie in that position with his grandparents.

"I'll talk to your father, Morgan, but I can tell you right now, you're only making things more difficult on yourself. You're just proving your father's point. You can't see what's best for Sammie."

Shored up by the two men in her life, and by her own heart, Morgan said, "I believe I do see, Mom."

Maybe she didn't always see others clearly, but she knew her own heart and she knew that no one would look out for Sammie more fervently than she would. Yes, she'd made some bad choices when she was younger. Yes, she'd been a little over-the-top where bucking her father was concerned.

She'd matured. She had her eyes wide open.

Morgan was smiling again by the time she walked up the stairs to Cal's class.

CHAPTER TWENTY-SEVEN

CAL STAYED BUSY that next week. He had papers coming in from both of his classes and while he had a month to get his grades in, he wanted his calendar clear the second the semester ended. The days until then—and until Morgan's next hearing—loomed interminably. And yet, he couldn't remember a time he'd caught himself whistling so much.

"What's with you?" his father asked on Tuesday night, a week after Morgan's first custody hearing— a week after they'd spent the half hour in her kitchen that had changed his life.

"What do you mean?" Cal was chopping onions.

Frank had come in after playing basketball with Sammie and taken hamburger out of the freezer. The two men were making homemade spaghetti sauce— something they hadn't done together in years—to go on the pasta they were having for dinner.

"You're whistling. Staying home every night. And you're going to bed earlier rather than locking your-self in that office of yours for half the night."

His group of young artists didn't start meeting again until the fall. He'd had his junior arts league meet-ing already this month. He'd arranged appointments for potential funding during his lunch hours—not on purpose, they'd just happened that way. The various university functions he attended didn't begin again until September.

And he couldn't very well go out. Not now that he was going to have a woman in his life in a few weeks.

"I didn't stay up half the night. And how would you know? You were in your room most nights before I started writing."

"Writing?" Frank's spoon stilled in the pot of freshly cut tomatoes and garlic as he looked over at Cal. "Writing what? You never told me you were writing. You said you were researching. For class."

"I never said it was for class. You assumed it was."

Frank stirred. A minute passed. "I might have assumed it was for class," he said, his tone less accusing. "What were you writing?"

"Nothing, Dad," he said. What on earth had loosened his tongue so much lately? Whatever it was, it had to stop. Safety lay in privacy. "Just typing up notes from the research I was doing."

"So you were researching." Adding a couple of tablespoons of white wine, some bay leaf and oregano to his sauce, Frank sounded appeased.

"Of course. I don't lie to you."

Another couple of minutes passed quietly while Frank stirred and tasted and adjusted and Cal browned his onions in a small touch of olive oil and added a pound of hamburger.

"But there's only one thing I know of that we don't talk about, and if your research wasn't for class, I'm fairly certain it had to do with Comfort Cove." Frank's voice was barren.

He'd just said he didn't lie to his father. "It doesn't matter, Dad."

"You're writing about what happened?" The sauce was put on a back burner.

"It's just notes."

"Do you think that's wise, Cal? To put things down on paper? What if someone gets ahold of your notes?"

What if? Cal lost his appetite. And his compulsion to whistle.

"Don't borrow trouble, Dad, please. I've been working on this for years and nothing has happened. Don't let that call to the nursing home bother you. Life is trying to look up for us. Let it."

Adding his ground beef to his father's sauce, Cal set the mixture to simmer and filled a pot with water to cook the spaghetti.

THE NEXT MORNING, before class, Cal remembered his words to his father about borrowing trouble when he listened to the voice mail in his office. Ramsey Miller needed him to call.

Guilt was a like a chronic disease in his gut, an albatross, an unwanted but very familiar companion. If it hadn't been for his testimony, his father would not have been a suspect twenty-five years before.

But Miller already had that testimony in his files. Cal's book dealt more with their lives after they'd left Comfort Cove, his own thoughts and memories and anger, and chronicled his research methods and findings, right down to dates and times of discovery. And not one piece of information had led to Claire Sanderson.

So there was nothing to worry about.

With his father's fearful reaction the night before fresh in his mind, Cal dialed Miller's number.

"I found something," Miller said.

No. Life did not work this way—all neatly tied up. "What do you mean?"

"Your book. Chapter two. You talk about a delivery truck on your street the morning that Claire Sanderson went missing."

"The truck I hid behind to sneak back to our place."

"You didn't mention the truck in your testimony to the police."

So that made him suspect? Or somehow cast further suspicions on his father?

Was it too much to hope that the two of them be happy? For at least a few days?

"I didn't deliberately withhold the information from them, if that's what you're implying," Cal said, hand in his pocket as he took the handset from his office phone over to the window to look out at the campus. "It's not like the truck means anything except that the guy delivered meat," he said now, remembering the truck, the writing on the side, as if he'd seen it the week before. He gave Miller the details. "It was at the neighbor's house every single Wednesday morning. Three doors down from us. They didn't buy their meat at the store like we did, and Emma and I asked our parents why. It was there every week, and it wasn't anything that had ever been a danger to us. The guy was known in the neighborhood. Believe me, there's nothing suspect about that truck. The police asked me if I'd seen anything unusual, but seeing that particular delivery truck in our neighborhood was normal."

"I understand. I read the book. You mention it only because you hid behind the truck as a means to sneak back to your house and into your backyard because you didn't want to go to school that day."

"I'd thrown up there the day before." A humiliation a guy didn't forget.

"I understand that the truck doesn't seem like evidence to you, but reading about it struck a chord," Miller said. "I remembered another abduction where a delivery truck had been seen in the area. That one didn't pan out in terms of a connection to Claire's disappearance—the child was found asleep in a tent in the neighbor's backyard. But I pulled records for other meat delivery routes. I ran that against reported abductions and had two hits."

What was Miller saying? "Does this mean my father is in the clear?"

"No. But it means there's a possibility of a break in the case. You say that meat delivery truck delivered to a neighbor three houses down?"

"Yes."

"Did your father have any association with them?"

"No. My... Rose Sanderson, Claire's mother, knew them, but not well, as I remember."

"Has your father ever had meats delivered?"

Here we go again. "No." Cal didn't bother to hide his frustration.

"I'm going to run cross-checks between the other two cases and the evidence we do have. I'll also be checking the records from the delivery company to see if your father's name comes up. If it does, I'm going to need to talk to him. Either way, I'll get back to you."

"Please keep me informed," he said. Miller hadn't had to call him. He could have called the nursing home first, looking for his father to ask about his meat truck associations. "And I'd like you to call me before you contact my father. At least give me a heads-up."

"I appreciate your position, Professor. I'll do what I can."

Which meant nothing at all.

"And all of this is because you want to find out what happened to the missing box of evidence."

"It's part of an ongoing investigation so I can't discuss details."

Cal frowned. "Do you have a body, Detective? Have you found Claire?"

"Look, Professor, I appreciate your help. I can't really say more, but I will tell you that this has to do with more than just Claire Sanderson. I was working on another case when I discovered the box missing."

"So it really isn't about my father?"

"I don't know that."

Frustrated, but appreciative that the detective was telling him as much as he could, Cal got off the phone with Miller and grabbed his briefcase. He had a class to teach.

And a woman to see there who, though they weren't seeing each other yet romantically, still made his world look a hell of a lot better than it ever had before.

"Okay, Frank's going to pick you up at school and drop you off at tryouts. I'll pick you up there," Morgan told Sammie as she dropped him off at school Wednesday morning. "You have everything you need?"

The boy, wearing his new sneakers and a University of Tennessee T-shirt and basketball shorts, all compliments of the Whittiers, smirked at her. "I'm ready, Mom. Frank said so. Quit worrying."

She was a mother. It was her job to worry. Which he'd realize when he got older.

"Just remember, the other boys are all older than you. This is only your first time trying out."

Looking at her with those expressive brown eyes, Sammie said, "Jeez, Mom, don't you think I'm going to make it?"

"I think you've got a good chance, Sammie. I just don't want you to give up if you don't."

"I'm not a quitter. That's what you've always said. We Lowens don't quit."

"That's right. We don't." She smiled at him. He was her son. For a while she'd almost forgotten what that meant. After years of fighting against her father's manipulation, she'd almost given in to it. And lost her son in the process.

Thank God for Cal. He'd been put in her life for a reason. A very good one.

And it wasn't just Cal. With Frank in Sammie's life,

her son had been almost a perfect child at home, and since she had no social life, she now had time in the evenings to spend on Mark Twain.

Wishing her son luck and giving him an extra long hug filled with all of the love she had stored up inside, she sent him off into his world and turned her car toward her own class.

WITH FINGERS THAT FUMBLED in his haste to not get ahead of himself, Ramsey Miller dialed a number he now knew by heart from the phone on his desk in the eighth precinct of the Comfort Cove Police Department.

Lucy had been on a case for a couple of days. She'd sent a text the night before that she'd wrapped it up— the body of the dead woman had led to the arrest of the woman's husband—and was taking a couple of days off.

"Yeah? What's up?" She sounded sleepy.

"Sorry to wake you."

"No, that's okay. I should be up, anyway. I have to get Mom's breakfast this morning." Lucy lived alone, but across the street from her mother who was not well. The woman who cared for her mother was good to Lucy, working unusual hours as they fit Lucy's schedule, so Lucy generally gave the woman time off on her own days off.

"She in bed again?" Ramsey asked. Did Lucy ever notice that her mother always took to her bed on Lucy's days off?

"Yeah. She had a spell last evening, apparently. Marie called just before she left."

Sandy Hayes could get around well enough if she stayed off the alcohol. And took her depression medication. She seemed to prefer having Lucy there to take care of her.

"Is she drinking?"

"No. I asked."

He was glad to hear it, not that it was any of his business. He'd never even met the woman. He'd only met Lucy once.

"I got a lead."

"What?" He heard the covers rustle and figured Lucy had just sat up in bed. "Where?" And then, more quietly, "Oh, Ramsey, did you find another one? Was it Claire Sanderson?"

She was referring to Ramsey's obsession with the Peter Walters case. He'd busted the fifty-five-year-old bastard on a child abduction case a year back. He'd been in time to save the kid, a three-year-old girl, from more than just a scare, but Walters had a big mouth and an even bigger need to brag, letting Ramsey know that he hadn't been able to save them all. Not one to have patience with cold cases, Ramsey had nonetheless found himself immersed in boxes of evidence that night—all local missing-children cases. His search had continued for most of that next week and he'd ended up finding information that tied Walters to another case from the Comfort Cove area. It didn't take him ten minutes of convincing to get Walters to tell him what he'd done with the body.

What he'd found made him puke. And Walters had a last laugh as he told Ramsey that, hypothetically, there could be more victims.

Ramsey had been a madman ever since, using every spare moment to try to prove that there had been no other victims. He'd searched the bachelor's house himself, enraged enough, when he found nothing, to tear up floorboards with his bare hands. Underneath them he'd found miscellaneous objects—children's clothing, a stuffed animal, a pink hairbrush. All in all, he'd come out with a box full of items that had potentially belonged to victims.

Going through old cases in a six-hundred-mile radius, he'd already matched four cases to Walters. In Massachusetts and out of state, too.

Walters was in prison awaiting trial on the most recent kidnapping, but since his victim was returned safely, he wasn't looking at the life sentence without parole that he deserved. And then he'd face trial on the kidnapping and murder of Kylie Jacobs. And on the kidnapping and murder of the other four victims Ramsey had tied him to. One of which had taken place in Massachusetts and would carry the death penalty. Ramsey wasn't going to rest until the man was dead.

It was during his investigations into cold abduction cases that he'd met Detective Lucy Hayes from Aurora, Indiana. He'd submitted a request for a box of evidence on an Aurora, Michigan, abduction that wasn't where it belonged; Lucy had checked out the box for a cold case she was following.

He'd called her. They'd exchanged case information and had been working together ever since.

"No," he said now. "I didn't find Claire. And I'm no closer to finding out what happened to her box of evidence. How does a box get up and walk out of a vault in the basement of a police facility? How did someone get in the door without a badge, get past security, carry out a box and not get picked up by cameras?"

Lucy didn't say anything. Probably knew he was venting. They'd been over it all before.

"But I did stumble on to something," he continued. Over the past months he'd grown accustomed to running things by her. He filled her in on the delivery truck.

"Here's what I'm thinking," he continued, speaking in low tones due to the bustle of police business going on around him. "This Frank Whittier had the girl in his car. Probably to keep her out of sight for the few minutes he waited on the truck. Then he hands her over and takes the payoff when the guy sells the baby. Either that, or the two of them are as sick as Walters and then I don't want to think about what they did with her." He told her about the two other abductions on meat delivery routes. "I'm checking now to see if there's any connection to Whittier and the other two kids. We figured Frank didn't do this alone. So maybe we've found his partner."

"Do you have the driver's name?"

"Yeah, but I haven't found the guy yet. I'm still tracking him down."

"This would mean that Claire wasn't one of Walters's victims."

"That's right." Which had become his goal in life—to rule out which children had been Walters's victims. Each time a case didn't match up, he was relieved. At the same time, he was driven to find every one of his victims and hang Walters for each and every one of them. He wanted closure for the families. He wanted Walters to pay. And he grieved every single time he hit pay dirt.

"But whoever took Claire and these other children did something with them," Lucy said, her voice echoing the sadness that haunted him.

"Yeah."

"Life sucks, doesn't it?"

"Seems to."

"Keep me posted."

"Yeah."

CHAPTER TWENTY-EIGHT

MORGAN WAS WAITING for Cal's call at ten o'clock Wednesday night. He hadn't said he'd call. They weren't in a relationship—yet—and didn't talk on the phone as if they were. But in the past, whenever he'd had reason to call, he'd done so at ten. The time seemed to work for both of them.

And today, he had reason to call.

At 9:57 p.m. her phone lit up, signaling his call. He was early. She liked that he hadn't been able to wait, either.

"Hi." She hadn't been able to talk to him after class. She'd had no valid reason to. And this close to the end of the quarter with papers being due, he'd had a lot of students hovering around him, needing his attention.

"How'd it go?"

"He made the first cut!" She'd been bursting with the news. "Can you believe it? He's not even five feet tall and he's that much closer to playing on the junior high team!"

"Congratulations!" Cal chuckled. "You aren't a proud mama or anything, are you?"

"Of course I'm proud. But I'm also very thankful for you and your father. Without the two of you…"

"Don't, Morgan. If you're going to start downplaying your part in this, I'm hanging up. He's your son. Take credit for his accomplishments. It won't kill you, I promise."

Sighing, but with a huge grin on her face, Morgan relented. "You should have seen him, Cal. The second I picked him up from tryouts, I knew he'd done well. He practically danced into the center and stopped to talk to every little kid who noticed him."

"What did you do to celebrate?"

"We stopped for pizza on the way home. His choice, of course. And then spent a couple of hours on the internet tonight, reading up on everything related to basketball that he could find. From stats to strategies to success stories of short players. He'd been wound so tight, he was actually tired at eight-thirty and went to bed at nine without any argument."

"When is the second cut?"

"Tomorrow. I was hoping your dad would take him again. I called a couple of times but he didn't answer. I figured I'd catch up with him in the morning. If he can't do it, I know Julie can."

"I'm sure he'll do it. I actually got him to agree to go out for a steak dinner with me tonight and then stop off for some new jeans. He added some new sweatpants to wear when he's playing with Sammie. And the whole night he was after me to call and find out how tryouts went. But I wanted to give you guys your time together."

"You could have called."

"Maybe I wanted to talk to you in private." Cal's

voice grew serious. "You have no idea the change your son has made in my father's life, Morgan. It's truly me who owes you, not the other way around."

"Or maybe neither of us owes anyone," she said, running her finger around a barely visible wood grain on the table. "That's how it works with…friends, isn't it? The give and take is mutual."

"Friends?"

"Well, I mean…"

"I have plans for us to be much more than friends, Ms. Lowen."

Her body flooded with desire. She swallowed. She should have brought in a cup of tea. Laced with every calming herb known to humankind.

"You have nothing to say to that?"

"I'm too busy thinking about tea," she said, grinning just a bit.

"Your herbal stuff?"

Squirming in her seat, she said, "Maybe."

"The aphrodisiac kind, I hope?"

"No!" The word came out far more strongly than she'd intended. "I'm sorry," she quickly added. "But you are more of an aphrodisiac than I seem to be able to handle, Professor, so just be nice and let me think about my tea."

"I turn you on, huh?"

"So much so that I am sitting fully dressed at my dining room table, with a fully padded, serviceable bra and white briefs on under my clothes. I couldn't take a chance on anything more comfortable."

"Or what?"

"Or what, what?"

"Why couldn't you take a chance? What would have happened?"

Her nipples were hard.

"I don't know and I was afraid to find out."

"I like the sound of that." Even his voice was sexy. This wasn't fair.

"You are still my teacher, Cal. And I have a custody hearing to worry about. I can't start a relationship right before the judge makes his decision, no matter who it's with. It would just feed the image of me that my parents have given him." She'd thought a lot about this. "And even if it didn't, being with you, in any capacity, would take my focus away from Sammie right now. I can't afford that. Not with my father as the adversary."

"Did your mother talk to him like she promised she would?"

"I have no idea. I haven't heard from either one of them. If Mom had something to report, she'd have called either way. The silence is actually making me nervous. I'm sure my father's plotting something again."

"Or maybe he's just taking some time to cool down and think and will do the right thing by you."

She'd like to hope so, even though experience told her differently. Still, Cal had met her father. He knew what she was up against. And Cal was a smart man. If he thought her father might bend, then maybe he was right.

"Maybe I'm just too close to the situation to read him clearly after all these years."

"Or maybe you do read him clearly, but this is an entirely new situation for both of you. Your father is wrong, Morgan. Apparently that's not something he's had a lot of practice with. But as you've said, he's not a bad man."

"No, just an emotionless one." Her father would do what he thought was right. But he acted with his head, not his heart.

THINGS HAPPENED IN THEIR own time and sometimes at exactly the right time, Morgan thought as she answered the phone the next morning.

"Hello?" She'd dropped Sammie off and had just pulled into the day-care parking lot.

"Morgan? It's your father."

She knew that from the number that appeared on the display. "Hi, Daddy."

"I'm calling to arrange a meeting with you today during the lunch hour," he said. "I have something to discuss with you."

"You want to meet at the restaurant?"

"I'd like you to come to my office."

He wasn't planning to just railroad her into his way of thinking, then. He could do that at the restaurant.

With a smile on her face, Morgan agreed to the meeting and went into the day care to greet her pre-schoolers.

There was no mistake about the timing of her father's request.

"COME IN." GEORGE LOWEN buttoned the jacket of his black suit as he opened the door of his inner sanctum to Morgan a couple of minutes before noon.

"Where's Nancy?" she asked, referring to the woman who'd been her father's personal secretary since Morgan was little.

"Early lunch." George closed the door behind them.

Ordinarily she'd have been intimidated by that closed door, by being alone with her father in his office. Ordinarily she'd have felt self-conscious about the casualness of her calf-length colorful cotton skirt and yellow peasant blouse, but today she had an entirely different feeling about meeting with her father.

She'd still pulled her blond hair up into a chignon, though. Some things just set her father off. Morgan's hair down, unkempt as he called it, was one of them.

She went straight toward the armchair she usually occupied.

"Let's sit over here," George said, motioning to the two maroon leather armchairs in front of his massive cherry desk.

"Is Mom joining us?"

"She's downstairs arranging lunch." So she was on the premises, but not present? Morgan studied her father, the stiff way he sat, the slight unsteadiness in the hands that reached for the single folder on top of his desk.

"What's going on?"

He put the folder on his lap, with his hands on top of it.

"I want you to know I don't blame you."

"For what?" What did the folder contain?

"You do your best. I believe that."

"What's going on, Daddy?"

"As your mother always says, you're a good girl."

Morgan stared at him. "I'm a grown woman."

He handed her the folder. "Maybe there's more I could have done with you, should have done with you...."

She held the folder, but was too confused by what he was saying to look inside.

"Tell me what's wrong."

He met her gaze, his brown eyes the same brown as hers and Sammie's. His face was lined. For the first time in her life, her father looked old to her.

"Your mother has made a point, Morgan. She's shown me that in one thing I was wrong. Your choices in men aren't your fault, Morgan. They're mine. Your mother says that girls are attracted to men like their father. She pointed out that you choose men who are as you see me—someone who will expect things of you, expect you to listen to them and believe what they say, without listening to you or what you need."

The concept of her father listening to her mother was novel to her. His admitting that he was wrong...? Unbelievable. But his conclusion about her choice in men was utterly wrong. "Look in the folder, Morgan."

Slowly, keeping an eye on her father, Morgan did as he asked.

After glancing at the letterhead, the papers had her full attention.

Her father had hired a firm she'd never heard of to do a private investigation.

Caleb and Frank Whittier were the names on the first line.

Her first reaction was anger. The kind that blinded you for a second. How dare he do this? How dare he bring Frank and Cal into their fight? How dare he have her friends investigated?

And then, although she wasn't proud of it, she read on. Only the initial paragraph of the report, at first. The part that gave the investigator's opinion that Frank Whittier was a danger to Sammie.

"Where did he get his information?"

"I'm not sure and I didn't ask. This guy does what he has to do. When we saw Sammie over the weekend every other word out of his mouth was about these men—Cal and his father, Frank. I had my regular team run a check on both of them. Your professor checked out, but they couldn't find any recent mention of Frank anywhere, so I hired someone."

"You couldn't just accept that they're good people?"

"No." Her father shook his head. "We found so much nothing that it bothered me. Frank has not owned a home in more than twenty-five years. He hasn't held a job that we could find. He hasn't even had a mailing address or a driver's license."

"Frank works as a janitor," she told her father. "He's a retired schoolteacher."

"He didn't retire from teaching, Morgan. He took a forced resignation after he was held for questioning in a criminal case involving a young child in his care."

Oh, God, no. The blood drained out of her face. It felt as though it drained out of her body. She shivered. And was afraid she was going to be sick on her father's plush beige carpet.

CHAPTER TWENTY-NINE

"TELL ME."

Morgan faced her father, feeling thankful for once that the man had enough money to move mountains and enough distrust to have the people she and Sammie associated with investigated.

"Frank is the prime suspect in the disappearance of a little girl, Morgan."

Her heart pounding, she asked, "Where?" But she knew. God in heaven, she knew. And she'd just made the biggest mistake of her life. "It was in Comfort Cove, Massachusetts, wasn't it?"

The abduction that Cal knew about, the two-year-old little girl. He'd said that he and his father lived in the town. That they didn't know the child well.

"Who was she?"

"Her name was Claire Sanderson. She was two years old. Frank Whittier was engaged to the girl's mother, Rose. Cal and Frank lived with Rose and her two little girls, Emma and Claire."

"You said he's the prime suspect. They didn't ever prove that he did it?"

"No, which is why he's free to prey on my grandson."

George had no evidence that Frank had hurt Sammie.

"Caleb Whittier stayed all night the evening that Sammie went missing because he needed to make certain that his father wasn't involved. Or if he was, so that he'd know what the police knew. He'd know how to protect his father. That's why, as soon as it was determined that Sammie ran away, he took off. Didn't you find it odd that he didn't hang around at least long enough to meet the boy he'd spent the night worrying over?"

She had found that odd.

"I suppose Mom agrees with you?" Not that she would admit if she didn't.

"Yes." Her father didn't gloat. She'd give him that.

"Think about it, Morgan. The man is their only suspect. I don't know all of the details of the case, but according to the papers back then, the child was seen in Frank's car after she'd gone missing. And when the police searched his car later, her teddy bear was stuffed under the front seat. He was the last person to have seen her. And even with teams scouring the area and everyone being interviewed, there was never a second suspect. Are you willing to risk your son's life with a man whom a school system considered unsafe to be around their children?"

Morgan knew Frank. And Cal. She couldn't believe either one of them would hurt a child.

But she didn't always see the bad in people, did she?

And Cal had lied to her about that little girl. He'd told her he and his father barely knew the child who'd gone missing in his hometown.

Could she afford *not* to believe her father's evidence? Had she put her son in the hands of a child abductor?

Morgan's entire emotional being shut down.

"Call your team, Daddy. Sammie's at school and then Frank is taking him to basketball tryouts. I'll call Julie and have her take Sammie there instead. And I'll let Frank know I'm taking care of the tryouts. I don't want to alarm Sammie at this point. And he's not going to miss those tryouts. I'll take off work for the rest of the day, but I don't want Sammie suspecting that there's something going on. Please tell your men to watch him like a hawk until I get there to pick him up. And then I'm bringing him home to live. You're right. He's better off there."

She just couldn't take the chance that George was wrong. He seldom was when it came to getting the facts.

"If that man's done anything to Sammie... If he's touched him..."

"I sure as hell hope he hasn't. There's nothing in my report to indicate that they were anywhere but the basketball court outside. Until yesterday when he took Sammie to a junior high school."

Sammie showed no signs of having been improperly touched. To the contrary, he was happier and seemed healthier than she'd ever seen him.

And he'd been seeing a counselor. If he'd been in danger with Frank, Sammie hadn't known about it.

So maybe she was right, and Frank had been wrongly accused.

But she couldn't take that chance. The bottom line

was, at the moment, she didn't trust her own judgment any more than her father did.

"I'm glad that you're finally doing what's right," George said.

"Just make sure someone is watching him until I get there, without letting him know there's anything amiss. I want him to be able to finish the tryouts."

"I've had men on him since Sammie ran away," George said. "And the second this report came through this morning, I put them on Frank full-time, too."

In the end, it paid to have an unemotional know-it-all for a father.

"I NEED TO TELL SAMMIE that he's going to be staying with you," Morgan said. She'd called the day care, Julie and Frank. She'd seen her mother. She'd read every word of the report on Caleb and Frank Whittier. She had two hours before she had to pick up her son from basketball. She was alone with her father again and ready to leave. "He'll be less likely to resist if I tell him that this is my choice."

"Okay." Her father's face hadn't changed at all. If he felt compassion for her, it didn't show.

"Promise me, Daddy. You'll let me tell Sammie. You aren't going to have one of your men show up to bring him home. They can watch Sammie but let me get him and bring him to you."

"I give you my word."

"I have to go see Cal," she said.

"I don't advise it."

"I know. And I suspect you're going to have someone following me, too, now, which is why I'm telling you up front that's where I'm going. I… We… I have to break up with him."

Her father's chin tightened. "So he got to you personally? I thought he was dating some art teacher at the university."

"It's complicated."

George straightened. "Life doesn't have to be so messy, Morgan. I hope you realize that now."

"After I see Cal, I'm going to pick up Sammie and bring him home to you and Mom," she repeated, keeping her mind on the facts at hand and refusing to let her father get to her.

After all, he'd just possibly saved her son's life.

At the door, she turned. "Thank you."

CAL WAS IN THE À LA CARTE cafeteria on the west side of campus having a late lunch when Morgan's ringtone sounded.

Since she almost never called him, it took him a second to realize what he was listening to. Dropping his burger on the paper wrapper in front of him, he grabbed his cell before he missed her call.

"What's up?"

"I need to see you." Her voice trembled as she spoke.

"Absolutely. When?"

"Now?"

He had a student meeting. He'd cancel it.

"Okay." He was already on his feet, throwing away the rest of his lunch. "Where?"

"Your office?" He couldn't tell if she was crying or not, but something was very wrong. And she'd called him.

"You're on campus?"

"Yeah. In the parking lot."

Whatever it was, he'd fix it. Somehow, some way, he'd help her. "I'll be waiting."

"Thank you."

He was sure she was crying as she hung up. Cal needed to hold her, to make her world happy once and for all.

He'd do it, too. No matter the cost.

The feeling was new to him.

STANDING IN HIS OFFICE doorway, Cal listened for Morgan's footsteps on the stairs. With his arms waiting to take her in, he met her halfway down the hall.

She slipped past him.

"You're going to want to close the door," she said over her shoulder as she walked into his office.

Her gaze was hard and there was no sign of tears. No sign of the warm, loving woman he knew he was going to marry. As soon as she'd have him.

Closing the door, he approached her again, but she held him off with one arm up in front of her.

"Don't," she said. "Don't come near me." He hardly recognized her voice.

"What happened?"

He'd missed the folder she had with her until she opened it and threw it on the floor at his feet.

And then he knew.

"Your father had me investigated."

But it wasn't the investigation that bothered him. It was Morgan's reaction. "You can't possibly believe any of the things he's telling you," he said.

The idea that Lowen might look at him had occurred to him, certainly. He'd thought about it in terms of the danger to Frank. It had never occurred to him that, if the truth came out, Morgan would choose her father's side over him.

"How can I not? You lied to me. You said you hardly knew that little girl who went missing."

He'd forgotten that he'd told her that. He'd been so vague that night, their relationship still so new....

"Morgan..." He reached out a hand to her, trying to look her in the eye. He'd lost a lifetime of opportunities for a crime his father didn't commit. He couldn't lose Morgan. "I should have told you. I admit, I deliberately chose not to. But Sammie—and you—were perfectly safe at all times, I swear. The suspicions, they're all lies, Morgan. But no one has ever believed us. My silence was due to a lifetime of being on the run, of protecting my father from the lies and suspicions that have all but killed him. And me. This detective in Comfort Cove, he's found another suspect. I'm waiting to hear from him and then this will all be cleared up."

Her expression hadn't changed. It was like she was completely closed off to him. Unable to hear him.

"Don't you see? For the first time in my adult life, I had a chance at a life. With you..."

"Did he do it?" she interrupted, her voice shaking.

"No."

"There's proof that little girl was in his car."

"I know. I'm the one who saw her there. I'm the one who told the police." He took a small step forward. She backed up immediately.

"Her bear was there. After she went missing. Can you explain that?"

"No." He'd never been able to explain that. "She had it at breakfast that morning. And then I left for school. Except I didn't go to school. I'd told my father that I didn't want to go, and why, but he was making me go anyway. I left and then made my way back home cutting through backyards. I was watching my father's car so I'd know when the coast was clear and I could go into the house again. That's when I saw Claire standing on the back seat."

"Tell me one thing."

"Anything." He loved her. Couldn't she see that? Didn't it count?

"Are you 100 percent certain that your father is innocent in Claire Sanderson's disappearance?"

"Yes." He wanted to be.

"Certain enough that you're willing to risk my son's life?"

He'd never left Frank alone at the house during the basketball practices. Because he had to drive Sammie there? Because he worried that his father might have a breakdown?

Or because, in the farthest recesses of his mind…

He took too long to answer. Before he found his voice, Morgan was gone.

MORGAN MADE THE WALK back to her car, opened the door, put on her seat belt, all automatically. Her body took over because her heart and mind were frozen.

She couldn't believe that Cal was covering for a predator. That he was an accessory to God knew what horrible atrocities.

A two-year-old girl.

She just couldn't fathom it.

Sitting in her car, she stared out at the sea of cars, the students that arrived and left.

She couldn't believe in herself.

Just last week Cal had told her about believing in herself. About his student who'd believed he could graduate even after so many failures. That student had believed in himself even when his father had stopped believing.

Had Cal made that student story up just to manipulate her? To get her to believe in him? To turn her away from her father?

She couldn't believe that, either.

How did you live with a mind that played tricks on you? A heart that wasn't discerning enough?

Dizzy and sick to her stomach, Morgan didn't turn the key in the ignition. Her glen called to her. She needed to lie in the grass and just go to sleep. She needed that so badly.

But she had something else to do. She had an hour left before she had to get Sammie and tell him that he was going to be staying with his grandparents.

He'd want to know why.

She had to figure out what to tell him.

That Frank, his new hero, was a very bad man? He wouldn't believe that. And maybe Cal was telling the truth. Maybe Frank had been erroneously accused.

But could she take that chance?

What if Cal's belief in his father stemmed from the guilt of having turned the police on to him in the first place?

One thing was certain. She was not going to tell Sammie what Frank was suspected of doing. Sammie was only ten. There were things he didn't need to know. Besides, Frank hadn't been formally charged. Sammie would be all over that.

Her head hurt. So badly.

Lying back against the seat, she closed her eyes. Tears trickled out of the corners. All she'd ever wanted was to love and be loved. Was that so bad?

And Cal. He'd been so sweet when she'd called. Right there for her. And he'd looked so stricken.

But he was protecting a man he wasn't certain was innocent.

And he'd introduced Sammie to Frank, not knowing if his father was a child abductor or not....

Her phone rang. Morgan almost ignored the call. She didn't want to talk to Cal. Or even her parents. But it could be Sammie. She grabbed her phone out of her purse.

And didn't recognize the number.

"Hello?"

"Ms. Whittier? This is Coach Safford. You need to come right away, ma'am. Sammie is missing..."

She went cold.

"…already called the police…"

Like a robot, Morgan started her car, put it in gear and drove out onto the street. She knew the school. Sammie had played Little League there. She knew the way and she drove.

But she also dialed the phone.

"Detective Martin, please."

Hands shaking, heart breaking, she waited. Turned a corner. And sped in between cars, crossing lines illegally, breaking the speed limit. A cop stopping her would be a blessing. He'd be able to get her there more quickly.

"This is Detective Martin."

"Detective? I'm Morgan Lowen. I don't know if you remember me, but—"

"Of course I remember you! How's Sammie?"

"He's missing…." Her voice broke. She tried to speak again, but choked.

"Calm down, Morgan. I need you to talk to me." The detective's voice was commanding, just short of sharp. "Tell me what's happened. Where are you?"

"In my car. Driving to Sammie's basketball tryouts."

"You shouldn't be driving, Morgan. Can you pull over?"

She shook her head. She had to get there.

"Are you pulled over? Morgan? Tell me what happened."

She was only a couple of miles away now. Clear road ahead. Blinking rapidly to keep the tears out of her way, she pushed farther down on the gas.

"I just got a call from Sammie's basketball coach.

He asked to use the restroom during tryouts and never came back."

"He ran away again."

"No!" She missed a stop sign. "Please! Sammie was at basketball tryouts, which is right where he wanted most to be. He doesn't have any reason at this point to run away. He just told me that he told his counselor he wants to live with me. You have to listen. We can't waste any time!"

The school was right ahead. And by the time she pulled into the parking lot she'd told Detective Martin about Frank Whittier and his association with Sammie.

"You said you're at the school now?"

"Yes." She climbed out of her car and ran toward the police cars gathered by the back door of the gymnasium with her phone still to her ear.

"Tell Detective Sanchez to call me. I'm going to have someone bring you in."

"Okay. And…" She saw the detectives through the crowd gathered around them. "Can someone please deal with my dad? I don't want him showing up here."

CHAPTER THIRTY

WITH HIS MEETING canceled, Cal locked up his office and went home. He'd had a dozen women break up with him. He'd never left work for them.

"What's wrong?" Frank asked, the second he walked in the door. His father appeared to be waiting for him.

"Nothing."

Frank studied Cal, leaving him feeling as though he was a little kid again, answering to a man who could read his mind. "I heard the Durango pull in."

"End of the semester, no meetings." Cal shrugged. "I've got papers to grade and no interruptions here." His gaze bounced off his father's and he opened the refrigerator, grabbing a bottle of water he didn't want.

"Tell me what's going on." Frank stood in the way of Cal leaving the kitchen.

Stepping to the side, Cal made to move around his father. The older man blocked him.

"I pissed Morgan off, okay?" he said, irritation covering for the cold fear piercing through him. He'd deal with this. He always did.

"Pissed her off, how? Seems to take an awful lot to rattle that girl. But that might have something to do with the call I had from her saying she didn't need me to take Sammie to tryouts. She said she had the day off. What did you do?"

He glared at the man, surprised to see that they were at eye level again. Frank was standing taller these days. "I don't know how, okay?" he lied. "She didn't give me a lot to go on."

"Then you need to go to her, son. Don't just let her walk out of your life. Not this time. She's the one."

"No, Dad, she's not."

"You can't just walk away every single time you get hurt."

"Oh, no? Isn't that we've always done, Dad? Run away?" He didn't mean the words, didn't mean to lash out.

But loving his father had cost him so much.

"I'm sorry," he said. "I'm sorry I told the cops I saw Claire Sanderson in your car. And I'm sorry I snapped at you."

He was seven again. And hurting. In twenty-five years the pain hadn't lessened in the least. It had just been pushed far back inside of him, waiting to explode.

"It's okay, son," Frank said, putting his hand on Cal's shoulder and giving him a squeeze. "It's me who needs to apologize. These past several years, I'd given up. You didn't deserve that. We'll work this out. I'll talk to Morgan...."

They both heard the car pull into the driveway at the same time.

"Maybe that's her now." Frank went to peer out the kitchen window.

Cal tensed. Had she come to see him? Did he have a chance to make this right?

And just how was he going to do that?

Frank turned, face white, eyes wide. Looked at Cal. "It's the cops."

"Mr. and Mrs. Lowen. Hi."

Morgan's parents, seated on the sofa opposite her, nodded a stilted greeting at Detective Martin as she entered the small family room at the police station where they'd been told to wait. There were three couches in the room. Morgan occupied one. Her parents another. Elaine Martin, in a light gray pantsuit, took the third.

"Are you sure that Sammie didn't run away again?" Grace asked the detective what she'd just asked Morgan and George. In her maroon skirt and jacket, Morgan's mother looked like she'd just stepped from a boardroom.

"We aren't certain, of course, and we have a team of officers and a dog out searching your property," Detective Martin said. "But under the circumstances, we're treating this as an abduction just to be safe. We're set to issue another Amber Alert and have sent bulletins to all of our precincts and cruisers."

She glanced at Morgan.

"We have Frank and Caleb Whittier in custody," she said, elbows on her thighs, hands clasped.

Morgan's heart leaped, whether from fear or some other indefinable thing, she didn't know. "They're here?"

"Not yet, they were picked up at home. They're on their way down. I'll be questioning them in a bit."

"Has Frank said where Sammie is?" she asked.

"Neither of them are saying anything. They've asked for an attorney."

"Is their attorney on his way, as well?" George bit out. "We can't wait all day to get information out of these bastards."

George's new security team had been fired. They had no explanation for how the boy had gotten by them.

Morgan didn't know what to think about anything anymore. Except that her son was missing.

"If Frank was at home, where's Sammie?"

Elaine Martin's eyes softened with compassion as they met hers. Her professionalism was easier to take. "We'll find your son, Morgan."

And here they went again. They'd find him. But alive?

"They never found Claire Sanderson."

"I've got a call into Detective Ramsey Miller. He's working the Claire Sanderson case."

"Still? A twenty-five-year-old case?"

"Apparently there was some new movement in the case a couple of months ago. Miller's been in contact with Cal Whittier. And from what I've been told, he also ran a check on Frank."

"What did he find?" Grace asked.

"That's what I have to find out."

She needed answers.

"Coach Safford said that Sammie had a call not

long before he asked to go to the bathroom," Martin said, glancing between the three of them. "He didn't think anything of it at the time. Sammie was on break and took the call. He didn't seem upset. The coach assumed it was you." She looked at Morgan. "He overheard Sammie tell another kid something about his mom. They're going to question the kid now."

Her stomach tightened.

"Did you call him?" Martin was looking at her.

"No." Morgan shook her head. She'd been with Cal. Telling him they were on to him. And then she'd been sitting in her car.

"What about you two?" Elaine looked at her parents. "Did either of you call Sammie this morning?"

"No," they answered in unison.

"We're checking Cal's phone records for recent calls," she said next. "If Frank has a personal cell, it's a pay-as-you-go."

"I told Cal that we knew who they were," Morgan said, wondering when this would all end. She just couldn't take any more. "He might have called Frank, who called Sammie. Maybe they were having him meet them somewhere and were just getting ready to leave when the police showed up."

"We're checking on that," Elaine said. "I'll let you know as soon as I hear anything. In the meantime, sit tight."

"Wait," George said. "What about ransom calls? Shouldn't we have lines set up?"

"Should I go home?" Morgan asked.

"We've got a team at your house," Elaine reminded

Morgan, who'd already turned over a key and given the police permission to enter her premises. "Any calls would come to your cell phone and it's here with you. Because of the circumstances, your relationship with the Whittiers, I'd rather you stay put, just until I can question them. I'm going to want to speak with you afterward to corroborate stories. Things are different this time since we have a suspect."

"Okay." Morgan was fine with staying.

Cal would be there soon.

Confused, wondering how she could even think about the man without going into a blind rage, Morgan turned her thoughts to the only thing that mattered. Getting Sammie home safely.

IT HAD BEEN A LONG time since Cal had been in a police station. He'd spent most of his years in a self-imposed prison to keep himself and his father away from the police.

Sitting with his father on one side of a table in a small, windowed interrogation room, he tried to find the absence of emotion that had seen him through life. Their attorney, Jim Brown, a man Cal knew from the junior arts league board, sat at one end of the table. Detectives Martin and Sanchez sat opposite Frank and Cal.

"We've already told our attorney that we'll cooperate fully," Cal said as soon as introductions were done. Martin had only acknowledged knowing Cal by a nod of her head. "My father and I have nothing to hide."

He wasn't going to wait to be interrogated, to let

them run this interview. He wasn't going to be trapped into saying something incriminating about his father by their twisted ways of wording questions.

"As I told Detective Ramsey Miller from the Comfort Cove Police Department in Massachusetts, my father and I have nothing to do with their missing box of evidence."

Frank's quick intake of air beside him was not comforting. Still, Cal couldn't worry about his father at that moment if he was going to save him for the years to come.

He should have told his father about Ramsey and the missing evidence. He should have told Morgan about Claire Sanderson and the suspicions regarding his father.

He hadn't. He'd done what he thought best, and it had all backfired. It was time to make things right.

He and Frank had been silent in the car on the way to the station, but they both knew this was somehow tied to Claire Sanderson.

Ramsay Miller had been poking around. Cal had been a fool to relax at all, to think even for a second that Miller would do as he'd said and inform Cal first if he found anything.

"We appreciate your willingness to cooperate," Detective Martin said.

"I assume Miller is on his way down?"

"I called Detective Miller," Martin said. "I haven't heard back from him yet."

"Neither my father nor I have been in Massachusetts, nor do we know anyone who has, nor have we hired anyone to visit the state for us. We have no use for the evidence stored in the Comfort Cove Police Department evidence room. As I've already stated, we have nothing to hide, just as we had nothing to hide twenty-five years ago. You already have our complete testimony on that score and Ramsey Miller is now in possession of the book I've been writing, which not only chronicles the events directly preceding and following Claire Sanderson's disappearance, but also includes every bit of my research on that and other abductions that have taken place. My father is in no way connected to any other case on record."

Frank sat up straighter. And Cal realized, hearing his own words, what he'd probably just exposed. To himself as well as to the rest of the people in the room. He'd not only researched other cases to try to explain Claire's disappearance and therefore exonerate his father, but he'd done the research to convince himself that his father wasn't living a double life.

"Mr. Whittier?" Martin waited until he met her gaze. Cal was having a hard time sitting still. He just couldn't live his entire life under suspicion, going after nothing for fear of losing it, losing what he had when he went after it.

He'd lost Morgan's trust by his own lies and omissions.

And that wasn't Martin's problem. He focused on the detective. *Give her what she wants and get out.*

"While we are indeed concerned about you and your father's suspected connection to Claire Sanderson and you're sitting here because of that connection, our primary concern right now is not Miller or Sanderson or missing evidence."

"What is it, then?" Frank spoke up beside Cal.

Martin looked at Cal's father, clearly suspicious. "Mr. Whittier, when was the last time you saw Sammie Lowen?"

"Yesterday afternoon. I took him to basketball tryouts. I saw him safely to the gym door. The coach was right there, checking the boys off his list as they arrived. Tryouts were closed. Before that, I saw him on Tuesday afternoon. My son brought him over for basketball practice. We were out in the driveway the entire hour and a half he was there. My son was in the house. Sammie's mother picked him up just after five."

"Have you seen or heard from him since yesterday?"

"No, I have not." His father said evenly. Calmly.

How in the hell could he be so calm? The first time in twenty-five years his father had any association with a child—as a favor to Cal—and the cops were going to try to make something of it?

Because of George Lowen.

Sanchez was watching the exchange between Martin and his father.

"My father has never done anything that would in any way hurt Sammie Lowen." Cal spoke softly. "I've been present for each and every practice. My father's been coaching him as a favor to me. Sammie made it through the first cut of tryouts because my father took the time to work with him and prepare him."

Elaine Martin glanced at him, but quickly returned

her attention to his father, brushing Cal's remarks aside.

"Think carefully about any contact you've had with Sammie, Mr. Whittier," she said, leaning forward. "We know that Sammie Lowen received a phone call this afternoon. We're checking his cell phone records and your son's, as well, as we speak. I don't want to find out that you've lied to me."

"I'm certain I have had no contact with the boy." Frank looked her straight in the eye.

"What's the complaint here?" Jim Brown spoke up. He glanced at Cal. "I know you said you wanted to speak for the two of you, but I'm uncomfortable with this line of questioning when we don't yet know why we're here."

Cal had filled Jim in as completely as he could in the minutes they'd had together regarding Claire Sanderson's disappearance and the subsequent hounding of his father.

"Sammie Lowen is missing," Martin said. She and Sanchez watched Cal and his father intently.

"Missing?" All of the fight went out of Cal. And then he jumped up. "Sammie is gone again? From where? For how long? Where's Morgan?"

Sanchez was on his feet and beside Cal before he'd known he stood. "Sit down, Mr. Whittier," he commanded, at which time Cal dropped back to his seat.

"Hold on, son. They need our help here."

"Anything you say can and may be used against you in a court of law," Jim reminded them of the rights they'd been read.

"Did Sammie run away again?" Cal asked. "That doesn't make sense. He had tryouts this afternoon. Second cuts. He wouldn't miss those."

"We don't know anything yet," Martin said. Cal didn't believe her. "But we're treating this as an abduction." She looked straight at Frank.

"Are you charging my client with anything?" Jim asked.

"No, sir, we aren't. But we've already received a warrant to search his home and intend to hold him until we've done so."

"I know where he is." Frank's words fell like a bomb in that little room.

And Cal's life burst into flames.

CHAPTER THIRTY-ONE

EVERY EYE IN THE interrogation room was on Frank Whittier.

"Where is Sammie Lowen?" Elaine Martin asked.

"I shouldn't have said it like that," Frank said. "If the boy's been kidnapped I'm wasting valuable time here. And his face being plastered all over the news a few weeks ago in conjunction with George Lowen was certainly an invitation to any lowlife who might want to try to make a quick buck."

"Mr. Whittier," Sanchez spoke, his voice low and menacing. "If you know where that boy is, now is the time to tell us. It only gets uglier from here."

"You don't have to say anything," Jim said. "Please be aware that anything you do say could implicate you."

"Dad, if you know where Sammie is, tell them. Now." Cal didn't need to think about that one. They lived right. It was the only thing they had going for them.

If his father was sick, in trouble, Cal would help him. Later. After Sammie Lowen was safely in his mother's arms.

"I just think I know where he'd go if he left on his own," Frank said. "I don't know who called him. But I can't imagine anything less than a catastrophe calling that young man away from second cuts. If he left on his own, you can bet it had something to do with that phone call. Last week, Sammie was over playing basketball the day his mother went to court for the custody hearing. He told me about someplace he'd seen, a place to hide. He said that's where he'd go if the courts took him away from her. But I got the impression he'd go there anytime he thought he was in danger. Maybe something in that phone call scared him, made him think he had to hide."

"Where, Dad?" Cal's throat was dry. Rough.

Frank looked at Elaine Martin. "I'll take you to the spot. Sammie trusts me and I'm breaking that trust. I want to be there for him if he's in trouble."

"Okay," Martin said as Sanchez nodded. Cal had a feeling they'd agree to just about anything that would get them to Sammie more quickly.

"And because I think my son deserves to see that his father is worthy of the trust he's placed in him all these years, I want him to accompany us, as well."

"You ride separately and he stays in the car with an officer," Martin said, without even looking at Cal.

"That's fine."

"Mr. Brown?" Martin looked at Jim.

"You realize that they think you took the boy," Jim said to Frank. "You leading them to him is evidence they'll use against you in court."

"I know."

Jim looked at Cal, who nodded.

"I'll have my phone on," the attorney said, and they all stood.

Morgan sat with her parents. She paced the small waiting room, thankful for its privacy. She wondered if Detective Morgan was with Cal and his father. And if Sammie was okay. God. Was her son alive?

Sammie's face had been all over the news just a few weeks before. Everyone knew now that he was George Lowen's grandson. She thought about ransom calls and kid mills, and the horrible things that sick people did to little boys. Sammie was small for his age.

And cute as could be.

He also had a big mouth. Would her son mouth off and get himself in trouble with his captors? Or would he be able to use his lungs to attract attention and save himself?

She almost hoped that Frank Whittier had taken him. Sammie knew Frank. He hero-worshipped him. He wouldn't be frightened.

Until…

What would Frank do with him?

Frank couldn't be responsible. There had to be some other explanation.

But what if he was?

The low rumble of her parents' voices as they occasionally conferred penetrated her thought processes, but nothing could soothe the horrible ache in her heart.

Had she really been stupid enough to put her son's life at risk? Was she really that incapable of reading people's motives?

"Mr. Lowen?" A uniformed police officer opened the door, a man in a brown suit and a tall, thin, older man standing behind him.

"Yes." George stood. "Michael. Thank you for getting this done so quickly."

Assuming the man was the private detective, or the new head of security for Lowen Enterprises, Morgan paid attention.

"Everything is ready," the man her father had called Michael said. "We just need your signatures."

That was her father, always ready, and because he was ready he could be counted on to save the day. Why hadn't she seen all this before?

"Morgan?" Her father called her over to the table in front of the couch upon which they'd been sitting. "I've got some friends with FBI contacts. If I have custody of Sammie, with legal rights to make calls and decisions, these contacts will do as they're told. We're going to get a lot more attention more quickly here. There are people who will pull strings for me just because they're afraid not to. I'm not proud of that fact, but at the moment, I will use whatever leverage I have to get Sammie safely back to us. You said you were going to bring the boy to our place, anyway, so I went ahead and had Michael draw up custody papers and courier them over here for us. Once I have it on paper that I'm Sammie's legal guardian, I'll begin calling in favors."

Even now, George Lowen was wielding his power. If she wanted the most assurance that she'd get her son back, she had to do as her father wanted. Give him his heir. She struggled to breathe. But she nodded. And moved to the table to sign her father's papers.

SITTING IN THE BACK of the unmarked sedan with Sanchez, Cal watched the similarly unmarked sedan in front of them, keeping his eye on the back of his father's head. Martin was riding with Frank.

For all of their blandness, their attempt to not draw attention, both cars were being driven by uniformed police officers.

Frank leaned forward, giving directions, Cal surmised, and Martin raised an arm, between Frank and the driver. Cal gritted his teeth, clenching every muscle in his body to keep himself from reacting.

They'd get through this. They'd go home together. And if need be, they'd move on. They knew the ropes.

He'd lost Morgan. Once Sammie was safely back in her care, there was nothing left for him in Tyler, Tennessee.

If Sammie made it back to her care. She'd brought Cal and Frank into Sammie's life. And now her father had reason to use that choice as another sign of Morgan's poor judge of character.

Frank had been a good influence on the boy. He'd never thought Frank's past would be used against Morgan. It wasn't like his father had an order to stay away from children. The man could work in a day care if he wanted to. If they'd hire him.

Frank just hadn't wanted to bring more suspicion on himself. That was why he'd made a conscious decision to stay away from children.

They were a couple of blocks from the junior high where Sammie had his tryouts. Sammie was familiar with the area, Morgan had told him, because they'd played Little League on a field there. And he'd been in the school for various functions, like a banquet where he'd received an award for being the player with the most catches in his age group.

Thinking of Morgan hurt like hell. But he knew it was nothing compared to the pain she had to be feeling right now. *Hang on, beautiful lady,* he thought, over and over. *Hang on. We'll bring him home to you.*

Cal was surprised when they pulled into the school parking lot. Martin got out and his father slid out right behind her.

His father was handcuffed to the detective.

The twosome approached the car in which Cal sat.

Sanchez rolled down the window and Martin stuck her head in. "Your father wanted me to tell you that there's a metal cover in the floor down the hall from the gym. It's normally covered by a big rubber floor mat. Sammie saw a guy go down there once a while back. He'd thought it would be a cool place to go to take cover. Something about army guys and hiding out. Then when the thing came up with his mom and he was at the school for basketball tryouts he remembered the hole. He told Frank that he'd be safe there if they tried to make him live with his grandfather. That way he could play basketball when everyone was gone at night."

Martin sounded doubtful.

"I'd have radioed ahead to have someone else check on his story, but he didn't tell me this until about sixty seconds ago. We're going in."

"Be careful, Dad," Cal said.

"Yep."

Martin moved forward and Frank walked beside her with his head held high.

Completely helpless, Cal sat in the backseat of the police car and watched his father walk away.

PAPERS SIGNED, MORGAN SAT, wavering between numbness and despair, waiting for word, any word, from anyone. She no longer had energy to pace the room. Or make conversation. When she'd put her name on the papers and watched as Michael notarized them, something vital inside of her had died.

She wasn't an optimist anymore. There wasn't always a brighter side.

And still, she cared about little else than her son's safe return. Whether he was in her custody or not, she would always be his mother.

Detective Rick Warner stopped by to see them. He told them little, only that they'd questioned Cal and Frank and had a potential lead on Sammie's whereabouts. They'd let them know more when they could.

Someone else from the department offered food. Morgan declined. Her parents ordered and her father added something for Morgan, as well.

She wasn't going to eat the salad he'd requested.

Cal and Frank had given the police a lead. What did that mean? What could it mean other than that her father's investigator had been correct in the conclusions he'd drawn from his findings? Frank Whittier had been a danger to Sammie. And Cal had not only lied to her, but he'd also knowingly exposed her son to the potential danger his father represented.

So why did she ache for him still?

Was she that messed up?

Maybe there just hadn't been time for her heart to assimilate the news that Cal wasn't a good man.

At the moment, the whys didn't seem to matter. Sammie was missing. She'd just given up custody of her son. And she needed Cal.

TENSE AND EXPECTING an interminable wait, Cal was shocked when less than five minutes later, his father and Martin, along with the officers who had driven them and those from a couple of squad cars who'd blocked off the area, came walking back out of the school, en masse.

He reached for the door handle. Sanchez stopped him. Not unkindly, but not gently, either. "Wait," he said as his arm shot out across Cal's body.

Straining to see what was going on, to see more than one of his father's shoulders, he wanted to take down the man beside him. Martin, who was in front of his father now, made a motion.

"Let's go." Sanchez opened the door, slid out and held the door open for Cal.

"What's going on?"

No one was saying much; the officers' focus was trained on the middle of their entourage. Once he was standing, Cal could see what they saw.

A little boy with tearstained cheeks—Sammie— was being held by his father, his small arms wrapped around Frank's neck. Frank's head was bent toward the boy, as though he was speaking to him. As Cal approached, the crowd parted and allowed him to walk right up to the pair.

And that was when it dawned on him that Frank was no longer in handcuffs.

"Something's going on." Grace, seated on the couch opposite from Morgan, straightened, staring through the window that led out into the hallway of the third floor of the police station.

Morgan didn't care about bustle in the hallway.

She'd cared even less about the dinner that had been delivered ten minutes before. Or the tea her mother had offered her.

She just needed Sammie safe. That was all. She asked nothing else of fate or God or any powers that be. Just that Sammie be safe.

The door behind her opened. Just as it had when Michael had come in. When the tea arrived. And dinner. And an officer asking them if they needed anything. And Detective Warner.

"Morgan?"

Detective Martin. She swung around.

And there was Sammie. In the arms of the man who'd abducted him?

"What...?"

"Hold on, Mr. Lowen." Detective Martin held her hand up in front of her and put it against George's chest as he approached with a menacing look on his face. Holding George back, she motioned Frank into the room.

"I think all of you need to listen to what this young man has to say," she said, pointing at Sammie. "And then, I hope, this will be the last time we see any of you. At least in this capacity."

"Sammie?"

Morgan didn't care what anyone had to say. She needed to feel her son, to know he was real.

Frank put the boy down and Sammie ran to her, his arms wrapping so tightly around her it hurt. Pain had never felt so good. "Oh, my God, Sammie," she said, and started to sob. She hadn't shed a tear in hours and now they were flowing as if a dam had broken.

Sammie was crying, too, and his tears put a stop to hers. Sammie hadn't cried the last time he'd come home to her.

Something was different. Something was wrong.

Avoiding the two men who'd entered the room with the detective and her son, Morgan looked at Elaine Martin. "Where was he? What happened?"

"Ask him."

"Sammie?"

Vaguely aware that her parents were standing at the couch across from them, Morgan held her son at arm's length, only so she could look into his sweet, earnest face. And accept whatever news he had to give her.

Sammie glanced back in the direction of the men behind Detective Martin.

"Tell her, son." Frank Whittier's voice.

And then, "Trust her." Cal. Her eyes filled with tears again.

"Talk to me, Sammie."

"I wasn't going to run again, Mom, I swear."

"You ran away?"

"Not really." His head dropped, his shoulders slumped. "I promised you I wouldn't and I guess I broke my promise, but it wasn't like before." He looked back up at her. "I don't want to leave you," he said, starting to cry again, though she could see he was trying as hard as he could to be the man he wanted to be. "I promised I wouldn't run away from you again and I didn't."

Sammie's back was to her parents so he didn't see when George sat down. But Morgan saw. And the knot in her stomach started to tighten again.

"Grandpa called me when I was at practice this afternoon," he said, his brown eyes wide, begging her to believe him.

Morgan looked, not at her father, or her mother, who would always support George, but at Elaine Martin.

The detective nodded. "The phone records were waiting for us when we got back."

"He told me that you'd agreed to give me up. That you thought it was best."

That was when Morgan looked at her father. "You promised…"

"You were going to see Cal," he told her. "You're so easily swayed. Your judgment betrays you. I wasn't going to let you change your mind. One way or the other, the boy belongs with me."

"What I wanted," she said, loud and clear, "was for you to let me talk to my son about my decisions. You promised."

"And I would have kept that promise if you hadn't gone to see Whittier. He was going to try to change your mind. And you'd just admitted that you were in love with him."

"I didn't say that."

"You didn't have to."

Conscious of the other people in the room, Morgan shook her head and focused again on the son whom she loved with every fiber of her being. "Grandpa called you and then what?"

"I just didn't know what to do," he said, the words ending on a high whine.

"I understand, sweetie, just tell me."

Morgan sat down, pulling Sammie into her arms. With his head cradled against her chest, in a way it hadn't been since before he'd started kindergarten, he said, "I figured that if, when I ran away from you, that made a court case for them to take me away from you, then if I ran away from Grandpa, that would make another court case for them to take me away from him."

Out of the mouths of babes. She'd heard the cliché many times. Now it seemed relevant.

Grace stood, crossed over to sit beside Sammie.

He glanced at her, then huddled back against Morgan, his back to his grandmother.

"I knew about this place in the boys' locker room off the gym. It had rubber mats over it, you know, for walking on when you get out of the shower, but one time last summer when I went in to pee, there was a guy working on the showers and he had the mat up and there was this big hole that went down underground. I thought I could hide there."

In the sewer? Morgan shuddered.

"After Grandpa called, I got scared and I thought of that place and I knew they'd never find me there and so I said I had to pee and I pulled back the rug only enough to get to the cover so it would fall back in place and I used a weight bar to open the metal cover and slid down inside and then closed the cover. But then—" Sammie's voice broke "—then I knew I'd been really stupid because I didn't have any food and I'd had to drop down in there and there was no way I could get back up to the lid. It was pitch-black. And... and then I remembered that I'd told Frank where I'd go and I knew that when he heard I was missing, he'd come bring me food. He came, but he didn't bring food. He brought the police."

Sammie could have died down in that sewer. If not for...

Morgan looked at Frank Whittier. "You found him?"

The older man bowed his head and then raised it again. "Sammie told me about the hideaway the day of your court hearing. We had our practice before he knew the result of the hearing and he mentioned that he had a place to hide if they took him away from you."

Even then her son had known where he belonged.

"You saved his life."

She didn't dare look at Cal. He'd lied to her. But

she'd had no faith in him, either. She'd listened to her father, the man who'd betrayed her, instead of to the man who'd actually cared for her.

"I just..." Frank was interrupted by the peal of Detective Martin's cell phone.

"Martin... Yes, Detective Miller... Yes, I did... Yes, I did... Yes... Well..." There was a long pause and total silence in the room as the detective listened. "Oh!"

Everyone in the room, with the exception of Sammie, who was still resting against Morgan, stared at the detective. And waited for her to speak after she hung up.

"That was Detective Ramsey Miller, from Comfort Cove, Massachusetts," she told the room at large. "He's currently looking into the Claire Sanderson abduction in connection with a current case."

She turned then, and faced Frank Whittier. "That book your son wrote about the abduction that he sent to Miller last week..."

Cal Whittier wrote a book? And sent it to a detective?

He was helping the police when she'd basically accused him of harboring a criminal?

"He mentioned a meat delivery truck in the book. It wasn't in any of the police reports. It was as normal to your son as the houses and trees, and he didn't mention it any more than he mentioned the houses and trees he hid behind as he made his way back to your house instead of going to school that morning."

"I remember the truck," Frank said. "It stopped

three doors down, every Wednesday morning. I don't remember seeing it that morning."

"It was there. Detective Miller has been working to track down the driver and they just brought him in this afternoon. He was interviewing the man when I called him earlier. The driver remembers seeing you, Frank," Detective Martin said, more emotion in her voice than usual. She stopped, looked at the Lowens. "Would you like to do this in private?"

"Under the circumstances—" Frank nodded toward Sammie "—no, I would like everyone to hear what you have to say."

Morgan glanced only at Frank. The man's expression was stoic. She couldn't read him. Did he want Sammie to hear firsthand that he'd done something wrong? Or was he that sure he was about to be exonerated?

"He said he saw Claire in your front yard when he first drove past on his way to make a delivery. He saw Cal, too. He was farther up the street. The little girl caught his attention because the front door was standing open and there didn't appear to be anyone else around. He was so bothered by a little kid like that, outside all alone, that after he drove around the block to make another delivery he went back by the Sanderson home before continuing with his route. That was when you came out, put your briefcase on the front seat, opened the back door to drop your suit coat on the seat, which is what allowed him to see that the backseat was empty, and you drove off. Which is exactly what you told the police you did. There was no sign of the child, so he assumed you'd taken her back in the house and all was well. He was running late at that point and continued on his way.

"He didn't know about the child going missing until a couple of days later. He was young then, and partied a lot, and was afraid that if he came forward they'd hold him as a suspect. He knew about the other delivery truck abductions. He said he couldn't lose his whole life for a crime he didn't commit just because he'd been trying to do a good thing. He figured they'd clear you when they didn't find more evidence. Unfortunately our world is full of people who turn a blind eye rather than risk the consequences of getting involved. Apparently this guy at least had enough of a conscience to follow the case and know that you'd never been charged."

"Frank didn't do it," Sammie whispered. Morgan heard her son. She saw Frank Whittier drop down to his knees, his hands on his head.

The older man shuddered and then, from his knees, glanced up at Detective Martin. "I'm exonerated?"

"Yes, sir, you are." Martin's eyes glistened with emotion.

And that was when Morgan saw Cal because he fell beside his father, hugging the older man.

Cal turned his head once. His wet eyes met Morgan's.

And that was when she remembered that she'd signed away her rights to the boy she held.

She glanced toward her mother.

Her mother looked at her. And then at George.

When Grace stood, Morgan knew that her mother was going over to her father's side again. Some things in life she could count on.

But she had Sammie to think about. Sammie to fight for. If her father could sue her for custody, she could sue him back. Sort of like Sammie had said.

"George, Michael didn't leave here until five," Grace said, her tone soft. Calm. But firm, too. "Too late to file papers tonight. If you don't call him, I will."

Hardly daring to believe what was happening, Morgan looked from one parent to the other. Her mother was not backing down. At all.

Her father still showed no emotion. Not even as he fell from his throne. "I'll call him," was all he said as he left the room. Grace went after him, and Morgan didn't think she would ever forget the words her mother said.

"I'm going to call him, too, just to be sure that George does the right thing."

As her parents walked out one after the other, Morgan noticed that Cal and Frank had already gone.

CHAPTER THIRTY-TWO

MORGAN MISSED THE LAST day of class. She was allowed to miss one class, so it didn't matter as far as her grade went. But it mattered to Cal. He'd put a lot of stock in that class, in that meeting.

He'd spent some time on the internet the night before when he and his father, after sharing a couple of beers and a pizza at one of the busiest places in town—just because they could—had returned home. He'd seen a couple of university job postings in Texas and Louisiana that appealed to him. Depending on the outcome of his meeting with Morgan that morning, he intended to apply for them.

Frank wanted to take some continuing education classes, recertify and see if he could put in a few more years of teaching, and possibly coaching, before he retired. He could do that anywhere.

For that matter, he could do it in Tyler, if he didn't want to move with Cal.

It was odd, knowing that Frank didn't need Cal anymore. His father could live on his own. Get a driver's license. Have an address. Hell, he could even buy a house, once he got a job so he could qualify for the loan.

When Morgan didn't show for class, Cal knew he had his answer. He applied for both positions.

A week later, he'd been offered both.

HER PHONE WAS RINGING. Sitting in the junior high parking lot the second week in August, reading a book while Sammie was inside at practice, Morgan grabbed her cell phone from her purse. Her son wouldn't be calling unless he was hurt.

She didn't recognize the number.

"Hello?"

"Morgan? This is Frank Whittier."

Her heart began to pound. "Hi, Frank, how are you?"

"Good. I'd like to speak with you. Is there a time we can meet?"

She told him where she was, where she'd be for the next hour, and he said he'd be there in ten.

Nine minutes later, Cal's Durango pulled into the lot next to her and Frank got out. Unlocking her Taurus, she motioned for Frank to get in.

And when he did, she couldn't stop looking at him. Not just because even in jeans and a polo shirt the man looked distinguished instead of old, but because he was Cal's father. "You look good."

"I've got a semester of classes ahead of me and then recertification," he said. "Life is good."

This from a man who'd been robbed of twenty-five years.

"Good." She smiled, glad to be with him. "What did you want to talk about?"

"First, Sammie."

Frowning, she tensed. What about Sammie? If her son had thought her overprotective before, it was nothing compared to the watchful eye she kept now that she fully accepted the responsibility that came with his being the grandson of a very rich man. But so far, there had been no complaints from the little man.

That she knew of, that is.

"Sammie said he'd called you," she said, in case Frank was worried that she didn't know. "I told him it was fine with me as long as he wasn't bothering you."

"He doesn't bother me," Frank said. "That's one great boy you've got there. Kind of reminds me of Cal. Before everything went wrong, I mean."

She didn't want to talk about Cal. Or think about him. But how did you stop thinking about a man who starred in your dreams every night?

"He's asked me if he can start coming by again, to play ball."

"Oh! I'm sorry, I had no idea that was why he was calling. He doesn't know about your classes, or realize that you'll be a lot busier now and..."

Frank was shaking his head. "It would be the highlight of my week if you'd allow him to come over," Frank said. "He told me he made the junior high team, but he's the smallest one out there. He could use the confidence boost some extra court time will give him. I got my driver's license last week and will be buying a car this weekend. With your permission, I could pick Sammie up from school one or two days a week and keep him until you're off work."

"Does Cal know your plans?"

"No."

"Don't you think you should ask him?"

"No."

"He might not want my son at his home."

"It's actually my home," Frank said. "We've been living there rent-free as payment for my work at the nursing home. The landlord has agreed to let me continue to stay as long as I want. I'll be working at the nursing home at least until I finish classes in December. And then, who knows?"

The older man grinned. And she saw Cal. "Maybe, in a few months, after I've got some order back in my life, I'll give Rose Sanderson a call. Cal says we should wait for them to call us. I can't say I disagree with him. They'll have been told about the update in the case and though the restraining order Rose got against me is long expired, it's probably still best that we wait. Awhile. And then if I don't hear from her, all bets are off."

Frank hardly resembled the hunched old man she'd met at Cal's house that first day. "I hope everything works out for you."

"So what do you say? May I tell Sammie yes? May your son come play ball at my house?"

Deny her son something he needed and wanted that she could provide for him? "Of course."

"Thank you."

She sat there, so close to Cal, and yet so far away, wanting to tell Frank to tell him hello. And not wanting to force herself where she no longer deserved to be. She'd made a huge mistake in judgment.

She'd betrayed them both. Frank might be willing to forgive her, but clearly Cal wasn't. He hadn't called. Not even after the semester ended.

And she didn't blame him. How did you trust a woman who couldn't seem to see a forest for the trees?

"I have something else to discuss with you."

"Oh. What's that?"

"My son."

Her hands started to shake.

"Do you love him?"

She stared at Frank.

"At the police station that day, your father said you were in love with my son."

"Yes, he did."

"So, are you?"

The guy needed his pound of flesh. He deserved it. "Yes."

Straight-faced, Frank nodded. "I hoped so. Because I'm certain he's in love with you."

"Not anymore."

"Now more than ever."

"He hasn't called. Or come by. Or…"

"Forgive me for saying so, but Caleb is a bit of a putz when it comes to the opposite sex."

"Frank, really, I'm sure he wouldn't want you doing this."

"I'm certain you're right, but my son's a putz in large part because of me. He's sacrificed twenty-five years of his life already, surely you don't want to see him waste any more time?"

"Of course not."

"Well, then, you can understand that neither do I. After all that Cal has done for me, I have to do this for him. And if he hates me for it—" Frank threw up his hands "—so be it. I can live with that. I can't live with the knowledge that he's so unhappy."

"Cal's unhappy?"

"He might not know it, he might think he wants to move to Louisiana, but he doesn't. He wants to move in with you."

Tingles ran through her body, and then came to an abrupt halt. Frank couldn't possibly know whether or not Cal wanted to live with her. That just wasn't something he'd discuss with his father—or anyone.

"Cal's mother died when he was too young to remember her. I never introduced him to another woman until I asked Rose Sanderson to marry me. She adored Cal. And he adored her, too. She was the only woman he'd ever known and she treated my son as though he was as much her biological child as Claire and Emma were."

"Emma? Oh, yes. Claire's sister."

"Yes. She was two years older than Claire. Four, the last time we saw her. Twenty-nine now. Cal tells me that he heard from Ramsey Miller that Emma is still living in Comfort Cove. Rose is, too. But I'm getting off topic here. After Claire disappeared and Cal said he'd seen her in my car and then they found her teddy bear there, Rose went a little crazy. She said some pretty bad things. And she threw us out. Cal could have forgiven her, I think, for turning on me. But he never understood how she could reject him so completely. I didn't help him to understand. At the time, I was too busy trying to figure out how to stay out of jail and make enough money to raise him. I was scared and heartbroken and grieving for Claire, and Cal somehow learned not only how to handle rejection, but to expect it. First his biological mother left him. And then Rose rejected him."

"But once he got older, started dating...I don't know a woman alive that would reject Cal now," Morgan said, and felt her cheeks get warm.

Frank's chuckle intrigued her. "You're wrong about that one. He's had at least a dozen relationships that I'm aware of over the past fifteen years. He knows how to charm them, but he gives nothing of himself. No heart."

Cal had told her almost the same thing that last night he'd been at her house. The night they'd decided they were a couple. One that would start seeing each other after the semester ended.

And the custody battle was over.

"My son has never given a woman anything to hold on to. And every single one of the women he's dated, being human, eventually breaks off with him."

"He never breaks it off?"

"Never. Except maybe that woman he was seeing about the same time you started coming around."

Kelsey.

"And he never, to my knowledge, has tried to make

things better, either. He expects rejection. He gets it. And he moves on."

He'd said Cal was moving to Louisiana.

That last day in his office replayed itself in her mind. The file she'd thrown at his feet. Her refusal to look at him. Or listen to him.

She'd just come from her father and...

"When Cal and I were at the police station, being questioned, he let it be known that he'd done research for that book he wrote in part to find out if there were any other unsolved abductions to which I could possibly be connected."

She turned sharply, staring at him. "He told you he doubted you?"

"No. He told Detective Miller that he knew I wasn't guilty because he'd done his own checking. The point is, he did doubt me, and that's okay."

"How can you say that? If he loved you, if he knew you well enough, he'd have believed in you and—"

"It's human to doubt," Frank said, staring her right in the eye. "It's healthy to doubt. The beautiful formula for humanity has two major counterparts, head and heart. The head brings doubts to keep you in check. The heart propels you forward to keep the head in check. It's a perfect system when we let it do its job. Cal let it do its job. He doubted me, but his heart knew I was innocent. He was compelled by his heart, he lived by his heart, and his doubts had him double-checking me just in case his heart was leading him wrong."

There was freedom in what Frank said. Huge freedom. If she could accept it.

"Where you were concerned, he listened only to his head when it came to our troubled past. He should have told you about Claire Sanderson before he asked you to bring Sammie to our home."

"He's really moving to Louisiana?"

"He accepted a position there."

"Did he tell you I rejected him?"

"No. He hasn't mentioned you at all."

Her thoughts tumbled around one another. Minutes passed.

"I've said what I came to say." Frank opened the car door, got out and closed it behind him. She watched him go.

CAL WROTE HIS LETTER giving notice to Wallace University, effective immediately. It was the fifth such letter he'd written. He knew he was giving them too little time to find a replacement. And yet, his decision to leave felt right. The job in Louisiana beckoned. He and his father would probably do well to have some time apart after so many years of being joined at the hip. They had to find their own lives.

In the fourth-floor office he'd grown quite fond of, he read the letter one last time, hit Print, put it in an envelope and tossed it in the intercampus mail bin on the edge of his desk.

"Excuse me, Professor?" The words came at the same time as a knock on his partially open door.

"Come in." He turned toward the door, knowing

that he'd just made the right decision to leave. He was hearing Morgan's voice, and would continue to do so as long as he stayed there.

"I was wondering if I could ask your opinion on something?"

The voice was still Morgan's.

And so was the body attached to the voice.

Cal didn't move. Except to say, "I'd be happy to try." He assumed she was seeking some kind of academic advice.

Still, he couldn't believe that she'd come to him for advice of any kind. He'd lied to her. And Morgan was sensitive to being misled.

It had been a few weeks since he'd seen her. She was thinner. Too thin. And still gorgeous. Her jeans and tank top were new to him. Her hair longer and loose. He liked it that way.

"I have a problem." She was staring at him. He liked it.

"I'll help if I can."

"I screwed up. I doubted where I should have believed and believed where I should have doubted and I don't know how to fix that."

His world stopped spinning uncontrollably. Just like that. There was no sound. No big ringing of bells. No huge bounding waves. No knock on the head.

Just, very simply, what had been grossly wrong was suddenly right.

He didn't have to think. His heart spoke. "I think the best thing to do is to understand that everyone makes errors in judgment. They're part of the human experience."

When she opened her mouth to speak, when he saw that her lips were trembling, he started to tremble, too. "Is there a way to make things right even when there's been a very severe error in judgment?"

Was she asking him to fix things between them? To unlie to her?

"The point of erring is to learn," he told her. "If you learn from your mistake, then you've made it right." The reason he marked papers, rather than just slapping grades on them, was so that his students could learn from their errors. They were in his classes to learn, not to get everything right. They didn't need to be there if they got everything right.

He gave the lecture every first day of class. Morgan had heard it many times.

She frowned, and Cal couldn't take any more. Standing, he held her in front of him, looking straight into the heart of her, hoping she could see the heart in him.

"I learned, Morgan," he said. "I swear to every power there is that I will never ever lie to you again. Not ever. For any reason."

"You learned?" She looked confused. "What did you have to learn? You know everything, Cal. Do you have any idea how hard it is to live up to the man you've idolized for years?"

"Probably about as hard as it is to live up to the woman who has more heart in one finger than you've dared to have in your whole life."

He thought he just might have a chance at life again when her brow cleared and she smiled a long, slow smile he'd never seen before. "Head and heart," she said.

"I'm not following."

"Your father said that the perfect balance in life is a melding of head and heart. You're head and I'm heart and I guess that means that together we make the perfect pair."

"My father?"

She nodded, still smiling. Like she knew the secrets of the universe. "Frank came to see me a few days ago."

"He did."

"Yeah, he says that you don't really want to move to Louisiana."

That was news to him. His father had done nothing but encourage him to make his own choices.

"He says that you love me."

Cal wanted to take offense, or be angry, or some other suitable male response. Instead, he smiled. "He did, did he?"

"Mmm-hmm, right after he made me tell him that my father had been right that day at the police station when he'd said I was in love with you."

Wait. He stared. Had she just told him she loved him?

"This is the part where you either kiss me or head for cover," she said. "Because if you're waiting for me to end things and let you off the hook, you're going to be waiting for a really, really long time."

He might be stupid, but he wasn't a fool. "Morgan Lowen, will you marry me?"

"I was kind of hoping you'd kiss me first. How can I marry a man I haven't even kissed?"

He pulled her up against him, letting her feel how hard he was. "Is that a yes?" he asked.

She moved against him. "I guess it has to be, huh?"

"Probably. Unless you're going to spend your whole life fantasizing instead of living."

"Nope. I learn from my mistakes." Her eyes clouded and she grew completely still. "Telling you I'm sorry will never be enough for doubting you, Cal. But I am sorry. I hurt you to the very core by giving credence to what my father was telling me rather than letting you explain your side of the story."

"You have nothing to be sorry for, love. You did absolutely the right thing. The thing I'd have had you do. You were protecting your son. I lied and that laid the groundwork for what came after. You didn't trust me because I'd betrayed your trust with those first lies I told you."

"You didn't really lie, Cal. You told the story your father had taught you to tell in order for the two of you to preserve some kind of life after he'd been unfairly persecuted. At the time, I was nothing to you but a stranger, really. You guys were in survival mode."

"Survival mode or not, I will never lie to you again."

"I know that."

"I love you, Morgan Lowen." He'd never said that to a woman before. Not even to Rose Sanderson, though he'd wanted to tell the woman who'd once been a mother to him that he loved her.

"And I love you, Caleb Whittier. Now are you going to kiss me or do I have to wait until the wedding?"

Like a good professor, he answered her question immediately. Thoroughly.

With a whole lot of passion.

Her college professor taught her that reality was far better than the fantasy worlds they studied. And that she had pretty damn good judgment, after all.

EPILOGUE

"IS HE ASLEEP?" Cal leaned over Morgan's shoulder to peek into Sammie's room one night in late August. Sammie had played his first scrimmage game that night—nothing official, just an end-of-summer practice game that his coach had set up with a neighboring junior high school.

"Yeah." Reaching for Cal's arms she wrapped them around her, covering his hands with her own at her stomach. "He's still got his jersey on."

"He held his own with boys who are all older and bigger than he is." Cal sounded like a proud papa.

"Thanks to you and your dad."

Cal gave her a squeeze and led her across the hall to her room. "Sammie's talented," he said. "And a hard worker. Wonder where he got that characteristic from?"

She smiled vaguely. She'd been too busy to go out with Cal all week because she'd been making her wedding dress. "About the wedding," she began, changing the subject.

"What about it?"

"I'm fine with having it at the country club, fine with Mom and Daddy paying our way, but I will not wear a dress that man purchased when I pledge myself to you for the rest of my life."

Cal's lips, moving all over her neck, were wreaking havoc with her concentration.

"It wouldn't have mattered, sweetheart, you know that, don't you? What you're wearing or who paid for it won't affect the meaning of that day. You'd look good in anything," he said, trailing his lips across one bare shoulder. "Besides," he added, "your father is your family, even if he is an arrogant ass."

"Who doesn't give a rat's ass about anything but money. And Sammie, because he wants to know that Sammie isn't going to blow everything my father has worked for his whole life. He wants control of Sammie so he knows that Sammie is well trained to take over for him someday."

She wasn't over it yet, the anger her father instilled in her.

"I can't speak to his caring," Cal said. "But I know that you care about him. He's your father. You care. That's enough for me."

"After what he did...the way he manipulated me... I—"

"He's family. He has faults, but we're on to him. And he did apologize."

Morgan could still hardly believe that George had actually called to apologize to her. It was only because he'd done so that she and Cal had agreed to her parents' request to give them a wedding, one befitting George Lowen's daughter, with all the requisite guests invited.

"I want nothing from him," Morgan said now. "He can leave everything he has to Sammie, but I wish he wouldn't do that, either. I want my son to earn what he has. To understand the value of money, which means understanding that there are things in life that are far more important than money."

"I think Sammie's already ahead of you on that one. He turned down Hayward."

"Because he couldn't play basketball there."

Taking Cal's hand, Morgan led him back out to the living room. She had to work in the morning.

And he was far too much of a temptation.

"When did you say Sammie was staying with your folks again?" Cal kissed her long and deep.

She kissed him back until her knees were about to give out on her. And then, at the last second, she dragged her mouth away from his.

"Tomorrow night, and you know it." Her chuckle was a bit rough. She didn't want to make love with Cal while Sammie was home until after they were married. But that didn't make her immune to his ability to make her crazy with needing him.

"We still on for steaks and wine in bed tomorrow night?" he asked, a warm smile on the lips she so craved.

"The wine and steaks are negotiable," she told him, smiling, too.

Her response earned her another long kiss at the front door. "It won't be long before you won't have to go," she told him.

"It won't be long before we move into our new house, you mean."

A home she and Cal and Sammie had all chosen together. The home he was buying for her as a wedding present. It was centrally located between Sammie's school, the day care where Morgan had been officially promoted to full-time teacher and Wallace. Cal had grabbed the resignation letter from his outbox and shredded it.

"Your mom called my dad today."

Morgan's stomach dropped. "She did?" What was her father up to now? Or more accurately, what had he put her mother up to?

"Wipe the frown off your face, worrywart," Cal said, running his finger along her lips. "Grace seems to be a new woman now that she's learned to stand up to your father some. She called to apologize for any stress or discomfort they'd caused him and to ask him if he'd like her to help him plan our rehearsal dinner."

"Frank's giving us a rehearsal dinner?"

"He is now. She also wanted to invite him over for Sammie's birthday dinner."

"His birthday isn't until November and we can have our own birthday dinner."

"Which we will, but we'll still have to have a dinner with them." With his arms around her, his hands locked at her back, he grinned down at her. "She also invited him for Thanksgiving and Christmas dinner."

"She's afraid she's going to be cut out, but if she gets your father on board…"

"Kind of what I was thinking."

"She's as bad as my dad, trying to manipulate us." She'd never, ever seen her mother be that way, though.

"I think she's desperate. She can't bear the thought of losing you and will do whatever it takes to be a part of your family. Truth be told, I feel kind of sorry for her."

With her mother's voice in the courtroom still ringing in her ears, Morgan wasn't as ready to forgive. But… "I'm not going to cut her out. I'm letting Sammie go over there, aren't I?" Because it was right. They were his grandparents. "It's just going to take some time, Cal."

"I understand. I just don't want you to fall into my trap and close your heart. People aren't perfect. They get hurt and make mistakes and—"

"So you're ready to let your dad call Rose Sanderson, then? You're ready to forgive her?"

Her response was a tight hug from her future husband. And then, a barely discernible whisper in her ear, "Thanks to you, I might be willing…."

"Soon?"

"I want to give them some time to contact us first. I really believe it's the right thing to do, considering the circumstances."

And because she didn't disagree with him, she let the subject drop. For now. But she wouldn't let it go indefinitely. Cal needed to come to terms with his past.

To let hurts heal.

And she loved him enough to help him get there.

Just like he'd helped her.

She pulled back, staring up at him.

"What's wrong? You look like you've seen a ghost."

"Not a ghost. Just my father in me."

"What?"

"I was just thinking that I wasn't going to let you off the hook over Rose and Emma Sanderson because I know you still have healing to do and…oh, my gosh, Cal, am I just like my father? Controlling and manipulative and—"

"You, my sweet, are just you. A piece of your father and of your mother, and mostly just the unique human being you were born to be. As to the rest, we all step into the lives of those around us, if we care enough. If we think we can help. Like I did with my dad all these years."

"And like Frank did when he came to see me."

"Right."

"So, maybe, in his own way, my dad cares. A little."

"I think he does."

"Okay, we'll go with that. Makes putting up with him easier."

"We've already won where your father's concerned, Morgan."

"How's that?"

"By agreeing to let him pay for our wedding."

"And how does that make us victorious?" They'd wanted a very small, very quick exchanging of vows that was private to them and Sammie and Frank and made everything legal as quickly as possible.

"Because by agreeing to the wedding, he's going to be there."

"And?"

"He's giving you away to me, and what more could either of us want from him?"

Morgan laughed. And hugged him. And knew, as she pressed her lips to his, that her professor had not only become her intended, and her lover, but he'd also become her very best friend.

* * * * *

*The next book in Tara Taylor Quinn's
new trilogy,*
IT HAPPENED IN COMFORT COVE,
*takes you to...Comfort Cove,
the Massachusetts town rocked
by a crime twenty-five years ago.
A crime some people have never forgotten....*

*A DAUGHTER'S STORY will introduce you
to Emma Sanderson. She's the older sister of Claire,
the child who went missing—
and daughter of Rose,
the still-grieving mother.
Emma, too, is looking for answers.
What she isn't looking for is love,
not after her fiancé's bitter and
profound betrayal.
And yet she finds it...in the most unlikely place
she could have imagined.*

*A DAUGHTER'S STORY by Tara Taylor Quinn
will be available in October 2012.*